P9-CLI-171

DIMENSION
WHY
HOW TO SAVE THE UNIVERSE
WITHOUT REALLY TRYING

"Warning: Do not try wearing a hat after reading this book, for your head may be a different size. Read in isolation, to avoid blowing out others' eardrums with laughter. If you value tidy, predictable plots and have no interest in time travel, intergalactic adventure, and the connection between baked beans and the fate of humanity, look elsewhere. Now. And give your copy to me. This is not only a must-read but a must-read-again."

—Peter Lerangis, author of the Seven Wonders series

HOW TO SAVE THE UNIVERSE WITHOUT REALLY TRYING

JOHN CUSICK

HARPER
An Imprint of HarperCollins*Publishers*

Dimension Why: How to Save the Universe Without Really Trying
 For information address HarperCollins Children's Books, a division of HarperCollins Publishers, 195 Broadway, New York, NY 10007.
www.harpercollinschildrens.com

Library of Congress Control Number: 2020933698
ISBN 978-0-06-293758-2

Typography by Chris Kwon
20 21 22 23 24 PC/LSCH 10 9 8 7 6 5 4 3 2 1
❖
First Edition

This book was written for the express enjoyment of one Molly C of Brooklyn, New York (but I hope you like it too).

"Ah! Young people, travel if you can, and if you cannot—travel all the same!"

—**Jules Verne**

"Don't swallow your gum."

—**Professor Rivulon**

It is said at the heart of the universe beats a question only one can answer.
And when she does, creation itself will unravel.

Philosophers agree this incontrovertibly proves that while there may be no silly questions . . .

. . . there are definitely dangerous ones.

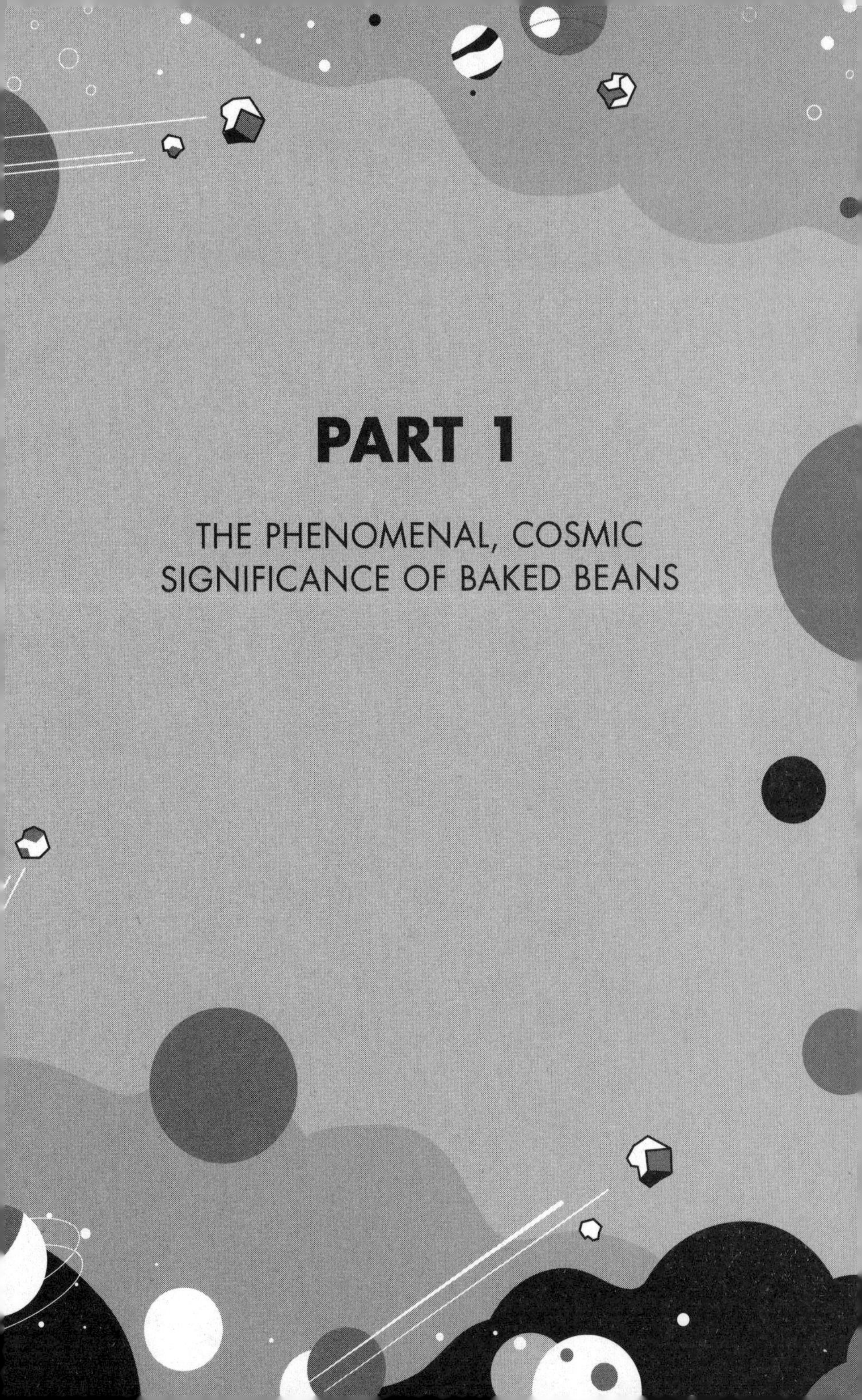

PART 1

THE PHENOMENAL, COSMIC SIGNIFICANCE OF BAKED BEANS

1

PHINEAS T. FOGG WAS bored. He didn't often get bored. He was intelligent (according to him) and rich (according to pretty much everybody), and when you're clever and have lots of money, it's rare to find yourself with nothing to do. The odds of this happening were somewhere around seventy-six thousand to one. That's in the *super unlikely* to *absurdly unlikely* range. And yet, here Phineas was, in the penthouse of his family's own building, in a room full of the most sophisticated and expensive gadgets in the galaxy, improbably bored.

Though Phin didn't know it yet, it was going to be one of those days when *super unlikely* to *absurdly unlikely* things happened a lot.

He'd been sprawled on the floor a good twenty-six minutes. His food replicator lay in pieces (he'd disassembled and reassembled it so many times he'd lost count), his favorite vortex manipulator was now an invigorating shade of green (he'd tried painting it blue, then pink, then polka-dot), and his Extraweb terminal—which accessed a super-vast, super-entertaining network of just about every interesting clip, article, program, or game one could imagine—lay dormant.

Some days, even cat videos lose their charm.

"I'm bored, Teddy," Phin said aloud.

"Let's play a game," said the large, slightly dingy teddy bear sagging in the corner.

"I don't want to play a game. We've played every game. We played Candy Planet. We played Connect Four Billion. We played Apples to Gravleks. I don't want to play them again."

"Let's play a game," said Teddy.

Phin shut his eyes. "I appreciate your persistence, but I'm really not in the mood."

"Let's—" began Teddy.

"Play a game," said both—one in a cheerful, slightly wobbly voice, the other in a very weary one.

In a galaxy full of incredibly articulate and intelligent robo-toys, Phin had an affection for Teddy, who wasn't a robot really, but a stuffed bear with a semibusted voice box. In the beginning Teddy could say three phrases, including "I love you" and "Where's my honey?" Now his internal circuitry was sufficiently degraded that only the third phrase, "Let's play a game," remained. But Phin knew Teddy loved him, even if he didn't say it every day.

Despite having zero confidence it would be any more exciting than lying down, Phin sat up, his antiseptic white jumpsuit bunching around his middle. Sometimes, Phin thought, you have to try something as radical as sitting up just to see if the universe will reward your boldness.

In this case, it worked.

A panel on the ceiling slid away, and a bulb whose sole purpose was to strobe red and look alarming dropped into the room and flashed.

Phin jumped to his feet. "The mail's here!"

He rushed to the chute and plugged in his PIN code. The mechanism hissed and whirred, unlocking one of the most sophisticated security systems money could buy. A door slid open. In the antechamber stood an unenthusiastic android, about four feet tall, with a screen for a face. Phin could tell the android was unenthusiastic by the way it crossed its arms and tapped its foot.

The words *You Have Received an Extraweb Gram* scrolled across its display.

Phin felt a mixture of excitement and melancholy, the same blend of emotions he experienced whenever his parents made contact.

There then appeared an image of two healthy, attractive people who looked a lot like Phin except older, tanner, and less bored. Phin's parents wore matching safari gear, complete with pith helmets and sub-ether goggles, making them both look a bit like android beekeepers.

"Hello, Phinny!" Phin's mother waved. He hated when she called him that.

His father grinned. "Hello, Phineas, we love you!"

"We love you so much!"

"Hi guys," said Phin. "How's the safari?"

"Absolutely brilliant," said Eliza Fogg. "We so wish you could experience it."

"If it weren't so incredibly dangerous," Barnabus Fogg added.

"Yes, if it weren't so dangerous, we would love it if you were with us."

"You'd just love it," said Barnabus. "The wildlife is incredible here on . . . El, where are we today?"

"Neptune the Second, near the Frillian Riviera," said Eliza. "There are giant serpents you can ride!"

"And flowers that spin cotton candy!" said Barnabus.

"That sounds amazing," said Phin, and he meant it.

Phin's parents had been enjoying a tour of the galaxy for the past eleven years. It had begun as a *Let's go on vacation before we have kids* kind of thing, then transformed into a *Let's make sure we see the eastern arm of the Milky Way before Eliza gives birth* sort of trip, then briefly a *Let's just pop home and have this baby so we can catch our flight to the Horsehead Nebula* situation. In fact, Phin had no memory of his parents that didn't involve an Extraweb Chat or Extraweb Call or Extraweb Gram like this one. Eleven birthdays, eleven Christmases, and twenty-two semiannual Child Appreciation Days had all gone this way: Mom and Dad off in some exotic location; Phineas alone, in his room, wishing he were with them.

"Do you think maybe next month I could come meet you? Say on Ursa Six?" Phin had his parents' itinerary memorized—no mean feat, as it was constantly changing and expanding, like one of those star-eating Newtonian blobs, but a lot more expensive.

"Next month?" said Barnabus.

"What's next month again?" said Eliza.

"My birthday," said Phin, patiently, lovingly, furiously. "I'm turning twelve."

There was an awkward pause.

"Let's play a game," Teddy offered.

"You said I could travel with you when I turned twelve," said Phin. He only reminded them of this every time they spoke. "Remember?"

"Phinny," said Mom.

"Phineas," said Dad.

"Phin," said Phin.

"You know we miss you, angel, but the galaxy is such a huge and dangerous place."

"Too dangerous," added Barnabus, "for a child. Why, your mother's been kidnapped six times this week alone!"

"It's true! And a space wizard shrunk your father to the size of a proton for an entire afternoon!"

"If anything ever happened to you," said Barnabus, his eyes glistening with real tears, "buddy, I just don't know what we'd do."

"If you're bored," Eliza added, "why not see if Goro wants to play Apples to Gravleks?"

Goro Bolus was not Phin's idea of a good playmate. He was Barnabus and Eliza's business partner, the Bolus in Fogg-Bolus, and in addition to being an adult, he was also the nastiest, creepiest adult Phin knew personally.

"I'd rather not," said Phin.

"Eliza, get Goro on the line," said Barnabus.

"No, don't—!" started Phin, but it was too late. Eliza punched up the conference line, and suddenly the bulbous face of Goro Bolus flickered onto the screen. Bolus was an Arbequian, which meant he resembled, in the opinion of most Earthlings anyway, a very large bean. He was short, even for his species, and wore a pair of unflattering spectacles. The incoming call had startled him, and Bolus scrambled to cover up some blueprints on his desk.

Goro Bolus always looked like you'd just caught him doing something evil.

"Goro!" said Barnabus. "Hey buddy, you busy? Got a moment to hang out with Phin?"

"Barnabus! Eliza! Uh . . ." Bolus tried a smile, which was clearly not his forte. "And, um, hello. Phineas."

"Hey, G-Sauce," said Phin, who knew Bolus loathed all nicknames, and that one in particular.

Bolus gritted his disturbing little teeth. "I'm afraid I'm in the middle of something a bit, um—"

". . . sinister?" suggested Phin, who didn't share his parents' unwavering trust in their business partner.

"Urgent," sneered Bolus. "Terribly sorry. Have to jump off. Lovely to see the Fogg family as always. Goodbye!"

His line went dead.

"He's so dedicated," said Eliza.

"What a guy," said Barnabus.

"It's fine," said Phin. His parents were always encouraging him to bond with Bolus, as if he were some kindly uncle and not the weirdo who ran the company while they traveled the galaxy. The one thing Bolus and Phin had in common was that neither wanted anything to do with the other.

"Hey," said Barnabus, his voice dripping with sympathy. "Hey, trust us, pal. Just a few more years. When you're older, you can come along."

"For now just sit tight, Phinny."

"In my room," said Phin.

His parents nodded solemnly, lovingly, maddeningly.

"It's really the safest place," said Barnabus.

"The safest place in the galaxy," said Eliza.

"Okay," said Phin.

After an exchange of air kisses and *I love you*s, the screen went blank. The postal android cleared its throat and held out a hand for a tip. Phin ignored it and closed the hatch.

Kidnapping. Space wizards. It all sounded so glorious, and Phin wanted to be a part of it.

Instead he was stuck.

Alone.

With Teddy.

He slumped into his chair, did a few spins for good measure, and sighed. Maybe his parents were right. After all, it was just as good seeing the roller-coaster serpents of Neptune the Second in high-def 3D.

Wasn't it?

"*Insanely safe*," said Phin, which was the motto of his parents' company, the Fogg-Bolus Hypergate and Baked Beans Corporation. "That's best. Isn't it, Teddy?"

"Actually," said a voice that was nothing like Teddy's, "I think that sounds awful."

2

A THOUSAND YEARS EARLIER, Lola Ray was standing in the security line at Newark Liberty International Airport, on the planet Earth, at the start of the twenty-first century, at just after eight fifteen in the morning. But she was trying to stay positive.

She had a backpack on one shoulder; an overnight duffel on the other; her infant sister, Mary, in her arms; and her slightly older but still-too-tiny-to-be-left-alone-for-ten-minutes sister, Gabby, wrapped around her right leg. She'd been up since five a.m. sister-wrangling, packing socks, and making snacks for the trip, and she was exhausted, hungry, and sore.

But she was trying to stay positive.

"Where is it?" Lola's mother said for the tenth or eleventh time, rummaging in their carry-on. "Hold this."

She handed Lola the family cell phone, or tried to, since Lola had no free hands, then tucked the phone into the crook of Lola's elbow.

"Yes, I know," Lola cooed to her baby sister, Mary. "Momma's gonna find Mr. Boop, don't worry."

Mary was screaming.

Gabby squeezed Lola's leg and shouted, "Drag me!"

The scenario was not unusual. Lola was used to looking after her siblings. She and Momma were a team. It was them against the world, especially since Papa had taken the research job in Vancouver. Lola was always ready to change a diaper or play Dora the Explorer. She was *the responsible one*, according to her mother, and *so good with the holy terrors*.

Lola took care of things.

She also took care of her mother.

Lola looked up from her screaming sister and squinted at Momma. "I think," she said in her most adult voice, "it's in your hair."

"My what?"

Shrugging the baby and cell phone into one arm, Lola reached up and plucked a rubber pacifier from the tangle of curls on her mother's head. She showed it to Mary and went "*Boop!*" on her nose before giving it to the baby to suck.

Momma sighed. "What would I do without you?"

It was an excellent question.

As the line shuffled a few steps closer to the security checkpoint, Lola imagined what *she* would do without her family. This flight to Vancouver had originally been a Lola-only trip. Summer vacation had just begun, and for the first time ever, Lola was going to travel alone, a just-her-and-Papa trip, no baby sisters, no Momma rolling her eyes at the comic books Lola liked to read. Just seven days of running around Papa's apartment complex, watching whatever she liked on Papa's iPad, and talking to him all about the obsession they shared—the TV show *Dimension Y. Dimension Y* was all about flying through time and space, having adventures, and saving the day. There were no sisters or pacifiers in *Dimension Y*, and Lola knew this because she'd seen every episode more than three times.

Then Momma and Papa had that big fight on the phone about Papa being gone for so long, and Momma had cried, and her voice had gone soft and plaintive—Lola had heard it all through the bedroom wall—and suddenly Lola's solo trip was turned into a family event, all four Ray women flying to Canada. "Won't that be fun?" Momma asked, and Lola had made herself smile. She was still smiling now.

When at last it was their turn, Lola handed back Momma's cell phone, as well as Mary, and pried Gabby off her leg. Momma went through first with the baby, then it was Gabby's turn, until at last it was just Lola.

She closed her eyes, and for a moment imagined she truly was on her own. Not just on her own, but a grown-up, about to jet off to an exotic location, to see the world.

The security guard beckoned her on with two fingers. She stepped to the line and presented her passport and ticket.

"Vancouver, eh?"

"Yes, sir," said Lola, who was unfailingly polite, especially to people in uniform. "It's my first time going to another country," she added, which was true. Her passport was crisp and blue, and had never been used.

The guard smiled. "It's a day of firsts. We've got a new X-ray gate. Supposed to be a lot safer."

"Safer?" said Lola.

The guard scanned her passport and handed it back. "Well, it hasn't turned anyone into a Bog Mutant *yet.*"

For a moment his comment puzzled her, then Lola remembered she was wearing her *Dimension Y* T-shirt, the one with the stencil of monstrous Bog Mutants crawling out of alien goo.

"You're into *Dimension Y*?"

The guard nodded. "Just started the two-part finale. Did you see it?"

"It's so amazing!" Lola said—so loud she startled herself. She wasn't used to grown-ups taking an interest in her opinions, let alone sharing her love for things like *Dimension Y.* Her father was the only adult she knew who watched it. "Sorry. I just binged the whole final season."

The guard pretended to cover his ears. "No spoilers!" he said, and smiled at her.

Lola moved forward and felt herself glowing. She decided then to rewatch the finale on the plane, if the plane had Wi-Fi, which Momma said it would. She'd wait until Momma was asleep and then use her cell phone. Maybe she'd have a few hours to herself after all.

Lola stepped up to the X-ray machine. She could see Momma and the girls waiting for her on the far side. The new X-ray gate, as the security guard had called it, was a bland gray archway with a few blinking lights up the side. A flashing sign on top said WAIT, then MOVE AHEAD.

Lola did.

"Hold still," said the guard on the other side.

Lola found it nearly impossible to hold still when someone told her to. She'd been standing in line for what felt like hours without any trouble, and now felt an overwhelming impulse to shimmy, jump, and do the Mashed Potato.

And worse, she felt a sneeze coming on.

"Hold on," Lola said.

"Hold still!" snapped the guard.

Lola could see her mother checking her watch, juggling Mary in one hand and her bag in the other.

"I think I'm going to—" she started.

Then Lola sneezed.

It was a heckuva sneeze.

When it was over, she opened her eyes and straightened, blinking. Something was wrong. She blinked again. Someone must have shut off the lights. There was a power outage of some kind, a blackout (she'd been through one of those during a hurricane a few years back).

But in movies, when the lights go out in a public place, everyone starts screaming or going *oooooo.*

No one screamed, no one went *ooooo*. No one was making a peep.

Lola was alone.

"Hello?"

Lola's voice echoed in what sounded like a very large, unfriendly space. She cleared her throat. Something dug into her hand, making her jump; then she remembered she was holding her passport. Reassured by its presence, she spoke again. "Hello? Is anybody there? What happened? Where did the lights go?"

As if to answer her question, a brilliant green beam of light swept through the emptiness before her. It seemed to search the dark, passing over unusual shapes that lurked in the void. Lola went cold.

"Identification!" said the thing behind the light.

Its voice was unlike any she'd ever heard, a cross between a bullfrog's croak and that feeling you get just after banging your elbow but before the shooting pain makes you go half crazy. It filled Lola with a sickening dread.

"Um . . . ," she said.

"*Identification!*" the voice said again.

Not sure what else to do, Lola extended her passport into the darkness.

A hand—she hoped it was a hand—snatched her passport away. It disappeared into the gloom behind the green light, which shone in Lola's eyes and was giving her a headache.

"Mmmm," said the voice. "Well, Ms. . . . *Passport*, if that is your real name. I'm afraid you're in an awful lot of trouble."

"Wh-what?" said Lola.

The thing with the dreadful voice stepped out of the shadows. Lola's mind split. One half wanted to scream, the other to go mute forever. Because the creature standing before her in this lifeless place was almost certainly—no, definitely—a Bog Mutant.

Its uniform read *Temporal Transit Authority*.

3

THERE WAS AN ALIEN in Phin's bedroom.

In *his* bedroom. With *his* stuff. Breathing *his* air.

And it was wielding a hair dryer.

"Identify yourself, alien!" he demanded, trying to sound imposing, which was difficult to do while hiding behind your bed. "And . . . stay where you are!"

The alien didn't respond. Instead, it cleared its throat and adjusted its grip on the hair dryer, which it leveled at Teddy's head.

Phin tried a different approach. "Okay. Then how about you tell me why you're pointing a hair dryer at my bear?"

"This isn't a hair dryer," snapped the alien. "It says *Vaporizer.*"

"That's the *brand name,*" said Phin.

"Oh," said the alien, and cleared its throat again. "Well, then why did you scream?"

"I didn't scream," said Phin.

"You definitely screamed," said the alien. "Piercingly."

Phin was so offended he almost stood up. But there was still a potentially dangerous hair-dryer-wielding alien in his room, and so he stayed put. "You surprised me."

"I'm sorry," said the alien, which struck Phin as a funny thing for a murderous alien to say. "It's just, I heard your conversation with your parents," it—she—went on. "I didn't mean to eavesdrop, I couldn't help it." She lowered the hair dryer ever so slightly. "It sounded kind of . . . rough."

"It wasn't," said Phin. "I love talking to my parents. They're awesome. They bought me all this." Phin gestured to the impressive collection of things.

"Okay," said the alien. "Why did you call me an alien?"

"Aren't you one?"

"No," said the alien. "Are you?"

Phin wasn't sure how to respond to this, so he decided to do what any respectable Fogg would do. He offered his visitor a snack.

"Would you like some baked beans?"

The alien, or whatever it was, sighed in what sounded like extreme relief. "That would be amazing. I'm absolutely *starving*."

"But first you have to promise not to kill me," said Phin. "Oh, and unhand my bear."

"I don't want to kill anyone." The alien's voice began to tremble, as if it were about to spew a poisonous venom blob—or, if it wasn't in fact an alien, just cry. "I want to go home."

Feeling pretty sure he wasn't about to be blow-dried to death, Phin came out from behind the couch.

"I'm Phin Fogg," he said, extending a hand to shake. The alien hesitated, then lowered the Vaporizer and stood. For an alien, she looked an awful lot like a normal human girl in an ugly T-shirt. The shirt had the words *Dimension Y* written on it, and a stencil of some naked security guards getting out of the bath, which was a bit weird.

"My name is Lola Ray," she said. "And I am seriously lost."

4

LET'S REWIND A BIT.

"I said," said the Bog Mutant. "You're in an awful lot of trouble, Ms. Passport."

The Bog Mutant pulled a notebook from his ill-fitting Temporal Transit Authority uniform. The uniform was just like any other uniform Lola had seen before—sort of blue-gray, drab, and ill fitting. But instead of being occupied by a person, it was filled with walking, talking green sludge. The seams bulged in odd places and didn't look particularly dry. The notebook in the Bog Mutant's gooey hand was also soaked, the pages thick and pasty. With its other gelatinous appendage, the creature extracted a pen, and though the pen was already slick with slime, it moistened the nib with its blunt green tongue.

"Okeydokey," said the Bog Mutant. "Let's do the questions!"

It cleared its throat, poised the pen just over its pad, and then, as if reciting from a memorized list (which it was), asked, "When did you come from?"

"Sorry?" said Lola. She was still not *quite* used to the sickening sound of its voice, but the sound was like an old friend compared to the sickly sight of its owner.

"No, no," said the guard, "You're supposed to answer the questions. You can say you're sorry later." The creature frowned. "I'm pretty sure that's how it goes. Questions first. Then accusations. Then tears and apologies. Yeah, that's right. So, Ms. Passport, *When did you come from?*"

"Oh. Uh, um . . . ," Lola replied intelligently. "I'm so sorry, Mr. . . ."

"Jeremy."

"Mr. Jeremy—"

The guard chuckled, a sound like pudding on the boil. "No, no. *Mr.* Jeremy's my father. Call me Jeremy!"

"Okay, uh . . . Jeremy," Lola tried again. "I'm so sorry, but I don't know where I am or how I got here." She glanced around the space they were standing in, which, as her eyes adjusted to the light, seemed more and more like an artificial cavern. It was as if they were standing in the storage basement of a large building—which is exactly what it was.

"I was in Newark."

"*Are*," said Jeremy, trying to make a note on his pad. "You *are* in Newark. Don't worry, tenses are hard. Especially with time travel. I had to take a whole seminar on it. Part of the training. Is. Are. Was. *Would-have-been-being-en.* I still have my flash cards, if you wanna see 'em."

"Did you say time travel?" asked Lola.

Now, here's the thing.

Lola had read hundreds of science-fiction books, had seen *Time Junkies* and *Quantum Blip: The Movie* on opening night. She'd rewatched the *Dimension Y: Clock-Smashers* miniseries more times than she could count. In those sorts of stories, it always took the hero a really long time to put it together that, *oh!*, aliens really do exist, or, *wow!*, there's suddenly a dinosaur in the bathtub, or, *holy cow!*, they'd been transported to Dimension Y. There was always lots of *But . . . ? You . . . ? How . . . ? What . . . ?* Lola always prided herself that if ever something truly fantastic happened to her, she'd be able to wrap her brain around it right quick. And indeed, she did.

"Oh!" she said with a kind of giddy pride. "I time traveled! I traveled in time!"

This, it turned out, was the absolute worst thing she could have said.

Jeremy nodded. "A confession! Oh, well, that makes things easy. Let's get you to prison, then. You'll now be liquefied for easier transport to the nearest Temporal Transit Authority detention center, where you will be horribly interrogated."

"Liquefied?" said Lola. ""But . . . ? You . . . ? How . . . ? *What . . . ?*"

"I'm under strict orders to incarcerate any known time

travelers, Ms. Passport. Just because you're the first one anyone's ever seen, that don't change the rules."

"Wait," said Lola. "You arrest time travelers, but I'm the first one?"

"There was bound to be one sooner or later." Jeremy shrugged. "Me and the guys, we've been waiting for a time traveler to show up for, oh, a little over a hundred years now. That's a pretty long coffee break." Jeremy chuckled that boiled-pudding sound again. "I know it sounds great, but it gets *really* boring. There's only so many games of pinochle a guy can play before he starts to feel pretty useless. It's great to finally put all that training to use. Now, if you'll just step up to the line and look into this light probe, you'll be melted automatically—"

"But wait!" said Lola. "I haven't done anything wrong! I didn't mean to time travel! I was just minding my own business and then I sneezed and then *bam*."

"Ignorance of the law is no excuse," said Jeremy, as if he were reciting something he'd read. Which he was.

Lola thought about how the responsible thing to do was to calmly explain how this was all crazy, that she was just an innocent bystander, and there had been a huge misunderstanding. Surely this Bog Mutant in a uniform would listen. Surely there was sense and logic in this world. Surely this Temporal Transit Authority was as reasonable as any other authority.

On second thought, Lola chose to be wildly irresponsible.

"Excuse me," she said. "Is that a zipper on your uniform?"

"Sure is," said Jeremy. "Buttons are tricky for me."

"Great. One sec?"

Before Jeremy could react, Lola yanked at his zipper. There was a startling *zzzzzzzzt!* sound, and then a big gooey splash like someone had emptied a garbage bag full of yogurt onto a concrete floor.

"Hey!" shouted Jeremy, who was now mostly a puddle.

Lola ran. Behind her, Jeremy the puddle cursed and shouted at her to come back. She leaped over boxes and dived around crates. She slid under piping and ductwork and passed what looked to be a pyramid of stacked metallic objects—like the canned-goods promotional displays at her grocery store. She ran through the storage basement, the beam from Jeremy's green flashlight receding behind her, growing fainter, until she lost track of it completely and was once again on her own.

She found herself in a gloomy stairwell and climbed up and up, coming at last to a door that opened onto a long hallway so white and clean it made her eyes burn. Picking a direction at random, she followed the bright corridor, her sneakers slapping against the polished floor.

After a while, having seen no one at all, Lola came to a large, vacant atrium. The ceiling arched beautifully overhead, gleaming and modern. The space looked as if it were meant to accommodate hundreds of visitors on a busy day.

Now, though, the great peaked foyer was empty and cold. Standing in the center was a statue. It was, upon consideration, the ugliest statue Lola had ever seen.

The bulk of the statue was a wide cylinder, about six feet high, with ridges along the side almost exactly like a tin can. Stepping closer, her breath loud in her ears, Lola saw that it was, in fact, a statue of a tin can. But why anyone would erect a statue revering a tin can—a can of baked beans, from what she could gather from the label painted on the front—was beyond her.

This is what the lettering said:

The Fogg-Bolus Hypergate & Baked Beans Corporation
"Insanely Safe!"
Est. 2399

Because it seemed like the sort of thing people did in these situations, Lola said the date aloud in a kind of awed whisper.

"Twenty-three ninety-nine?"

In a daze, she turned, hoping to see something that would make her feel better. Bay windows lined the far wall. They were circular, like portholes, and daylight streamed through. Lola looked out to get a sense of where she was, to get a vantage on her situation. What she saw didn't improve her mood.

Newark had seen better days, and that was saying something.

New Jersey in the future—for that's what Lola felt certain she was in—was a vast and barren wasteland. Where once had been highways there was now rubble and dust. Twisted scaffolding reached out from the ruin like claws, and who knew what these structures had once been, or been part of. The horizon was a jagged gray line, and nothing stirred save wisps of swirling dust. It was the emptiest place Lola had ever seen, and all at once she felt so terribly alone.

Her mother. Her sisters. Even her father. If this was the future, that meant they were all . . .

Lola decided not to think about it. Not thinking about it helped, but not by much.

She had only a moment to console herself before a new sound made her jump. Something squeaked and groaned back the way she came, and other sounds, strange and mechanical, echoed from deep within the building. Something big, perhaps the building itself, was powering up. Or powering down, Lola couldn't be sure. Thinking fast, she made for a set of panels on the far wall. One of these was open, revealing a small space just large enough to hide inside. She climbed in, closing the door and blocking out the light, the statue, and the view of the ruined world.

She held her breath. She listened. Something thumped below her. She thought she heard a door swing open somewhere. Then, so close it made her yelp, something went *click* and *buzzzzz* in the tiny compartment. Lola lurched.

She was moving.

The compartment was moving.

The pressure in her stomach told her she was hurtling upward. She was in some sort of elevator, though not an elevator for people—it was too small for that; Lola had to tuck in her knees just to fit. It was some sort of dumbwaiter, hurtling up through the lonely structure, a shiny skyscraper built on the ruins of a desiccated city in a strange and frightening future.

What Lola didn't know was that the dumbwaiter went all the way up, to the penthouse in fact, where the building's sole occupant, the heir to the Fogg-Bolus Hypergate and Baked Beans Corporation, resided.

5

"THE DUMBWAITER OPENED IN, I guess, your hallway?" Lola was explaining.

She and the boy, Phin, were now in what she supposed was Phin's kitchen. It looked fancy and sleek, clean yet cozy, nothing like her railroad kitchen at home—which was cozy in a different sort of way. Once the whole hair-dryer standoff was over, Phin had led her here and offered a seat at the breakfast bar. He'd promised her baked beans, but instead seemed to be performing an elaborate and delicate science experiment.

"Go on," Phin urged, warming up the nuclear reactor.

"I heard a voice, so I followed the sound down the hall until I saw you talking to your parents. I didn't know what to do, so I hid behind the bear." Lola glanced out the window. The wasteland stretched as far as she could see, which was now pretty far, but from this height, Lola could just make out the spires of a distant city. "Is that really New Jersey out there?"

"What's left of it since the Great Pork Fat Meltdown of 2415," said Phin, and didn't elaborate. Instead, he powered down the particle accelerator, switched off the nuclear reactor, added a dash of nutmeg, and spooned the baked beans into a happy little blue bowl.

"Here you go," he said, and passed Lola her lunch.

"Thanks." The beans smelled fabulous. Lola looked around for anything resembling a spoon. She reached out to touch the bowl, and a small blue spark arced against her finger. "Ow!" She flexed her hand. "Do beans always do that in the future?"

"Hmm? Oh, no," said Phin. "Probably static cling. Anyway."

He pulled up a stool and rested his chin on his fists, contemplating the Lola creature sitting before him. Questions raced through his mind like zero-G roadsters. Time travel was impossible. Everything he'd read on the subject said so, and he'd read extensively about pretty much every interesting thing there was to read about. And this Temporal Transit Authority—he'd never heard of it, and he'd heard of pretty much everything. The implications were staggering.

Being a good but basically self-centered kid, there was one thing that Phin just couldn't come to terms with, and that was how all this related to *him*.

"The one thing I don't understand—"

"There's just *one* thing?" said Lola. "Hey, you don't by any chance have, um, *spoons* in the future, do you?"

"The thing I don't understand is why you didn't set off the alarms. Even if you just *wham-bang* materialized in the basement, there's only supposed to be one person in this building, and that's me. We have the most sophisticated security system in the galaxy. The post office won't even send carbon-based life-forms here anymore, just androids. And not their best ones either." Phin furrowed his brow. "You should have been vaporized the second the system detected you. And I don't mean blow-dried."

"People have been trying to vaporize me a lot today," said Lola. Her stomach was making all sorts of impolite sounds. "Spoons? No? They went extinct, or . . . ?"

"Hold on," said Phin, twirling on his stool and pressing a big button on what Lola had assumed was the microwave, but was in fact a communication hub for the penthouse's security system.

"Well, howdy, buckaroos!" said the flickering cowboy face that appeared on the wall-mounted screen. "Gee whillikers, I hope yer having just the most rootin' tootin' day!"

"Uh . . . hello, Bucky," said Phin, mortified he'd forgotten to switch the personality settings to something less childish. "Bucky, what's the current status of your security protocols?"

"Well, butter my butt and call me bread!" said Bucky, the ultrasophisticated security mainframe. "You know, now that you mention it, partner, all my security protocols have been disabled! Now ain't that funnier than a donkey in a ten-gallon hat?"

"They're *disabled*?" Phin's mind reeled so hard it nearly fell over. "Who disabled them?"

"Sorry, partner. I'm not at liberty to say. But the system's been down all morning!"

"This is . . . *inexplicable*," said Phin.

"Is it?" said Lola, who was wondering how rude it would be to just slurp straight from the bowl.

"Weeeooo, that sure is a ten-dollar word, Mr. Fogg!"

"Well, turn them back on, Bucky!" Phin felt a rising panic. With the security protocols disabled, they were exposed, vulnerable . . . *anything* could get in.

"I'm afraid I can't do that, little doggies. Whoever overrode my system put a block on any new commands. The barn doors are stayin' open!"

"But *why*?"

"Well, can't says that I know," said Bucky, "but you could ask the robot."

There was a very long, unhappy silence.

"What robot?" said Lola, glancing around the kitchen.

"Why, the giant Kill-Robot coming up the elevator. Should arrive at the penthouse in about thirty seconds or so. Golly, he's a big feller! Got all sortsa lasers and ion cannons and whatnot. And he don't look too happy neither!"

Phin looked at Lola. Lola looked at Phin. These were, as is said in old novels, quite meaningful looks. Phin's meant, *You did this, didn't you, you bear-throttling girl-alien! You're the scouting party, and now the doors are open and the horribly dangerous world outside is about to get in!* And Lola's meant, *You left the door unlocked? That is the most wildly irresponsible thing a person can do! What are you, a child?*

"Bucky," said Phin, still staring at Lola in a way that made her nearly—*nearly*—lose her appetite. "Can you scan the Kill-Robot's subroutines and tell us its intentions?"

"I sure can, but I don't think you'll like the answer!"

Phin shut his eyes. "Please?"

"Welp," said Bucky, making a kind of lip-smacking sound. "I see a whole lotta death and destruction, particularly for any living thing in this penthouse. Yep, yep, there's lotsa fire and screaming and just a whole buncha *kill kill kill*. But then, that's a Kill-Robot for ya! Clue's right in the name!"

"What . . . do we do?" asked Lola.

"I was going to ask you the same question," said Phin.

And Lola saw in Phin's eyes that he was utterly terrified, which made her feel a bit bad for thinking poorly of him. And Phin saw, with almost an imperceptible degree of relief, that Lola was also terrified, and was not in league with the Kill-Robot at all, but instead was a perfectly nice girl-person who was very far from home.

"All righty, buckaroos," said Bucky. "I'm just gonna go

ahead and shut down until this is all over. Sure was nice knowing y'all!"

Phin's brain cycled through everything he'd ever seen or read about similar situations and drew a big, useless blank. Finally, at last, something was actually *happening* to him and he had absolutely no idea what to do. Lola, meanwhile, was getting ready to run—it had certainly worked so far. But there was no place to run to.

"Well—" she started.

And that's when the penthouse elevator went *ding*.

6

IF YOU ASK THE engineers of the Quazinart Home Appliance Company, they'll tell you it took decades to perfect the All-in-One D-Lux Home Kitchen Suite. Countless late nights, false starts, dead ends, missed anniversaries and children's softball games, and then, at last, breakthroughs. It was a work of aesthetic and technological genius, that all-in-one kitchen. A masterpiece of convenience and efficiency. The Sistine Chapel of the home-goods world.

But it only took two point five seconds to destroy it.

Phin and Lola cowered behind the counter as fire and destruction roared around them. Ballistic missiles and searing death rays pummeled the walls. The floor shook; chunks of plastic and wiring fell from the ceiling. Smoke choked the air.

"Attention, victims!" bellowed the enormous Kill-Robot (which, by coincidence, was itself part of the Quazinart Home Destruction and Mayhem line). "Show yourselves or be obliterated!"

“What does it want?” Lola shouted over the roar.

“I think that’s obvious,” said Phin.

They were huddled shoulder to shoulder. Phin clasped a wooden spoon that had tumbled from a smashed pantry cabinet. Lola cuddled the bowl of baked beans, which she’d grabbed without thinking and now clung to for dear life.

“Well, it’s clearly here to kill *you*,” said Phin.

“Me? It’s *your* apartment!”

“But nothing’s *ever* tried to kill me before,” shouted Phin. “You already had someone try to liquefy you today! I’m just noting a pattern is all.”

Lola had to admit he had a point, but she wasn’t ready to concede.

“Hey!” she shouted in the direction of the Kill-Robot.

“What are you doing?” Phin shouted. Nothing he’d ever read on the subject of surviving Kill-Robot attacks involved casual conversation. “That’s not . . . Don’t talk to it!”

Lola waved him off. “Hey! Kill-Robot! Yeah, I’m talking to you!”

The hail of ballistics ceased. The quiet was deafening. Dust and debris settled through the air like snow.

“What?” said the Kill-Robot.

“We’re just trying to figure out which one of us you’re here to kill,” said Lola.

“Kill-Robot is designed to kill all!”

“Yeah, we get it,” she called. “And I mean, you’re doing a

great job. But you must have been sent here to kill *one* of us, right? I mean, you don't just go around getting in elevators and killing whatever's at the top, do you?"

The Kill-Robot would have liked to do exactly that, but in this case, there had been explicit instructions. The Kill-Robot's processors whirred as it tried to sort out the quickest answer. It was not designed for thinking. It didn't like it. It wanted to get back to the smashy-blasty part.

"Well?" said Lola.

"Kill-Robot was sent to kill Phineas T. Fogg, son of Barnabus and Eliza Fogg!"

"Ha," said Lola with a smug smile. "I *told* you."

"Great," said Phin. "I feel much better now."

The interlude over, the Kill-Robot began firing again. The floor-to-ceiling unbreakable windows shattered, letting in a howling wind from outside. The gale whipped the apartment into a frenzy. Large fissures opened in the ceiling, threatening to crack at any moment. The counter they were hiding behind was getting critically close to losing its structural integrity.

There was nowhere to go, there was nowhere to hide. Lola closed her eyes and prayed for a commercial break. She would have settled for a *To be continued* with a *Next time, on Lola's Life . . . !* But no such luck.

Lola tried to think, and decided that if she were going to die, she shouldn't die hungry.

She snatched the wooden spoon from Phin's hands.

"What are you doing?" said Phin.

And then, with a slightly demented look of triumph, she said, "*This.*"

Lola took a big, heaping, steamy bite of baked beans.

And everything went *BOOM.*

And Now a Brief Aside on the History of Baked Beans

If you are reading this book sometime in the early twenty-first century, chances are you have no idea how special baked beans are.

You may think they are merely one of the most delightful side dishes ever invented, a sumptuous blend of savory and sweet, perfect on their own or with hot dogs or barbecue.

And you would be almost completely wrong. For baked beans are, in fact, one of the most miraculous things in the universe. Whether by fate or chance, this simple snack holds the secret to faster-than-light travel.

How it happened was this.

Sometime in the twenty-fourth century, just as humanity was making its first tentative, awkward contact with other species on other planets, Phineas Fogg the First, Phin's great-great-great-great-grandfather, was the owner of Fogg's Space Haulage and Trucking. Fogg's ships were some of the fastest ever built, but on the galactic scale, they moved at a snail's pace. Even his speediest vessel, the *Jules Verne*, only traveled 99.7777 percent the speed of light, which meant with pedal to the metal it would reach Alpha Centauri, the star nearest our own, in just under five years.

"Too snuggling slow," Fogg would growl, as this was an era when *snuggling* briefly became a very dirty word, for reasons the chronicler won't go into here.

So Fogg set out to develop a way to blip instantaneously across great distances. Rather than building faster ships, he conceived of portals in the fabric of space, allowing ships to pass from one star system to another in the blink of an eye. He called his invention *hypergates.*

But there was a problem. In every test, in every experiment, the portals were too unstable. Their wormholes would warp, wobble, and collapse. "Like trying to build the Lincoln Tunnel out of lemon custard," Fogg spat and flicked his own nose, which in his time was a very rude gesture.

Then, one night, something wondrous happened.

Fogg was alone in his lab. It was late, and he was tired. At the end of his rope, and with dangerously low blood sugar, Fogg went to the pantry for something to eat. Finding a can of humble baked beans, he heated himself a pot on a Bunsen burner and sat down to enjoy a steaming bowl.

Legend has it that when Fogg stood to fetch a ginger ale from the refrigerator, he knocked over his bowl, spilling its syrupy contents all over his model hypergate. "Snuggling snuggle snugs!" Fogg spat. "Maximum snuggles to the whole universe!" he bellowed, and flicked his nose so hard it sprained.

But then something happened. The hypergate twitched. It hummed. The beans began to swirl, to churn and bubble, and with a terrific blast of light, a portal opened.

Fogg watched in amazement.

The portal held.

It was one of those happy accidents that pepper the history of human achievement. By knocking over his baked beans, Phineas Fogg the First had created instantaneous interstellar travel.

Later tests revealed that the makeup of baked beans, the interplay between liquid syrup and semisolid bean, the blend of acids and lipids, of salt crystals and protein, was precisely the perfect substance for stabilizing wormholes. "All this time I wanted a quantum solution," Fogg told reporters, "when what I needed was a quantum *sauce*."

Fogg partnered with the galaxy's biggest supplier of baked beans. This happened to be Bolus Foods, a culinary canning company located on the planet Arbequia in the Oomy-Ummy Quadrant of the western arm of the Milky Way. And so the Fogg-Bolus Hypergate and Baked Beans Corporation was born. Within ten years, massive hypergates a mile wide were erected above all the most popular and important planets, and by the time Phineas the First retired, there wasn't a known species who didn't use his hypergates on a daily basis. Fogg-Bolus had united the galaxy with fast, safe, affordable travel.

As a food item, baked beans remain popular as ever. They are still spicy-sweet and sumptuous. Some now claim they can detect a slightly infinite aftertaste, a tickle on the tongue of other worlds, and an unfortunate aftereffect of gas giants. But still baked beans are eaten with delight by thousands of species across the galaxy, just as they should be.

And so this is why when Lola Ray, whose DNA tingled with quantum energy left over from her journey through time, took a bite of that most unusual and unique substance in the universe . . .

. . . everything went *BOOM.*

7

THERE WAS AN EXPLOSION.

Incredible, mind-churning white light.

Then there was darkness.

Phin really didn't want to open his eyes. He was certain he was dead, and if he could still feel things like the pounding in his temples and the aches all over his body, he figured the afterlife wasn't going to be a picnic. Better to stay flat on his stomach with his eyes shut for as long as possible.

"Phin," said a voice, a deep and burly voice, a voice of infinite wisdom and compassion. "Phin, get up."

"Nope," said Phin. "No thank you. I'm fine here."

What did he remember? A Kill-Robot, Lola eating a big spoonful of baked beans. Then the blast, a white light that obliterated his senses. And now this. Just pain, a voice, and the smell of lilacs.

Which . . . was a bit weird.

Phin opened his eyes. He saw green. Not the nasty artificial green of teleport lights and computer screens but the warm, cheerful green of grass waving in a meadow on a breezy September afternoon. He smelled and recognized—though he'd never smelled it before—the end of summer, the first crisp in the air. It was a feeling of promise, of goodness. The smell of a happy life.

And then, cutting through it all, mildew.

"Teddy?"

Phin looked up. He was lying on his belly in an enormous field. His white jumpsuit was covered in dust and scorch marks, but the world around him was pristine and alive. Hills dotted with lilacs and sunflowers rolled off infinitely into the infinite distance. The sky was a perfect blue with one or two wispy clouds. And he was alone, save for his favorite stuffed bear.

Teddy stood over him. It was an odd thing to see, partly due to the angle, and partly because he'd never seen Teddy standing before, let alone smoking a pink plastic pipe, the kind made for blowing soap bubbles. Teddy stood with one paw on what could be called his hip and puffed away, blowing little pinkish spheres into the atmosphere.

"Phin, my boy, we don't have much time," Teddy said in a voice that was nothing like his usual one. It was the wise and loving voice he'd heard a moment before, but now tinged with impatience.

Phin hefted his aching form into a sitting position.

Somewhere, birds were chirping, but otherwise all was quiet. His ears still rang from the din of the attack, but the Kill-Robot, his kitchen, and the city were gone.

And so was Lola.

Phin blinked. "Is this real?"

"It might be," said Teddy. "You are standing, or rather sitting, in the Probability Field. Where everything may or may not be. Everything here somewhat is, and somewhat isn't. It's only probable, though not likely."

"That doesn't make any sense," said Phin. "But I'm with you."

"You might be," said Teddy.

Phin pushed on. "What happened? How did I get here?"

"How you arrived is less important than what you must do when you go back."

"I'm going back?"

"Afraid so, my boy." Teddy blew a few more thoughtful bubbles. "In a moment you'll regain consciousness back in your kitchen, or what's left of it. The good news is, that nasty Kill-Robot's circuits were fried by the explosion, so you'll be quite safe. At least for the time being. *Time* being the operative word."

Phin rubbed his temples. He had a splitting headache and this conversation wasn't helping.

"Phin, look at me," said Teddy. Phin obliged. "When you

return to your world, you will have a most difficult task. I can't say whether you will succeed, or whether success is even possible. But you must try. Phin, you must try to save the universe."

It took a moment for this to sink in, but when it did, Phin felt a rush, or several rushes—first fear, then confusion, and finally excitement. All this time, all the waiting to join his parents on an adventure, and here he was, being tasked to save the universe! Tasked by a talking teddy bear, but still. He jumped to his feet.

"Yes! I knew it! I knew I was meant for something great! Oh, this is so amazing. And it totally makes sense. After all, I'm a genius and I've read pretty much everything about everything, so of course it's up to me! Haha!" He did a little dance, which would have been embarrassing if anyone other than Teddy were there to see.

Teddy scowled and bopped Phin over the head with his bubble pipe, bringing Phin's jig to a halt.

"You are not the most important person in the universe, Phineas T. Fogg!" Teddy bellowed. He straightened and cleared his throat. "But. You have just met her. Let's take a walk."

Phin and Teddy began to stroll through the Probability Field. The grass was soft under Phin's bare feet, so much softer than the carpets in his penthouse. If this was what the outside was really like—so temperate and beautiful—Phin couldn't imagine why his parents wanted him to stay indoors all the time. He felt a little crinkle in his heart, thinking of them. Something very bad was happening. Someone had tried to kill him and could be after them as well.

"You're thinking of your parents," mused Teddy.

"How did you know?"

"I didn't. It's just very likely."

"Probability Field," said Phin.

"Possibly," said Teddy. "Now listen closely, Phin, because what I'm about to tell you is of universal importance."

Phin listened.

"Almost a thousand years before you were born, a perfectly ordinary girl stepped into an X-ray machine at an airport security check, and something remarkable happened. She was thrown centuries into the future. But the moment she left, an energy signature radiated out into the universe, an energy signature that very few beings would recognize. After many hundreds of years, it traveled all the way to a distant dimension, apart from our own . . . where it was detected by some very powerful and malevolent entities. These beings are known as"—Teddy paused for dramatic effect—"*the Phan*."

"The . . . *fan*?" said Phin. "Like"—he waved his hand, stirring a light breeze—"like . . . oscillating? Three settings? That kind of fan?"

"No, not *fan*. *Phan*," growled Teddy, running low on his near-infinite patience. "With a *P* and an *h*."

"Oh," said Phin. "Okay. Go on."

"The Phan knew—"

"Wait," said Phin. "Why do they call themselves that?"

"It's . . . no one knows," growled Teddy. "That's just what they call themselves, *all right*?"

"Fine," said Phin. "Sure, okay. No need to get grumpy."

Teddy rubbed at his fuzzy temples. "Now where was I . . . ? Oh yes." He resumed their stroll. "The Phan knew that a being who had traveled through time would possess something they desired."

"What's that?" asked Phin.

"A secret," said Teddy. "Knowledge so powerful it could unravel the fabric of reality itself."

"Oh," said Phin, thinking he was keeping up but not quite. "So what's the secret?"

Teddy glared at him. "I don't know. It's a *secret*."

"Oh," said Phin. "Right."

"For centuries the Phan plotted, making themselves ready for the day the girl would rematerialize at some point in the future. Using their influence, they set up a special organization, the Temporal Transit Authority, to monitor all of space for the day the girl appeared."

Teddy paused to pluck a possible dandelion from the possible ground and brought it to his button nose.

"Hold on two microseconds," said Phin. "If Lola is so special, why did the Kill-Robot come to kill *me*? Or was that just an unbelievably huge coincidence?" Thinking he had Teddy dead to rights, he added, "That sounds very *improbable*."

"Quite possibly," said Teddy, unflustered. "But you see, Phin, the Phan need *you* as well. Or rather, they need something you and your family possess. To *gain access* to Ms. Ray, the Phan will need to bring themselves across to *our* dimension. And to do that, they will need a gateway. Or rather, a network of gateways powerful enough to bridge the gap between their dimension and ours."

"*Hypergates*," said Phin.

"Almost certainly," said Teddy. "And I'm afraid that's not all. They've enlisted the aid of a very nasty person. A person who can give them access to those hypergates. A person with something to gain by the hostile overthrow of the Fogg-Bolus Corporation."

With a flourish, Teddy blew on the dandelion, releasing its seeds. They floated and dipped, and then began to do something very un-seedlike. They rearranged themselves in a distended circle in the air just above Teddy and Phin. The air inside began to shimmer, and an image resolved itself.

The image was of an Arbequian, with upsetting little teeth and a pair of unflattering spectacles. He sat behind an oak desk that was far too large for him, before which stood two Temporal Transit Authority Bog Mutants who seemed to be delivering some kind of report. The Arbequian was half listening, staring out the window, steepling his little fingers.

He could not have looked more evil.

"Goro Bolus!" said Phin.

"Yes," said Teddy. "Your parents' partner and thirty-three-percent shareholder in the Fogg-Bolus Corporation."

"I knew it!" said Phin. "I *knew* that guy was up to no good. I should have *told* my parents. They should have *listened* to me! And now . . . and now . . ." Phin thought he might hyperventilate. "I'd like to pass out now," he said.

"You already are," said Teddy. "Passed out, that is."

"Then I'd like to pass in. As quickly as possible."

Teddy took Phin by the shoulders lovingly—that, or he was preparing to give Phin a headbutt.

"Phin, the very fate of the universe is at stake," said Teddy. "You must keep Lola from falling into the hands of Goro Bolus and the Temporal Transit Authority. If she does, all of us are doomed." He squeezed Phin's shoulders tighter. "The both of you must get off this planet and as far away from Earth's solar system as you can."

"But, but . . . ," Phin stammered, a sudden hollowness eating at his gut. "I've never been off Earth. I've never even left my apartment!"

Teddy's eyes narrowed, his soft, fuzzy mouth set hard. "Old friend, your life has been leading to this. You have taken an interest, Phineas, in the world outside your door, and now you must use that knowledge to fulfill your destiny."

The hollowness in Phin's stomach didn't disappear, but

it was joined by a second feeling. A sort of warm, tremulous wave, which moved up his spine and into his heart. It was the feeling of someone believing in him, someone trusting him, someone relying on him. It was the feeling of getting exactly what you've always hoped for—and it was terrible.

"Teddy," said Phin, "do you know . . . will we make it?"

"Probably," said Teddy, "not."

And with that, someone pinched Phin's nose so hard, he woke the heck up.

8

"OUCH!" SAID PHIN, SITTING bolt upright in what was left of his kitchen. "Ow ow ow!"

"Wake the heck up!" shouted Lola. She'd been shouting it over and over and had such a good momentum going, it was hard to stop. "Wake up! Wake up!"

"I'm up!" said Phin, rubbing his sore nose "I'm up. I'm up. I'm . . ." He was up all right, and right back where he didn't want to be. The air was thick with the scent of ionized particles and melted plastic. "I think I'd like to pass out again."

"Well, you can't," said Lola. "We have to get out of here!"

Phin glanced around, surprised not to be under fire. "What happened to the Kill-Robot?"

The Kill-Robot in question lay sprawled on the linoleum, its red eyes dark. Small hisses and clicks emanated from its metallic shell.

"That's what I'm trying to tell you," said Lola. "I ate the beans, and there was this big flashy explosion, and whatever it was knocked you unconscious and shut down the

Kill-Robot, apparently." Lola glanced over her shoulder at the slumbering battle machine. "But according to Bucky, it's rebooting and will be back online in—"

"Two minutes and thirty seconds, ya'll!" chimed Bucky.

"He's been doing that like once a minute," grumbled Lola.

Suddenly Phin snapped to attention as if someone had slapped him. "The elevator!"

"Has been disabled!" Bucky said cheerfully. "As have all delivery shafts and maintenance ports."

"We can't get downstairs," said Lola, who'd learned all of this while Phin was unconscious and didn't want to go through it all again.

"I know what to do!" said Phin.

With a plucky snap of his fingers, Phin leaped to his feet and dashed into his bedroom. Lola didn't think it would be much safer in there but followed nonetheless, casting a wary glance at the dormant Kill-Robot, which seemed to be twitching more than it was a moment ago.

What she found in the bedroom did not reassure her. Phin was in the corner, throttling his teddy bear. Teddy's head bobbled back and forth on his thick neck.

"Talk to me, you stupid bear!" he shouted. "Tell me what I'm supposed to do!"

"Um," said Lola.

"Let's play a game!" said Teddy.

"Two minutes until Kill-Robot reboot, cowpokes!" offered

Bucky over the penthouse's public address system.

"Phin?" said Lola.

Phin dropped to the floor, defeated. Teddy flopped onto his side, his friendly expression unchanged.

"I don't know what to do," Phin said.

"Okay, well," said Lola, "neither do I. So at least we're on the same page there."

"Lola, you don't understand." Phin got to his feet and began to pace. "I had a vision! Teddy said my whole life had been leading to this. That I'm supposed to save the universe."

"He . . . did?" said Lola, eyeing the stuffed toy. On top of everything, the one person who seemed to be on her side had gone totally bananas, which was pretty much on par with the rest of her day. "And how are you going to do that?"

"By rescuing you," said Phin, taking her by the shoulders much as Teddy had done with him moments before in the Probability Field.

Lola blinked, stunned for several reasons. "O-oh. Thank you, Phin."

"But first we need to get off this planet."

"Okay," she said in a less misty-happy way. "Wait a minute, *what*? How?"

"Fellas?" said Bucky.

"Show yourselves, victims!" came a thunderous robotic voice from the next room. The sound of reinvigorated ion-cannon shots began to pound the walls. "I will find you!"

"We'll need a ship," Phin was saying. "And a hypergate to get us out of this solar system. Also snacks. Should we bring snacks?"

A blast from an ion cannon blew the wall behind them into chunks.

"Phin," said Lola, "I think before any of that, we need to escape this *room*!"

"Escape?" said Bucky. "Well, heckfire and horny toads, why didn't you say so?"

And with that a door in the far wall slid open, revealing a perfectly good escape pod.

THE ESCAPE POD WAS on the large side for an escape pod, but that's still not very big. Phin and Lola clambered into what amounted to the rear hatch. Inside were two rows of seats facing a transparent view screen, much like a windshield. Below were the controls and steering wheel. It all reminded Lola of something, but she didn't have time to think what.

"What are you doing?" Lola asked Phin, who was fishing in what amounted to the glove compartment.

"I'm looking for a manual."

"You don't know how to fly this thing?"

"I didn't know it existed until a second ago!" Phin snapped. "Although I did a whole analysis last year about how there was almost certainly a hidden compartment in my room. I gotta say, feels pretty good to be vindicated—"

"Phin!"

"Oh, look! There's an on switch."

Phin turned a small knob on the control panel, and the escape pod hummed to life.

"Allow me entrance, puny targets!" the Kill-Robot bellowed from the next room, along with a lot of other nonsense about burning, flaying, and boiling them alive.

Something nagged at Lola's mind—apart from the obvious imminent death. "Are we forgetting something? Oh! Wait!"

"What? Where are you going?" Phin called.

To his horror, Lola leaped out the back hatch and disappeared into the smoky chaos of his room. Before Phin had the chance to scramble after, Lola clambered back aboard, lugging someone behind her by the mildewed paw.

"I thought we shouldn't leave him," she said, positioning Teddy in the back seat.

"Teddy!" said Phin. "Lola, I could kiss you, but that would be incredibly gross."

With a flourish Phin yanked a lever on the dashboard and the rear hatch snapped shut. At that same instant the Kill-Robot smashed into the bedroom behind them. The rear window of the escape pod was swathed in a constellation of red laser sights.

"Destroy! Destroy! Destroy!" said the Kill-Robot.

"What are you waiting for?" said Lola, as Phin was clearly waiting for something.

Phin was looking through the windshield at the far end of the escape pod's launching track, where the emergency breakaway wall was all that separated them from open sky and safety. He cleared his throat, a small sound, barely audible in the cacophony.

"Have you ever wanted to do something your whole life and then when you get the chance to do it, you're not so sure?"

At least, this is the very meaningful and vulnerable thing Phin would have said if Lola hadn't reached around him and smashed the big red button marked JUST GO.

With a tremendous roar, the pod exploded out of its dock and burst, wheeling and reeling, into the sunlight far above the wastes of New Jersey. It spun, twisted, dipped, got its bearings, and then rocketed straightaway toward the Hudson River and the stratosphere beyond.

"*I've been waiting for this moment my whole life . . . ,*" thought the little escape pod.

Phin and Lola were too busy screaming in delirious, utterly mad relief to think anything at all.

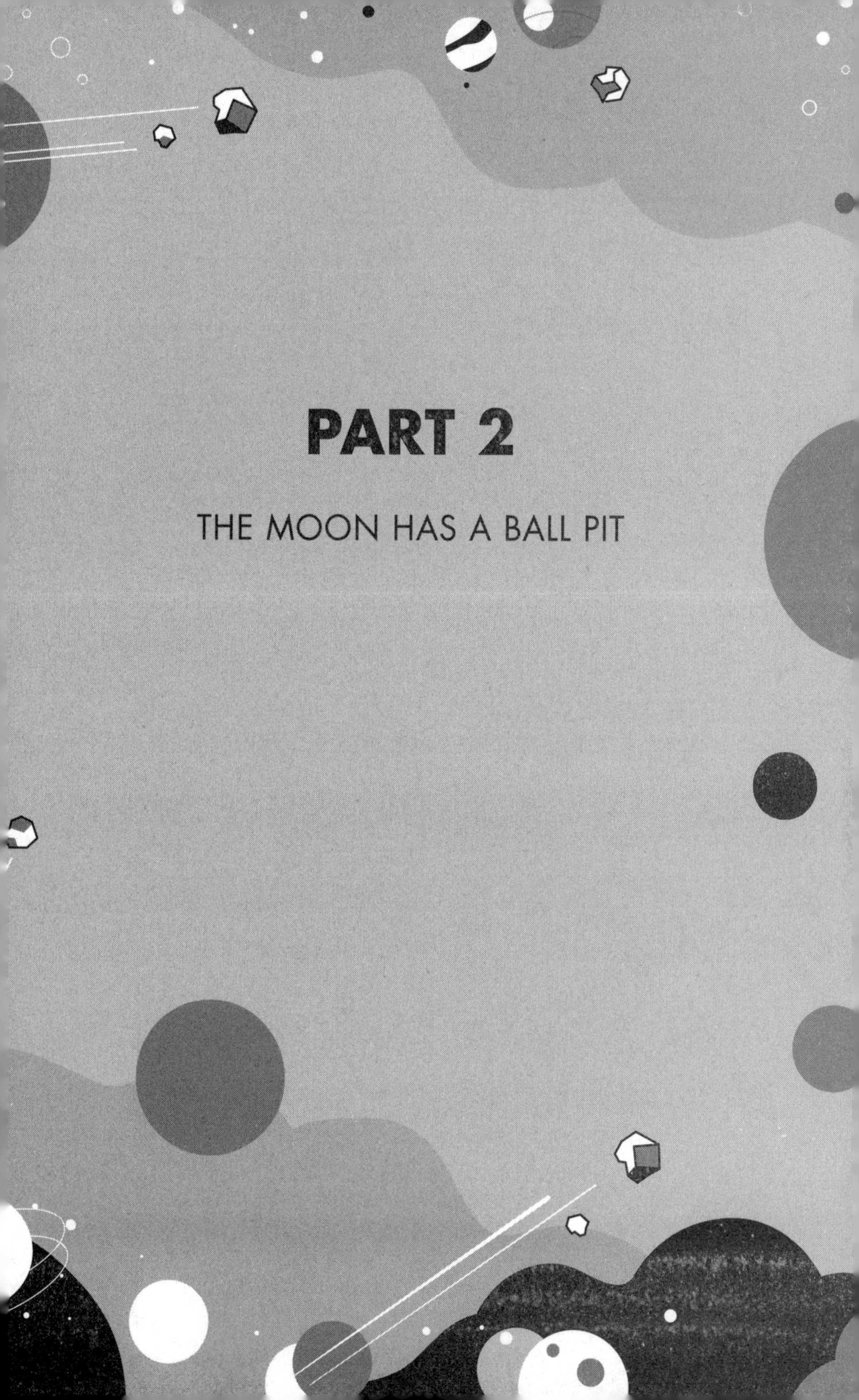

PART 2

THE MOON HAS A BALL PIT

10

LOLA SETTLED INTO THE back seat as the escape pod hurtled through the sky. Her muscles jumped and twizzled, but, by degrees, she caught her breath. The thrum of the engines was soothing, and soon they'd left the wastes of New Jersey far below and were arcing gracefully into the clouds. From the window she saw the new cities of Earth stretching up and down the eastern seaboard, glad that whatever had happened in New Jersey—that Great Pork Fat Meltdown or whatever Phin had called it—at least spared the rest of the planet.

By now she'd figured out what the interior of the escape pod reminded her of: it was almost exactly like her mother's old Volvo station wagon—right down to the worn leather seats and the Christmas-tree-shaped air freshener dangling from the rearview telepathic interface. She remembered the last time they'd all driven together as a family—to take Papa to the airport. She remembered the ride back, Momma behind the wheel and very quiet, and her sisters, who were too young to understand anything, screaming and fighting and laughing. She remembered thinking how very much she wanted to be alone right then. Just to be by herself and miss her papa without anyone needing anything or asking for anything.

Now she was truly alone, and she missed them all so keenly the back of her eyes stung.

But just then the little escape pod shuddered and lurched, and they broke through the cloud cover. The deep black of space closed around them like a great pair of wings, and out the window, the sky became brilliant with stars, a cookies-and-cream swash the likes of which she'd never seen from the ground. She was in space. She was *in space.* And all at once the wonder and terror of where she was and what she was doing flooded her veins, and she let out a wild laugh.

"What's so funny?" asked Phin.

"Nothing, it's just . . . ," she said, feeling a bit embarrassed. Lola cleared her throat. "Have you ever seen the show *Dimension Y*?"

"Never heard of it."

Of course no one would remember a television show that must now be centuries old. She swallowed.

"It's just," she said, "whenever they showed outer space it was always just this flat black plane with stars. I never realized it was so . . ." Lola searched for the word. *Big* wasn't it. *Three-dimensional* was closer, but not really. She stared out the window at the void into which they were rushing—not a black matte backdrop but a swirling ocean of light and dark, navies and indigos, and pink-yellow-blue planets hanging like teardrops.

It was just . . . *everything.*

"Sorry," she said, catching herself. "This must be like an everyday thing for you."

When Phin said nothing, she glanced at his profile.

"Not exactly," he said.

He was seated in what Lola would have called the driver's seat, though the pod seemed to be steering itself. A tablet rested on his lap, and whatever he was doing looked complicated. Charts and tables swirled on the tablet's surface, illuminating Phin's features, spooky in the gloom.

"Where are we going?" she asked.

"To Luna. We can use the hypergate there to get as far away from Earth as possible."

"What's Luna?"

Without looking he pointed out the window toward the silvery wedge floating off to their left.

"You mean the moon?"

This time he looked up, his expression one of utter astonishment at just how stupid she was.

"It's not *the* moon," Phin spat. "It's *a* moon. There are billions of planets in the galaxy, Lola, and most of them have moons. You can't go around calling Earth's moon *the* moon like it's got some kind of special privileges."

She sat back, stung. After a long, smoldering silence, she said, "You know, hey, where I'm from it's called *the* moon. And," she added, "where *I'm* from, people don't act like jerks just because other people don't know things that there is no possible way *they could possibly know.*"

She'd told him good—as the oldest of three siblings, she was excellent at arguing.

Phin did look a bit stunned, but he gathered himself. As an only child, Phin was excellent at disregarding any opinion other than his own.

"Well," he said, "you might be interested to know that while you're back there gawping, I am trying to chart a route for us. Which should be easy, but all I've got is this stupid little tablet, and the reception out here is practically zero, and if I were at *home* with all my *stuff* and a *decent Extraweb* connection I could do it in a snap! But because I'm *here* and my home has been *destroyed* and stuff, it's a whole heckuva lot *trickier*, especially when I have to pause every ten minutes to explain things to an under-evolved, know-nothing, temporal pain in the neck like you!"

The silence that followed was practically volcanic.

"You haven't been to outer space before, have you?" said Lola.

"As it happens . . . no," he finished meekly.

Lola crossed her arms and smirked. "I knew it."

Phin turned on her. "Well, *what is it*, then?"

"What is . . . what?" said Lola.

"*It*," said Phin. "You know exactly what I'm talking about."

Lola wasn't sure how to reply to this. "I . . . huh?"

"The *secret*." He said this in a tone at once hushed and snarling. "You've got a secret, haven't you? Don't lie."

Lola's mind trilled through all the secrets she had or could possibly have. None of them seemed relevant to the situation at hand. She'd once stolen gum from Mr. Patel's bodega. She secretly thought the *Star Wars* prequels weren't that bad. She didn't floss. What could he possibly mean?

"Phin, what are you talking about?"

"Teddy said—I mean," he corrected, stumbling, "I dreamed or . . . had a vision or . . . went to this *place* when I was knocked out. And I saw Teddy. And he told me that you . . ." He trailed off, shook his head.

"What? What is it?" said Lola.

"Well, he told me you have this *secret*. And there are these things from another dimension, the *Phan*. Like with a *P-h*. And they're teaming up with Bolus, this nasty guy who helps run my parents' company, so they can break through into our dimension—and it's all because of you. Because you've got some secret knowledge that they need. At least, that's what . . . my . . . bear . . . said."

"Oh," said Lola. "Oh," she said again, hoping it would help somehow. It didn't.

She felt that uneasy, slightly seasick feeling you get when

you find out someone has been talking about you behind your back, only a million times worse.

Lola didn't know what these *Phan* people wanted with her. How did they even know who she was? She certainly didn't have any secret knowledge.

"I don't know," she said at last. "I honestly don't know."

Phin stared at her hard. Then his expression softened. "Okay."

"Okay?"

"Yeah, okay."

"Good," said Lola.

The engines hummed along, oblivious to the tense silence they were underscoring. Lola felt tears prickling the backs of her eyes again, and swallowed them. After a while she glanced at the back of Phin's head, the pinch of his shoulders. She suddenly realized she wasn't the only one having a frightening and confusing day.

"Hey dummy," she said.

Phin looked around. "What?"

"Boop," said Lola, and booped him on the nose with Teddy's paw.

Phin blinked. He made the face of a boy who's just been booped on the face with a teddy bear paw. (You know the one.) He cleared his throat, then looked back at his screen, trying, and failing, to suppress a blush.

11

MEANWHILE, IN THE SMOLDERING cavern that had until recently been the radically overpriced and underinsured Fogg penthouse, a lot of very unpleasant people gathered. They were all unpleasant to different degrees and in different ways. Four of them were unpleasant for being monumentally stupid. These four happened to be Bog Mutants, a species of dim-witted and soggy-brained gelatinous creatures bred for the sole purpose of performing menial, unpleasant, or dangerous jobs that nobody else wanted to do. These four Bog Mutants happened to work for an organization called the Temporal Transit Authority, and even as Bog Mutants go, they were dumb.

All of them were named Jeremy. All Bog Mutants everywhere are named Jeremy. This keeps things simple, as all Bog Mutants look alike (even to each other) and it's very difficult to tell them apart. Furthermore, all Bog Mutants everywhere are born—or, more accurate to say, they *bud*—from a single supermassive fungus core, which lives in darkness at the heart of a hollow asteroid not far from Alpha Centauri.

This supermassive fungus core is called Mr. Jeremy.

The fifth unpleasant creature in the room was perhaps the most unpleasant of all. In fact, all things being equal, the fifth unpleasant creature, who was now tapping his little foot and sniffling angrily, was, on last check, the most unpleasant thing in our galaxy. His name was Goro Bolus, 33.3 percent shareholder in the Fogg-Bolus Hypergate and Baked Beans Corporation. He had been tasked by interdimensional beings he'd never met to do a number of unsavory things, one of which was take over the Fogg-Bolus Hypergate and Baked Beans Corporation. This job involved subterfuge, kidnapping, and murder, three things that came easily to this nasty and egomaniacal little bean.

"Well," snapped Bolus, peering from behind his unflattering little spectacles. "Did you find anything?"

"I found this," said Jeremy, holding up a piece of debris that was in no way relevant to the investigation at hand.

Bolus gritted his teeth. "Did you find anything *useful*?"

"What about this?" said another Jeremy, offering a comb. "You could use it to comb your little beard."

There was a sixth person in the room, who, by comparison, was less unpleasant than the others, but still wasn't the kind of gal you'd want at your birthday party. Her name was Gretta. She was tall, and smartly dressed, and wore very stylish glasses, and carried a sophisticated tablet on which she was taking notes. Her skin had the pale glossy sheen—and shade—of lime pudding. She was, to the best of her or anyone else's knowledge, the only female Bog Mutant in existence, and furthermore she was, for reasons no one had ever adequately explored, extremely intelligent.

Gretta was also the director of the Temporal Transit Authority, the organization whose sole reason for being was to locate and capture time travelers—of which there had only ever been one. Like Bolus, Gretta knew her direct superiors were strange interdimensional beings with unfathomable motives of their own. Unlike Bolus, Gretta wasn't motivated by blind greed.

"Readings indicate there was a massive discharge of quantum energy in this vicinity less than two hours ago," she said, scrolling through her tablet's interface. "It was most certainly *the* girl."

"Hmm." Bolus stroked his wispy little beard. "And the Kill-Robot?" The robot's fate wasn't all that important, but still, the thing had been expensive, and you don't get to run a multizillion-dollar corporation without knowing how to get a good return on an investment.

"Its electronic brain must have been fried in the shock wave, hence its . . . well, rather optimistic leap," said Gretta.

(The Kill-Robot had, apparently, thrown itself out the escape hatch in an attempt to pursue its target, and now lay in several hundred pieces on the rocks below. Kill-Robots aren't particularly intelligent, but are at least supposed to know they can't fly. The sales rep from the Quazinart Home Appliance Company had apologized for the malfunction, and had asked Bolus if he'd tried turning the Kill-Robot off and then turning it back on again. Bolus had the sales rep vaporized, and found the process immensely satisfying.)

"Which one of you actually saw the girl?" Bolus asked, addressing the quartet of Bog Mutants.

"Um," said one, "I think it was Jeremy."

"Are you sure?" said another. "I thought it was me."

"That's what I said," said a third, who was so dim he didn't even realize he wasn't the Jeremy who spoke in the first place.

"That one," said Gretta, pointing to the littlest of the Jeremys. This Jeremy had recently been sloshed out of his uniform by an Earth girl with very quick fingers, and by the time his brothers showed up to pile him back in, some of his less viscous bits had evaporated. He now stood a few inches shorter than the rest, which was convenient for singling him out, but awfully embarrassing for him.

"My boy," said Bolus, grinning and patting Jeremy on a soggy shoulder.

"What about him?" said Jeremy.

"Tell us how you met the girl," said Gretta, who didn't like Bolus touching her agents.

Jeremy shrugged, his body rippling in his suit. "Well, er, Mr. Bolus, sir, me and the boys were just sitting around drinking coffee and playing pinochle"—Jeremy looked very much as if he wished he were still doing just that—"when the call came in. *Illegal temporal dislocation*," he said, sounding out the long and difficult phrase. "Someone had to take the call. Figured it was a false alarm. Those happen every hundred years or so. Teleport goes weird, or someone forgets to wind their watch and then it's *oh look out fellas, we got a time traveler!* Usually the person of interest is disintegrated for wasting Authority time. But still, no harm, no foul!"

Bolus's menacing grin tightened like a vise. "Well, it's a good thing you didn't disintegrate *this* one, officer, because *this* time traveler is the real thing. The only time traveler *ever*, and that makes her very important to our benefactors."

Jeremy scratched at his ear. A bit came away and became part of his finger. It seemed like he'd just been told he'd done a good job, so he smiled.

"We should take a look at the security footage," said Gretta, tapping a few keystrokes on her tablet.

There was a click and hum and then a poorly rendered cowboy appeared on the wall-mounted video screen. "Well, slap my face and call me Fanny, hello there everybody! Sure getting a lot of visitors today!"

"Security System," said Gretta. "I need—"

"Name's Bucky!"

"Hey, a cowboy!" said one of the Jeremys, and clapped.

"Bucky," said Bolus. "Do you remember me?"

"Why, I sure do," Bucky said with cheerful country

enthusiasm. "You're the fella who overrode my security protocols so that big feller with all the guns and stabby parts could get in. Howya doin'?"

"We need to see the security footage of this afternoon," Bolus explained.

"Specifically the girl who was here," Gretta added.

"Well, no problem, just two shakes of a donkey tail!"

The image flickered, wobbled, and was replaced by a screenshot from earlier that afternoon. Two children cowered behind a countertop. One of them Bolus knew well—the son of his idiotic partners, the interminably-on-holiday Foggs. The other was a girl. Just a girl. A girl his associates—Bolus called them his "associates" when in fact they were more like his lords and masters—had been awaiting for a very long time.

"There," Gretta said, tapping the image. "Is that her?"

Jeremy hesitated. Being praised earlier had been a first-time thing for him, and he really wanted it to happen again. But he wasn't sure which answer the little bean man wanted to hear.

"That's her," he said hesitantly, "that's the girl. She's quick too." Jeremy waited for praise, but none came. He tried adding more detail. "Uh, her name's Passport."

"Passport, eh?" Bolus tugged at his beard. "Well Ms. *Passport*. We are going to see each other very soon."

A little while later Bolus and Gretta were alone in the elevator as it fell away from the penthouse.

"This could be it. After all this time," said Gretta. Her entire life had been dedicated to the cause of the Temporal Transit Authority, and now that her purpose was nearly fulfilled, she felt a strange mixture of elation and wariness. Neither of these things showed on her smooth and impassive features.

"Make sure you wipe the security system's memory," growled Bolus. "None of this can get back to me."

Gretta tapped her tablet. "It's done."

"Send out a press bulletin. 'Fogg Penthouse Destroyed by Gas Leak' or something. Very tragic."

Gretta rankled. She didn't like Goro Bolus, the creepy little bean man with his creepy little beard and ugly glasses. And she especially didn't like him ordering her around. But working with Bolus was part of her job, and it wasn't her place to question her superiors. The Phan needed Bolus, just as they needed Gretta and her army of Jeremys.

"I have a report from the penthouse's manifest as well," she said. "The escape pod is a Volvo Rescue Wagon, outfitted with a Majulook SuperFake cloaking device. I'll send out an all-points bulletin. Perhaps the local authorities will spot them." She hesitated. "What are you going to do about the Foggs?"

Bolus grinned. It was unsettling. "Barnabus and Eliza have no doubt received an alert their apartment was destroyed and will attempt to contact their son." He steepled his little fingers. "I'll reach out—as a *concerned friend*. Let them know their boy's gone completely mad with shock, and possibly gas poisoning, and is quite likely," Bolus added with a wicked sneer, "*hallucinating*."

"That's . . . a good idea." Gretta had to admit the little bean was ruthlessly cunning.

"Of course it's a good idea. Our time has nearly come, my dear. All the planning and waiting, the searching and scheming. Soon we will have our reward."

"Duty is its own reward," said Gretta.

"Well, you're welcome to it," said Bolus. "I have bigger things in mind."

Though he was a small creature, Goro Bolus's brain was considerably more powerful than those of most other life-forms he was likely to meet. His neurons fired billions of times per second, calculating, planning, rejiggering his schemes to best utilize the recent events.

But there was something puzzling about this whole situation.

"What are the odds, Gretta," said Bolus, "what do you think the odds are that the very girl you've been tasked with finding should appear in the very home of the very boy I need to kill?"

"Seventy-six billion to one," said Gretta, showing him the results on her Probability App, "In the *ludicrously unlikely* range. But then, the forecast did call for a *partly-to-super-unlikely* weekend."

Bolus shook his head, pondering this. "It's almost as if the universe is trying to make things easy for me."

He laughed a pompous, chortling little laugh. Goro Bolus was smart enough to appreciate such phenomenal luck. He was also the sort of jerk who actually believed he deserved it.

Gretta shivered.

12

IN THE EARLY DAYS of Earth's space program, the planet's first major spaceport was in Newark. Great launch towers cast their shadows across Newark Bay, and interstellar cruisers crisscrossed the sky over Brighton and Bayonne. High above, Earth's first fully operational hypergate hung like a shimmering hoop earring, its eye a swirling, bubbling, reddish-brown vortex of baked beans.

Then came the Great Pork Fat Meltdown of 2415. A glitch and some bad wiring caused the hypergate's reactor core to go nuclear. The explosion reduced most of New Jersey to a smoldering radioactive wasteland, destroying electronic equipment and every last digital record on the planet. Humanity was returned to the Dark Ages, and it took nearly a generation for the world's technology to be redeveloped.

Another consequence of this disaster not often acknowledged was that the millions of alien species who'd been tuning in to Earthling television broadcasts suddenly lost their signal and were unable to find out, ever, how their favorite shows ended. It was as if a million viewers across the galaxy cried out . . . as their programs were suddenly silenced.

Earth's next spaceport was built on Luna (where there was less to destroy, should something ever go wrong again). As humanity spread across the galaxy, New Jersey—now looking a lot like the surface of the moon—remained uninhabitable until the Fogg family, intent to prove that the radiation had long abated, built their personal skyscraper on its ruins. Phin's home stood as a monument to the disaster, as solitary as its lone occupant. That was, until today.

Phin explained all of this to Lola as they approached the moon's glittering surface. The spaceport spanned thousands of miles, encased in a great transparent dome so large Lola could make out clouds and weather systems swirling beneath its surface. Suspended above it all was the hypergate. Hundreds of miles in diameter, the enormous space ring rotated slowly in the dark, its rim aglow with tiny lights. Within its ring a great whirlpool of baked beans seemed to tunnel through space itself.

"Beautiful," said Lola.

"Yes," said Phin, trying very hard to seem like he saw this sort of thing all the time. "I guess it is, isn't it?"

He punched a few buttons on the console and the Rescue Wagon began to descend.

"Aren't we going through the hypergate?" Lola asked.

"No, we're too small. It'd be like"—Phin struggled to

find a twenty-first century metaphor—"like trying to take a scooter on a freeway. We'd get torn apart. We'll need to board a larger vessel." He adjusted their descent, pitching their nose lower. He was slowly getting the hang of this driving thing, which was much more fun (and really, less complicated) than the online simulators. "That hypergate is going to take us so far from Bolus and his army of jerks, they'll never find us."

"But where will we go?" Lola asked.

Phin waggled his eyebrows at her. "Anywhere we want."

Lola tried not to smile, then gave up trying. *Anywhere.*

Down, down they fell, toward the dome's commercial traffic gate. For the first time since they rocketed out of the Fogg penthouse, Lola felt a bit of vertigo.

"Don't puke," said Phin.

"Shuddup," said Lola.

"Seriously, don't puke in here."

"Stop saying *puke*!" said Lola, and shut her eyes.

Just then the pod filled with a deafening sound, a horrible tinkling, ringing, thunderous melody pouring out from hidden speakers all around them.

"What's that?" Lola said, her nausea forgotten.

"Oh no," said Phin. "No no no." His fingers whirred over the controls. "How do you block it? End end end!"

A message began to flash on the windshield. It read *Incoming . . .*

"What is it?" Lola shouted. She searched the sky above them, the crisscrossing lines of space traffic below, searching for whoever or whatever was attacking them. "Is it a space torpedo? Are we going to die?"

"It's not an attack!" said Phin. "It's . . . a ringtone!"

Lola gawped at him.

"A *what*?"

Phin swallowed. His expression chilled her to the core.

"My parents are calling."

With a trembling finger, Phin pressed a small green icon marked *Answer*.

The noise stopped. Time seemed to hold its breath. Lola expected small holographic images of Phin's parents to appear on the dash, since that's what happened in sci-fi movies.

This is what happened instead:

The control panel before her vanished. As did the ship. As did space. As did everything save for Phin and Lola, who suddenly found themselves on the veranda of a luxurious hotel suite overlooking the blue crystal beaches and ultra-black sea of the Frillian Riviera.

"Whaaaaa . . . ," said Lola.

The sky was a mottled pink, dotted with small, lukewarm stars. They were seated—or appeared to be seated—at a small iron table set with a sumptuous brunch. There was coffee, Neptunian eggs Benedict (which is like the Earth version except three feet tall and it sings to you), frothy mimosas, and a copy of the Neptunian Sunday *Times*. "Appeared" to be seated because all of this, from the basilisk stucco to the smell of freshly brewed coffee, was an extrasensory holographic projection. Phin and Lola were in reality still seated in their Volvo Rescue Wagon, and this out-of-body experience was merely a (very) long-distance phone call.

Across the table sat two pleasant people in matching pink bathrobes. Both held drinks, were splendidly tanned, and looked extremely concerned.

"Phinny!" said Eliza Fogg.

"Buddy, what's going on?" said Barnabus.

"Hey guys," said Phin, taking in his surroundings. "Nice brunch."

"Phineas, we are worried sick about you!" said his father, putting down a mimosa. "We're so glad you're okay!"

"Oh, baby, I wish I could hug you right now," said Phin's mother, tears soaking into her avocado face peel. "My poor sweetheart, you must have been terrified!"

Phin smiled a tight smile. In truth, he felt guilty. If you'd asked, he'd have told you it simply hadn't occurred to him to call his parents after the Kill-Robot attack—which would have been bad enough. But in truth, it *had* occurred to him. He just hadn't wanted to.

"What happened?" Eliza asked. "We heard there was some kind of gas leak."

"Thank goodness you're all right. Are you all right?" asked Barnabus.

"Gas leak?" said Phin, a cold wave rolling through him despite the temperate (if synthetic) air.

"We've been trying to reach you for hours," said Barnabus. "Your mother hasn't touched her breakfast, she's been so worried."

Lola was only half paying attention. Her shock at suddenly finding herself projected onto a distant planet had subsided quickly. In fact, she'd already found something new to shock and mystify her. Namely, the eggs Benedict.

"Um, Phin," she whispered. "The eggs . . . uh, I think the eggs are singing to me . . ."

"*Whatever Lola wants . . . ,*" the Neptunian Eggs Benedict crooned, "*Lola gets . . .*"

"Relax," Phin said to her. "The eggs aren't singing."

"Good," said Lola. "I thought I was losing my—"

"It's the hollandaise," he added. "Mom, Dad, listen. It wasn't a gas leak. We were attacked by a Kill-Robot!"

His parents winced. Phin wasn't sure what kind of reaction he was expecting, but it certainly wasn't wincing. They winced with compassion, concern, a deep-down-to-your-core love, but still . . .

Barnabus turned to his wife. "Space madness," he whispered.

"Gas poisoning," she mouthed.

"What?" shouted Phin. "I'm not mad or poisoned! It happened! Tell them, Lola!"

Lola straightened, cleared her throat, and tried to ignore the hollandaise, which had transitioned smoothly into a medley of show tunes. "Hello," she said. "It's nice to meet you, um, Mr. and Mrs. Fogg."

"Hello," the Foggs said in unison, if uncertainly. "Phin, who is this?" asked Eliza.

"Mom, Dad, this is Lola."

Lola waved.

"She's from . . ." Phin thought of the best way to explain this without getting too sidetracked. "Hoboken."

"Ah," said Barnabus.

"That explains it," said Eliza.

"Sorry?" said Lola.

"*Gotta dance!*" sang the hollandaise.

"Lola, tell them what happened." Phin's eyes were pleading. He'd seemed less uncomfortable when he was being shot at. She swallowed.

"Well, uh, Mr. and Mrs. Fogg, what Phin says is true. We were attacked by a giant Kill-Robot. It was sent to kill Phin. It even said so."

"Excuse me," said Eliza, "but what exactly were you doing in our apartment?"

"Phin, who is this young woman," said Barnabus, "and what are her intentions?"

"Guys!" said Phin. "Please listen to me! The Kill-Robot was sent by Goro Bolus! He's out to get us! He's in league with some super-evil interdimensional beings!"

"Phin," Eliza Fogg said quietly. "Honey, it's not that we don't believe you. It's just . . . we think you may not be thinking straight."

"Who told you all this?" said Barnabus.

"It was . . ." Phin hesitated. "Well, it was Teddy."

"Your bear."

"Yes."

"Who only says one phrase."

"Yes. Well, he could talk quite a bit in the . . . um . . ." Phin floundered. "You see, Teddy could talk in the . . . uh . . . Probability . . . the Probability Field."

"The Probability . . . what?" said Eliza.

Phin steeled himself. "I was sent there by a quantum shock wave, caused by Lola eating a spoonful of baked beans." He cleared his throat. "At least, I'm pretty sure that's what happened. She's from the twenty-first century, by the way."

There was a long, pregnant pause. So pregnant it was having triplets.

Phin felt ridiculous and pleading, while his parents were wincing again, in the way you might at the little old man in the park who barks at trees.

Then something that no one expected to happen, happened.

"Hey!" shouted Lola Ray, and clapped her hands like

someone trying to wake a sleepwalker. The Foggs jumped. "Hey now! You've got to believe him! He is your son!"

The whole table stared at her. Even the hollandaise was taken aback.

"Things are really not okay!" Lola fumed. "Things are really messed up and someone is trying to kill your son and probably you and absolutely me, and if Phin says the fate of the universe hangs in the balance, then I believe him. Because right now in this whole stupid galaxy he's the only person who hasn't tried to vaporize me or blow me up or just been super rude. He is, you know, actually a pretty good guy. It turns out."

She was on a roll now.

"So you guys need to wake up and start acting like *parents*! You heard your apartment was blown up and you ordered *brunch*. Brunch! The most unnecessary meal ever! This is a full-blown crisis and you are wearing *bathrobes*!"

The breeze trilled through the tinkling trees, and far off, the surf roared. Eliza Fogg set down her tea.

"Excuse me, little girl, I don't know who you think you are . . ."

"I'm Lola Ray!" said Lola. "And you two ought to be ashamed of yourselves."

Lola had never, ever in her life spoken to adults that way, especially not rich ones, and especially not rich ones in their bathrobes. Her face was hot and she was trembling, but she refused to break her stare.

"Uh," said Phin, as shocked as his parents.

The Foggs, slack-jawed, seemed to decide this girl was as loony as their son, and so could be ignored.

"Honey," said Eliza to Phin. "You can stay at the summerhouse for the time being. You'll be safe there."

"We want you to go there now," said Phin's father.

Phin didn't respond.

"You need to do what we say," said Barnabus.

"Can't you see we're worried about you?" said Eliza.

Phin took a sharp breath, and then, very calmly, he said, "I'm sorry, I love you guys."

The Frillian Riviera zipped out of existence around them, and Phin and Lola found themselves back in the humming interior of their ship, hovering above the gleaming dome of Luna.

"What happened?" said Lola, blinking.

"I hung up."

"Oh."

Lola swallowed. She peeked at Phin out of the corner of her eye. She wasn't sure what to say. She tried this:

"I'm sorry I shouted at your parents. That was, um . . . You see, my mom has been a bit . . . and I . . . well."

"No," said Phin, his voice quiet. "I mean, thank you."

"Oh," said Lola.

He shifted the ship into gear, and Lola felt them accelerate.

"So," she said. "Where's the summer home?"

"Cape Cod. I've never been there," said Phin. "I'll have to check it out someday."

In a few moments, they had landed on the moon.

13

"ARE YOU COMING?"

Phin was standing at Lola's door, holding it open. Their view screen had dimmed as their tiny ship had been automatically guided into a parking space. Lola blinked in the fresh glare and peered over Phin's shoulder at the space station beyond. They had docked beside a floating gangway, which was attached to a long concourse. Everywhere Lola looked, flashing entranceways opened onto antechambers full of colorful objects and lights. People strolled past, some on little scooters that seemed to be hovering a few feet off what passed for the ground around here. Above their heads, directional signs and marquees floated without any visible means of support, directing guests to *Terminal 6,000*, say, or luring them to visit Razelplex Theta, where apparently you could get two-for-one drinks after twelve.

But more astonishing than any of this was the assortment of totally nonhuman creatures walking, flying, sliding, and bobbling about, minding their own business, asking each other directions, and window-shopping. Lola saw what looked like slugs outfitted with monster-truck tires. She saw eyeballs the size of refrigerators crawling about on spidery legs. Lobster men in neon jumpsuits went claw-in-claw with their lobster partners, and a pair of enormous blue bears, walking upright in luxurious floor-length overcoats, argued over whether there was time to grab dinner before their flight.

"It looks like Comic Con," observed Lola as she stepped out onto the gangway.

"I don't know what that is," said Phin. "But come on."

She followed him toward the concourse, and as she did, she happened to glance behind her. Lola gasped, shocked to find that their little escape pod had vanished, and in its place a monstrous battle-ready dreadnought was docked, at least three hundred yards long, outfitted with turrets and cannons and a nasty pointy prow ready for ramming anything foolish enough to get in its way. It was huge and terrifying.

"Where's our ship?" Lola asked. She'd started to get used to its homey little interior, and plus, they'd left Teddy in there.

"That *is* our ship," said Phin.

"But, but," said Lola. "It's . . . *bigger on the outside*!"

"Oh," said Phin, as if he hadn't noticed. "Yeah. That's the Majulook SuperFake cloaking device. Makes the escape pod look like whatever you want. I set it to Terrifying Warship."

Lola considered this and saw the sense in it. People were much less likely to try and blow you up if they thought you were piloting something that looked big and fearsome.

"Will Teddy be okay in there?" She hurried after Phin, who was already several yards ahead.

"He'll be fine. We'll be right back, anyway. We've just got to book a spot on the first ferry out of here."

They stepped onto the concourse proper. The crowds streamed past them in all directions. The hubbub and murmur of a thousand languages assaulted Lola's ears, just as the strange aromas of an alien spaceport—very few of which were pleasant—invaded her nostrils. It was all so overwhelming she could barely move.

Conveniently, Phin was also not moving. Lola would have thought he was cowed by the magnificent and crazy alien stuff that was in evidence all around them, except that his expression was totally relaxed, and his hands were in his pockets. He appeared to be just . . . waiting.

"What are you doing?" she asked.

"Just . . . waiting," he said. His eyes followed the alien travelers that passed by. A few of them glanced his way, and then looked away. No one paid them any more mind than that.

"Um . . . ," said Lola.

Since she was new to this place, indeed to this millennium,

she decided to follow Phin's lead. And so they waited. Phin's brow began to knit again. He removed his hands from his pockets and folded his arms across his chest. After a minute of this, he began to tap his foot. Finally, in a tone of utter exasperation, he said, "Uh, *helloooo!*"

He addressed this to no one in particular. Or rather, he seemed to address it to everyone on the concourse. A pink sloth-like alien in a top hat blinked at him, then strolled on its way.

"Hello!" Phin tried again. "I'm waiting!"

"What's going on?" said Lola, utterly perplexed. "What are you waiting for?"

"For help, obviously."

"Help? With what?"

"We need to buy a shuttle ticket," said Phin. "Which I'd be happy to explain to someone if they'd just ask."

Slowly, Lola realized what was going on. As new and strange as Luna was to her, it was also new and strange to Phin. Not because it existed in this incomprehensible and bizarre future, or even because it was filled with aliens. But simply because it was outside his extremely narrow and limited experience of life. It was new to him because it lay beyond his front door.

"Do you . . . ," Lola began, not sure how to say this without sounding rude. "Do you think that someone's just going to volunteer to serve you?"

"Of course they will," said Phin.

"Why?"

"Well . . ." He blinked. He hadn't thought it that far through. "Well, at home, when I need something, a service drone or the computer asks me what I need, and I tell it. And then . . ." He finished with a little shrug,

"I don't think that's how it works here," said Lola. "I don't think that's how it works in most places."

"Nonsense," said Phin, worrying the lapel of his jumpsuit. "I'm very important."

"Yes," said Lola. "Okay, yes, I'll give you that. But . . ." She glanced around at the concourse of busy aliens, "No one here knows that. Or," she added, trying to be delicate, "even cares."

Phin went pale. His paleness gave way to a sickly green. And then finally, to an angry orange-red.

"Why don't we—" Lola began.

"I NEED," Phin shouted, "A FERRY TICKET."

And he held out his hand.

"Well, then, go buy one, ya crank!" someone shouted.

"WHERE?"

"A TICKET KIOSK, IDIOT!" someone else shouted back with equal annoyance.

"WHERE IS A KIOSK?"

"Goodness. FOLLOW THE SIGNS!" said a passing sluggoid, who then pointed to a sign marked *Ticket Kiosk*.

"THANK YOU!" said Phin, and he smiled at Lola. "You see?"

"What a jerk!" the sluggoid mumbled as it slithered away.

"That was . . ." Lola blinked. "That was incredibly rude."

"But it worked," said Phin. "Come on."

They followed the signs for the ticket kiosk, which guided them around a corner and up a hovering platform to another level. An illuminated arrow pointed toward a dark passage. It read FOOD THIS WAY. Lola's stomach grumbled.

"Do you . . . ," she started, but then she noticed the arrow was pointing not toward a doorway at all, but toward an enormous mouth set into the wall, complete with tombstone-sized teeth and an orca-sized tongue, beyond which tapered a dark wet gullet, waiting for something tasty to step into it. "Never mind," she said.

"Oh, I should probably mention," Phin said, "whatever you do, don't talk to yourself."

"What?" said Lola.

"If you happen to run into yourself, don't talk to her," he added.

"Wait, *what?*"

"Forget it, we're here," said Phin, who had come to an abrupt stop in the middle of the concourse.

There was no kiosk. Instead, jutting up from the floor was a blunt column with a large red button on its top. A stencil of what Lola assumed was a space shuttle had been emblazoned on its surface.

"Hold my hand," said Phin, and before Lola could say *what* again, he'd clasped her fingers and activated the short-range teleport.

14

PHIN AND LOLA SHIMMERED into existence within a not-very-exciting room. The room's only feature was a glass barrier, behind which sat a grumpy-looking Earth woman in a frumpy dress. Above her was an electronic screen displaying departure times and destinations all over the galaxy, like Sagittarius Minor, Singularity City, and something called the Horsehead Colonies.

In the corner was an ordinary potted plant, the kind you see in waiting rooms everywhere.

The alien who had just bought his ticket walked out through the only door—which was marked *Concourse*—which closed behind him with a little *hiss*.

"Is this real?" said Lola.

"Well, I've always theorized that the universe itself is a giant simulation," answered Phin, not at all helpfully. "In fact, we may all just be information projected onto the surface of a black hole—"

Lola groaned. "We get it, you read a lot. I mean is this like another phone call or something?"

"It's a ticket office," said Phin. "It's real."

"In that case, you better let me handle this."

"What, why?"

Lola, who was not rude, wasn't sure how to tell Phin that he was, so she just smiled pleasantly and approached the woman behind the glass.

"Hello," she said. "How are you? We'd like to purchase passage on the next available shuttle please."

"Where to?" snapped the potted plant.

Lola blinked. She looked back and forth from the woman, who had not spoken, to the plant in the corner, which apparently had.

The frumpy woman sniffled, took out a hankie, and blew her nose.

"Oh, uh. Hello, um . . . plant," said Lola.

"You're doing great," Phin whispered.

"Shut up," said Lola. "We'd like to go to . . . um, Phin, where are we going?"

Phin put his hands in his pockets and whistled. "So many choices. Anyplace far, really. Ooh, the Carbon Towers of Yasmine 6 are supposed to be very nice this time of year," he said, considering the board. "Or what about the Mega Black Caverns of Ursa 27-B? It's almost time for the annual super bat migration. GateAdvisor says it's just beautiful."

"Two tickets for whatever shuttle is leaving soonest," said Lola to the potted plant, and then, remembering Teddy, "Wait . . . three, I guess."

"We'll need a voucher for our Rescue Wagon as well," Phin put in. "Now." He glanced at Lola, who was giving him a disappointed look. "I mean . . . now, *please*."

Overhead, unnoticed by our heroes, a small black security camera narrowed its single eye.

"The next departing shuttle leaves in fifteen minutes for Singularity City. Cash or credit?" asked the potted plant, sounding like it didn't give a flying rhino what their answer was.

"Credit," said Phin, and handed Lola an ordinary black credit card.

"Place your card on the panel for identification," said the potted plant.

A panel on a robotic arm unfolded itself from the wall. Lola glanced at the plant, which was of course expressionless, and then at the frumpy lady behind the barrier. The frumpy lady sniffed, took out a hankie, and blew her nose again. She was, Lola realized, not a real lady, but a cheap plastic one.

Not sure what else to do, Lola pressed the credit card to the panel. A little screen above it read *Confirmed: Account Holder Fogg. Credit rating: Just Super Fantastically Amazingly Good.*

At this, the security camera above gave an expression of utter shock and excitement—to the extent a camera with only one little eye can.

"Your account has been charged. Would you like a receipt?" said the plant in its same bored, overworked, underpaid tone.

But before either could reply, a panel in the ceiling slid away, and a bulb whose sole purpose was to strobe red and look menacing dropped into the room and began to flash its little heart out.

An instant later, several hundred other panels slid open, and much more menacingly, disintegrator guns snaked out on maneuverable robotic arms and aimed themselves at Lola and Phin.

Lola yelped. "What's going on?"

"STAY RIGHT WHERE YOU ARE," a voice boomed from speakers located somewhere behind all the flashing lights and guns. "BY ORDER OF THE TEMPORAL TRANSIT AUTHORITY, YOU, PHINEAS T. FOGG, AND YOU, MS. PASSPORT, ARE TO BE TAKEN PRISONER FOR THE CRIME OF TIME TRAVEL AND ATTEMPTING TO FLEE ARREST." The voice then added, somewhat uncertainly, "I MEAN, WE'RE JUST ASSUMING YOU'LL ATTEMPT TO FLEE. MOST PEOPLE DO."

The exit door marked *Concourse* burst open and a team of Lunar security agents, deadly and faceless in their black battle armor, tromped into the room with weapons at the ready. These too were pointed at Lola and Phin.

The potted plant gasped. The frumpy lady sniffled, took out a hankie, and blew her nose.

"See where politeness gets you?" said Phin.

"Maybe you should try talking them to death," said Lola.

"No bantering!" snapped the largest Lunar security agent.

"Ahhhh!!" said the potted plant as it flew through the air and smashed into the face of the nearest security agent, knocking him over.

"Throwing people at other people," said Phin as they dodged a hail of blaster fire and ran toward the door. "That's super polite."

"I'm sorry!" Lola shouted at the potted plant as they made their escape.

The potted plant groaned, half pinned beneath the fallen security agent, its pot smashed to bits, its leaves crumpled and covered in soil. Though no one knew it then, the potted plant would go on to receive a sizable workplace-injury settlement from the ferry company, retire early, and spend the rest of its days quite happily in a sunny bistro just outside Baton Rouge.

15

ALL THROUGH THE CONCOURSE, lights flashed red and alarming.

"ATTENTION, NEW BAYONNE VISITORS," a voice boomed over the PA system. "WE HAVE A PAIR OF FUGITIVES LOOSE ON THE CONCOURSE. BE ON THE LOOKOUT FOR THESE CHILDREN."

The walls shimmered and images of Phin and Lola huddled behind Phin's kitchen counter appeared. The same image appeared on the floors and panels and just about everywhere you looked.

"It's us!" said Lola, legs pumping.

"Ugh, I hate that picture," puffed Phin.

Out on the concourse, everyone had stopped to stare at the images flickering before them. Some of the more observant ones were turning to watch the two familiar-looking children running like all get out, and the army of security guards chasing them down a set of escalators and over a decorative fountain.

"What do we do?" shouted Lola. "Apart from, you know, running?"

"I know exactly what we should do!" said Phin, who hoped he wasn't lying.

The guards were gaining. They were shouting things like "Halt!" and "Stop or we'll shoot!" Some of them just went ahead and shot anyway. A beam of pure destructive energy whizzed by and exploded a kiosk of sunglasses.

A flying pair of nifty shades practically fell into Lola's hands. She put them on.

"Should I buy these?" she shouted.

"What on Luna is wrong with you?" Phin snapped.

"I don't know!" she shouted. "I just have the intense urge to buy something. Isn't that weird?"

Phin didn't get the chance to answer. A disintegration beam whizzed between them and disintegrated a juice bar.

In a moment the guards would be on them.

"Wait!" Phin shouted. "Look over there!"

"Where?"

"That ball pit!" He pointed to a fast-food eatery complete with inflatable play palace.

"The moon has a ball pit?" said Lola.

"Yes!" said Phin. "And that's where we're going to hide!"

Together they ducked under a series of tables and moved serpentine through the eatery. A beat later the security team rushed into the food court, tumbling over each other in a clatter of weaponry and armor.

"Where'd they go?"

"Search the place!"

"Can I search the play palace?"

"Yes, Dave, you can search the play palace. For crying out loud . . ."

The kids were huddled behind a padded column in the middle of the ball pit. Thankfully it was well past lunchtime, and there were no children in sight.

"Move over," said Phin. It had suddenly become awfully crowded.

"*You* move over," said Lola.

"No, *you* push over," said the second Lola.

"Both of you be *quiet*," said Phin, then realized what he'd just said and did a double take. Actually, a triple take.

"Lola," he hissed. "Don't look now, but there are *two* of you."

To Phin's right was a Lola. To his left was a Lola. Both identically Lola-ish, both looking the way Lola usually looked, which was shocked and amazed.

"Cool!" they said together.

And Now a Brief Aside on the Importance of Checking Your Voice Mail

It takes a tremendous—an almost godlike—amount of energy and effort for anything to travel between dimensions. Effectively, you'd have to burn up an entire solar system just to do something as simple as place a personal call from one universe to another.

Which is exactly what the Phan had done.

It happened awhile back, before Phin was born. A telephone rang.

It was a very nice telephone in a very nice office. The telephone was deliberately old-fashioned, in keeping with the retro decor. It sat on a pedestal before a great domed window, which looked out on the sprawling wasteland below. On either side of it were his-and-hers mahogany desks, entirely bare except for a pen or two, and an ever-growing stack of mail in their respective in-boxes.

This particular phone had not been chosen at random.

The Phan had chosen it because of all the people in our universe, the owners of *this* phone could help the Phan break through to our dimension, which was part of their ultimate plan. The Phan were therefore very eager to speak with them.

The telephone, flying in the face of sanity and physics, rang.

It rang again.

Its cheerful little bell filled the vaulted room, clamoring against the sumptuous paneling, beating against the leather furniture, fluffing the shag carpet.

It rang and rang and rang.

And after the eighth ring, it went to voice mail.

"*Hi there!*" said the cheerful recorded voice of Barnabus Fogg.

"*Hello!*" said the voice of his wife, Eliza Fogg, with the same happily relaxed tone.

Together they said: "*You've reached the office of Barnabus and Eliza!*"

"*We're not in right now!*" said Barnabus.

"*But if you leave a message . . . ,*" continued Eliza.

"*We'll get back to you!*" they finished with all the delight and warmth of a happily married couple, deliriously in love, setting off on their first real vacation together.

"*Oh, and if this is urgent, please dial 999-alpha-zeta-bravo-61245,*" Eliza added.

They both went, "*Beeeeeeeep.*"

Then a voice never before heard anywhere in our universe, and certainly never recorded by any device known to anyone, ever, spoke.

It said, "WE ARE THE PHAN, SUPERINTELLIGENT BEINGS OF ANOTHER DIMENSION, AND WE . . ." The owner of the voice seemed to realize it wasn't speaking to an actual person. “Oh, for Pete’s sake,” it said. “They’re not in.”

There was a barely audible sound just off mic.

“I don’t know!” the voice snapped. “It’s some kind of answering machine. Hello? Hello? If you’re there, pick up.”

A pause.

“Really, if you’re there, pick up. We had to melt a star to make this phone call and we really want to speak to you.”

The office was silent.

“Unbelievable,” said the voice. “Phone call from another dimension and they can’t even be bothered to answer!”

The sound on the other end of the line rumbled again.

“Yes, I’ll leave a message, just let me, will you? Okay, here it goes. We’re calling because—”

The answering machine went *beep*. Whatever message it was that the Phan had worked so hard to get across the irrational distances between worlds was cut off.

Five years later—for that was how long it took the Phan to muster the energy to place another phone call—a different telephone rang. This telephone belonged to the emergency contact number Eliza and Barnabus had left in their away message.

And it was right down the hall.

“This is Goro Bolus,” said Bolus, answering his own phone since his secretary was at lunch.

“Oh, thank goodness you picked up!”

The voice Bolus heard was so strange and so powerful, it would have melted his brain if the interdimensional being it belonged to wasn't speaking at a polite volume.

"We can only keep this channel open for a few minutes," it said, "so listen up."

Bolus sat in his chair, frozen by the immense power and energy flowing through the receiver. In words, and without words, the Phan explained their plan. When they hung up, he was left with no clear memory of the conversation, only impulses, desires, and promises of absolute power.

After that, Goro Bolus was a new bean. He'd never been a particularly kind bean, but now his heart burned with an alien desire and his brain, enriched by its experience, pulsed with dastardly plans.

But now a question, a question that beat in the souls—if they could be called souls—of his masters, echoed through the dark chambers of his mind, more insistent than a ringing phone, more afire than a burning star.

It asked *How . . . ?*

How . . . ?

How . . . ?

16

"LOLA, YOU HAVE SIMPLY got to buy . . . those . . . *sunglasses*."

Phin said this in a whisper, but a whisper full of urgency, fear, and frustration.

"You think so?" said Lola.

"They're not really my style, but I do sort of want them," said the other Lola.

The three of them—the two Lolas and one Phin—were crammed together behind a padded column among a sea of colorful plastic balls in the center of the ball pit at Fun Time Ultra Sunshine Rapid Food Emporium, trying desperately not to move. The Lunar security agents tromped back and forth through the food court, searching for them, radios squawking. The column that they were now hiding behind supported the domed plastic roof of the ball pit and was almost too narrow to hide Phin and both Lolas, meaning Phin now had two sets of elbows in his ribs, and two heads of ruffly hair whipping in his face whenever the Lolas turned to speak to one another. One Lola wore the pair of obscenely priced sunglasses she'd picked up off the concourse floor. It was the only way to tell the two apart.

"Isn't that weird," said one Lola, "I'm usually not a compulsive shopper."

"But it's never too late to become one!" said the other.

"*Lola*," Phin hissed. "You've been *consumercated*."

"What?" the Lolas said together. He shushed them.

Phin, who guessed they had no idea what he was talking about, explained—quickly, quietly, urgently.

"Places like this—malls, concourses, anyplace where you can buy things," he said, "have microscopic nanobots in the air. They're called consumercators. They replicate consumers. The idea being," he rushed on before they could interrupt, "that a person is much more likely to make a purchase if a friend tells them they should, and much, *much* more likely if they *themselves* tell them they should."

The Lolas considered this. They *did* feel weirdly compelled to buy the sunglasses.

"They activate when you pick up a tagged item, which those sunglasses must be. If you just buy them, she'll go away," Phin said.

"Who will?"

"You," said Phin. "Or you. Or not really go away. You'll just kind of . . . be one person . . . again." Phin's brow furrowed itself extravagantly. "Look, I don't know exactly how it works, it just does. This is why I told you not to talk to yourself, remember? If you acknowledge your consumercate, they'll stick around until you buy something."

As if to illustrate the point, Phin plucked the sunglasses from Lola's nose. In an instant, a second Phin blipped into existence behind the padded column, making a bad situation worse.

"Hey," the new Phin said, "those sunglasses look great on you. They'd look even better if you were eating a Fun Time Ultra Sunshine Rapid Food Meal. Don't you think?"

"He's not hungry," said one of the Lolas, then, turning to what she thought was the original Phin, "are you?"

"Then *you* should buy a Fun Time Ultra Sunshine Rapid Food Meal!" said the new Phin. "It comes with an extra-large QuasiCola. I mean, you really can't beat that deal. You really can't beat it, I don't think."

The first Phin shut his eyes and counted to ten.

"What are you doing?" asked a Lola.

"I'm *not* acknowledging him," Phin grumbled. "And I'm thinking about how I have zero interest in making any purchasing decisions at this time."

The other Phin waited patiently for a moment, and then, as if he had better things to do, he shrugged and disappeared in a little poof of smoke.

"See?" said Phin. "Now please go buy something so we can get rid of . . . you . . . and get out of here!"

The Lolas looked at each other.

“Okay,” said the Lola wearing the sunglasses. “Sit tight.”

Craning to see if the coast was more or less clear, she eased her way out of the ball pit and back toward the Forever Nine Hundred and Twenty-One kiosk, where they sold the same brand of eyewear.

“I hope she makes it okay,” said the remaining Lola.

“I hope she has cash on her,” grumbled Phin.

“We do,” said Lola. “You gave us your credit card, remem—?”

And she vanished in a poof of smoke.

A second later Lola, still wearing the stupid sunglasses, hurried back behind the padded column.

“She’s gone,” she said.

“Yep,” said Phin.

“I’m going to miss her.”

Phin shook his head. “Okay, we’ve got to figure out a way to get back to our ship.” His brow did a different kind of furrow now, this time in thought. The security agents had done their sweep of the food court, but now stood with their backs to Lola and Phin, guarding the exit. Phin scanned the mostly empty dining area until his eyes caught something that made them twitch.

“Lola,” said Phin in an intense whisper. “How strong are your knees?”

“I don’t know,” she whispered back with equal intensity. “Um, normal strength?”

“Then come on.”

The pair picked their way across the court, keeping low. Stealthily they approached one of the few remaining tables still occupied. Hunched over the remains of a large lunch were a pair of enormous blue bears, the same pair Lola had seen earlier arguing about whether there was time for a pre-flight meal. Evidently, there had been time for several meals. Both bears were visibly gorged on honey mead and seafood. A dozen empty steins lolled amongst platters of caviar and salmon. One of the bears had shrugged off his overcoat and draped it across the back of a nearby chair. As quietly as he could, Phin took hold of the coat. It was surprisingly heavy, made of a rich navy fabric with dozens of brass buttons that threatened to clatter as he eased it, inch by inch, off the chair, cringing for a moment as the nearest bear hiccuped, belched, and lay his ursine head down for a nap.

“We’re stealing his coat?” Lola hissed.

“They won’t miss it,” said Phin.

“What they’re going to miss is their flight,” Lola mumbled, considering the slumbering bears.

“What now?” she asked once they’d reached the relative safety of an organic tofu stand.

“Now, I’m going to get on your shoulders, we’re going to put on this coat and walk right out of here past those guards.”

“What? Why don’t *I* get on *your* shoulders?”

“Really?” said Phin.

"Yes," said Lola. "Why not?"

"It's just . . . that's honestly not the part of the plan I thought you'd object to."

"Well, I'm objecting," said Lola. "I don't know if I can even carry you!"

"You said you had normal-strength knees!"

Lola glared.

A moment later a tall but unwieldy person in a long navy overcoat and garish sunglasses tottered by the security agents guarding the exit of the food court.

"Afternoon, gentlemen!" said Phin.

"Weird," said one of the agents to his partner.

"What is?" said the other.

"I could have sworn," said the first, "that guy's stomach just called him a jerk."

"Mall food," said the second agent, and shuddered.

"Okay, you can put me down now," Phin said some time later. "I can see the Rescue Wagon."

Lola knelt so Phin could climb down. She stood, blinking, rubbing the feeling back into her shoulders and knees.

"Next time, *you* be the feet." She looked around. Inside the coat she'd been able to see very little, relying on Phin's whispered directions. Now they had reached a stretch of concourse that indeed looked familiar, though the Rescue Wagon was nowhere in sight.

"Where's the ship?" said Lola.

"There!" said Phin.

"Behind the mastodon?" said Lola.

Where their ship had been parked, a mastodon now stood sunning itself in the Lunar afternoon. It blinked at Lola and shook its big woolly head.

"It *is* the mastodon," said Phin. "It's the Majulook Super-Fake cloaking device. I must have left it on shuffle."

Lola processed this. "So how do you know that's *our* ship, then?"

"Well, it's where we parked it, and I doubt anyone else brought a mastodon to the moon."

Given everything she'd seen today, a mastodon on the moon seemed pretty reasonable, but Lola took his word for it. The pair scrambled up the gangway, entered a hatch in the side of the mastodon, which waved at them with its trunk, and climbed inside the Rescue Wagon.

The ship was just as they left it, with Teddy in the back seat. Lola gave him a hug.

Phin shut the door, careful not to catch the big overcoat's tail, and checked the ship's controls. Then he hesitated. He turned around in his seat to consider Teddy, then turned back to what had caught his attention.

The ship was, in fact, *not* just as they left it.

"Come on, let's go!" said Lola. Though she felt much

safer back inside the Wagon, the sooner they were away from there, the better.

Phin hesitated. There was a *thing* on the dashboard. Not a dangerous-looking thing, but still, a *thing* that had no business being there. It was small, flat, and lavender. A five-by-seven little postcard, just sitting on the dash of their super-secure Rescue Wagon, which no one could have possibly entered while they were away. Phin checked the computer and confirmed that, indeed, no one had.

Frowning, he picked up the little postcard, holding it away from his face as if it might turn out to be radioactive.

"What is that?" Lola asked. "It looks fancy."

"I think," said Phin, scanning the small, neat text, "it's an invitation."

"Someone sent you an invitation? How did they know you'd be here?"

"No," said Phin. He fixed Lola with a look of grim concern. "Someone," he said, "has sent *us* an invitation."

17

FUN FACT: THERE IS an old adage in the galaxy that goes like this: *If someone offers you tea, best think twice before saying yes.*

No one knows where this adage comes from; its origins have been lost to time. Further, no one really knows exactly what it means—presumably it's a metaphor—and there are entire university courses dedicated to exploring what "tea" might represent and why you should think twice before accepting it.

There are also courses dedicated to deciding whether or not this "fact" is fun at all, or just a bit of nonsense taking up space.

Lola reread the invitation for the tenth or twentieth time:

> ***To: Phineas Fogg and Lola Ray of Earth***
>
> ***You Are Cordially Invited to Tea***
>
> ***Time: Whenever You Arrive***

Location:

Orion Arm

Alpha Centauri System

Proxima Centauri

Satellite B,

North Entrance

Attire: Casual

We Look Forward to Meeting You Properly,

The Triumvirate of Pong

"I have a question," said Lola.

"Just one?"

"What is the Triumvirate of Pong?"

She blew some foam from her macchiato, which the Rescue Wagon's onboard Conveen-U-Slurp beverage downloader had made for her. Lola believed one couldn't really tackle a problem without coffee, and this particular problem required an extra espresso shot. The macchiato tasted vaguely of motor oil and space dust, but she assumed it was caffeinated and so slurped it thirstily.

They had been puzzling over the invitation for an hour, sitting in the Rescue Wagon, Lola wrapped in the big cozy overcoat, Teddy propped between them. To the outside world it appeared as if a mastodon was contentedly sunning itself in a one-hour parking spot. Phin had used the Majulook cloaking device to fabricate a parking ticket on the end of the mastodon's trunk—but this had been unnecessary, since no meter reader wanted to tangle with a mastodon, never mind cared where it was parked.

"I don't know," said Phin.

"Wait, really?" said Lola. "I thought you sort of knew everything."

She hadn't meant to sound sarcastic, but clearly she had, as Phin gave her a nasty scowl. He'd been scowling pretty much nonstop since they'd discovered the invitation, and now his scowl was so deep it might have had spelunkers climbing through it.

"I don't know what it is because it isn't anything," he said. "Who's ever heard of the Triumvirate of Pong? No one! It's just some made-up nonsense."

"Well, for something made up, they have some very fancy stationery," said Lola. "And more important, how do they know who we are? I mean." She meditated over the steam from her mug. "You're rich and famous I guess. But how do they know *me*? Who here knows me? I mean, no one, right?"

"No one but the people trying to kill us."

"Yeah," said Lola, shaking her head, "but *these* people aren't trying to kill us. They've invited us to tea!" She considered her coffee. "I never liked tea, really."

"Give it to me," said Phin with finality, reaching for the invitation.

"Why?"

"Because I'm going to throw it out the window. It's probably just an advertisement for something. Triumvirate of Pong breakfast cereal or tea cakes or something like that."

"What?" Lola jerked away, nearly spilling what remained of her macchiato. "You can't throw it away! We need to go!"

"Go where?"

"Here," she said, indicating the location marked on the card. "Alpha Centauri. Satellite B. The North Entrance. Whatever that is!"

Phin threw his hands up in exasperation and turned to face the window.

"Phin," she said, "these people, the Triumvirate of Ping—"

"Pong."

"Whatever. They *knew* we'd be here. They knew *I'd* be here! In the future! With you! Maybe they know how I *got* here." Her voice softened. "Maybe they know how to get me home."

"Maybe they're elves! Maybe they're ravenous triple-headed pythons!" Phin said, not meaning to raise his voice but absolutely raising it nonetheless.

"Why are you shouting?"

"Because we don't know who they are! It could be a trap! It could be anything!" He snatched the invite from her fingers. "And you just want to shuffle off to Alpha Centauri and ring their bell?"

"Yes," Lola said. "That's exactly what I want to do. Look." She met Phin's eye, refusing to be cowed by his tantrum. "Someone is trying to kill us. And we need to get away from them, yeah? Well, of all the places to run to, why not *there*? Why not this Satellite B? Phin," she said, "I want to go home."

"Do you?" he said. "Why? I don't."

"That's different."

"How so?"

"Because . . ." Lola struggled to find the words. "Because I miss my family!" She missed them. Even her sisters. She missed her home. She missed normal things, like the moon being called the moon and robots almost never trying to kill you. "I can't just run forever."

Phin crossed his arms. "Why not? Sounds good to me."

"Why are you like this?"

"Because I don't know what's going on!" he shouted, and then, more quietly, "I don't know what I'm doing."

The blush had engulfed his entire face now. He hadn't meant to be so honest.

"Isn't that the point, though?" Lola asked.

Phin blinked. "Huh?"

"I mean, isn't that the *point*? To explore? To go into the unknown? Here's something *new*. Something you *haven't* read about. It's a question without an answer! It's the inexplicable!" Lola grinned at him, and then she said something that would have knocked Phin's socks off, if he ever wore any. "I know you're not afraid," she said, "so what is it?"

He looked at her. Her eyes were wide, questioning, but sincere. She wasn't making fun of him. She believed he wasn't afraid, even when he'd just told her the opposite.

But sometimes all it takes is someone seeing you the way you want to be seen. Suddenly, Phin wasn't afraid at all.

"Right," he said. "Fine. We'll still need to hitch a ride to get there, though. The Rescue Wagon is too small and too slow to make the journey on its own."

Lola grinned. "Okay! So what do we do?"

"Just buying a ticket's out. They don't have flights to places no one's ever heard of. We'll just have to sneak onto a craft that's headed in that general direction." He tapped his chin, then brought up the ship's computer. "Bucky, are any ships leaving for Alpha Centauri? It's not Satellite B, but it's as close as we're likely to get."

The UI's voice crackled from the dashboard speakers. "Well, twiddle my chits and slap my chicken, the luxury liner SS *SunStar* will be passing through the Alpha Centauri system on its way to Sirius Jinx."

"Hmm," said Phin, scrolling through the vessel's flight plan. "That could work. But there's no way we can get on board without buying a ticket, and we know my card's been flagged." He glanced at her. "And judging by the fact you're not carrying six duffel bags, I'm going to assume we don't have enough hard cash."

"Phin," said Lola. "Come on, there's got to be a way! We've got to go!"

Phin pushed back from the screen. "Unless you've got two tickets to the SS *SunStar* sitting in your pocket, there's no way we're getting on that ship."

Just for the heck of it, Lola peered into the navy overcoat's ticket pocket. She sniffed. She set down her coffee. She cleared her throat. She peered into the ticket pocket again.

"What?" said Phin.

"Yeah," said Lola.

"What?" Phin said again. "Wait . . . no."

"Yeah," said Lola.

"That's just . . ." Phin shook his head. "I mean, that's just *unbelievably* . . ."

"It is," said Lola. "Very."

From the pocket Lola produced two first-class tickets to board the SS *SunStar*, all expenses paid, with unlimited pool access and a complimentary caviar and salmon buffet.

18

THE SS *SUNSTAR* IS one of the most luxurious ships in the galaxy. The pride of Sun-Liner Space Cruises, it boasts three hundred first-class cabins, thirty-five megasuites, twelve full-size holodecks, a dozen zero-G swimming pools, a handful of five-star restaurants, and more hors d'oeuvres per square foot than any other cruiser in its class. Rather than rocketing through hypergates, long-distance dark matter steamers like the *SunStar* proceed through space at a leisurely two hundred and eight times the speed of light, turning the instantaneous jump from Luna to Alpha Centauri into a week-long excursion with unbeatable views of the galaxy. For the discerning trillionaire in no rush to get where he's going, it's really the only way to travel.

Lola lowered her sunglasses as she craned her neck to look up at the still-docked ship gleaming in the Lunar sunset. To her eye, the *SunStar* resembled an ocean liner more than a spacefaring vessel. It had three smokestacks along its spine, rows of circular port windows, and half a dozen lounge-chair-packed decks.

Lola thought of the *Titanic*—and then immediately wished she hadn't.

"Just follow my lead," said Phin as they made their way along the pier.

"Why," said Lola, "do people always say that? Why can't they just talk about the plan ahead of time?"

"And remove all the drama?" said Phin.

"You don't actually have a plan, do you?"

"Nope! But I will in a moment," he said. "I hope," he added, flipping up his collar in a way he imagined looked brave and dashing.

Lola was about to respond when something bumped into the back of her knees. To onlookers, it appeared to be a large leather steamer trunk with the letters *VRW* stamped on the side in a repeating pattern. The fact that it skittered along under its own power on squealing little wheels, and seemed to follow its owners wherever they went, wasn't unusual (plenty of luggage did that). But what no one could have known was that the trunk was in fact a Volvo Rescue Wagon, expertly disguised by its Majulook cloaking device. Lola would have found the transformation impressive if the thing didn't keep bumping into her.

The trunk seemed to wait patiently as she regarded it with a wrinkled brow. The luggage was all part of their disguise, like the oversize overcoat, which Phin now wore, and the kiosk sunglasses, which Lola had perched on the top of her head.

"I hope Teddy is okay in there," she said, tapping the trunk's lid.

"He's fine. It's all fine. Just do what I do," said Phin. He slapped on a grin, brought himself to full height (which still looked awfully short in the coat he was wearing), and marched up the gangplank. Lola had no choice but to follow.

Most of the passengers were already aboard, but a harried-looking porter waited to take their tickets. This porter was called Lucky, a nickname he'd acquired in the casinos of Singularity City, where he'd lost his savings and then some betting on the wrong sloth in the 300th Annual Frickle East Ultraslow Single-Meter Races, when by an amazing upset, Speedy McCree beat Fuzzy Lightning with a record-breaking time of three hours, forty-five minutes, and twelve seconds. Now penniless and miserable, Lucky worked for Sun-Liner Space Cruises to pay off his considerable gambling debts, and if you think that made him a touch ornery and suspicious, you get a gold star.

Lucky was required to wait at his post until final boarding call. He had been harassed and abused all afternoon by impatient and jetlagged rich people who were not used to standing in line. He was underpaid, overtired, and in no mood for shenanigans. Staring warily down the gangplank, he now saw two oddly dressed children hurrying toward him—one in an oversize overcoat, the other in a pair of gawdy kiosk sunglasses—followed by an enormous steamer trunk. He knew that shenanigans of some kind were exactly what was in store.

"No," he said when they reached him. "No. What do you want? Whatever it is, you can't have it. Go away."

The children were grinning. Their luggage seemed to wait patiently.

"Are we too late? I don't think we are," said the boy. "I told my wife if we didn't hurry, we'd miss final boarding call!"

"*Wife?*" said the girl as if he'd just called her a hairless triple-headed zumbuloid.

Lucky stared at them. The children stared at each other.

"I mean . . . ," said the girl, recovering. "Yes, I, uh . . . I told my *husband*"—the word seemed sour in her mouth—"we had plenty of time. And I was right!"

"Why, you're always right, my . . . *love*," said the boy, struggling with that last bit. "You're such a good, um, *spouse*."

"Buzz off, kids," said Lucky, checking the time. "I've got to close this gate in a minute."

"*Kids?*" said the boy. "Did you hear that, my little moon petunia? I told you these new bodies made us look too young."

Lucky's eyes narrowed. "New bodies?"

"Yes," the boy said with a chuckle. "We're test-driving some new bodies. What do you think? I told my wife they were too childish. But those are the times, I suppose.

Everything's got to be young, young, young!"

"Right," said Lucky. "And you are?"

"Ah! Our tickets," said the boy. He patted his overcoat—somewhat dramatically, Lucky thought—then, smiling in satisfaction, pulled two *SunStar* tickets from an inner pocket. "Here you are, my good man."

Lucky considered the tickets. There was no doubt they were the genuine article, complete with holographic interface and a diamond-plasma watermark. "This ticket is in the name of His Royal Ursine Majesty, the Archduke of Sagittarius. And this one"—he raised the second ticket to the light to double-check its authenticity—"is in the name of his wife, the Duchess of Sagittarius."

"Yes," said the boy without hesitating. "That is we. I mean I. I mean both of us. We are they. Them."

"I'm a duchess," said the girl, though Lucky couldn't quite make out if it was meant as a question or a statement.

"The Archduke and Duchess of Sagittarius," said Lucky, "are phenomenally important people."

"Why thank you."

"They are also seven feet tall," said Lucky, "and blue. And bears."

"Ah, *were* seven feet tall," said the boy who claimed to be the archduke. "And blue."

"And bears," finished the duchess.

"But as I mentioned, we're trying out some new bodies."

"For our vacation," the duchess added.

"You've got to be kidding," said Lucky.

The boy's face auditioned a few expressions, then settled out outrage. "Now you see here . . . *Staff*," he said, reading Lucky's uniform, "if that is your real name—"

"It isn't."

"Are you accusing us of not being who we say we are?"

"Dear, your blood pressure," said the girl, grasping her husband or whatever's arm.

"Why, I'll have your *job*, you worm! Who's your supervisor?"

Here, Lucky hesitated. He badly needed this job, or else the bookies of Singularity City were going to remove his knees and mail them to his mothers. "Look, uh, there's no need for that," he said. "I'm just . . . with the new bodies, it all seems kind of . . . unlikely."

"Now, now, dear," said the girl, stroking her traveling companion's fuming brow. "It's an honest mistake. We do look awfully different from our pictures."

"If maybe you have some alternate form of ID?"

At this question the girl stopped stroking, and even the boy's fuming seemed to pause in hesitation.

"Um, right," said the girl. "It's just . . . our luggage was lost."

"What's that?" said Lucky, indicating the steamer trunk.

"You can't honestly think," the boy rushed in, "that the

Archduke and Duchess of Sagittarius only travel with *one* steamer trunk."

"Why, *this* trunk is just for my sunglasses!" said the girl. "The rest of our luggage—"

"At least twenty or thirty bags total," said the boy.

"—was lost. You know how airports are."

"Spaceports," the boy corrected.

"Right," said the girl. "Lost all our luggage. Had it all sent to, um, Hoboken."

"Where's that?" said Lucky. "Never heard of it."

"It's an awful place," said the boy.

"Well, it's not *awful*," said the girl.

"Hellish. No one should go there. Not even to retrieve their luggage."

"Look," said Lucky, who was now as much out of patience as he was out of cash. "If I was a gambling man, and I used to be, I'd lay a-million-to-one odds you are not who you say you are."

Something flashed in the boy's eye. "A gambling man, eh? Well, I'll bet you two million credits you'll let us on board."

Lucky blinked. "You what?"

"You heard me," said the boy, now taking a small black credit card from a different pocket and tapping a few icons on its touch-screen interface.

"Okay," said Lucky, crossing his arms. "I'll take that bet. You can't come on board."

"Well, how about that. I lost. And you've just won two million credits." The boy gave the credit card a final tap. "Enjoy them!"

The personal data tablet in Lucky's pocket beeped. He checked it. Someone had just anonymously transferred two million credits into his private bank account, which was, to Lucky, a small fortune.

His eyes bugged so wide Lola swore she heard them pop.

"You're welcome!" Phin called as the porter pushed past them and ran full tilt down the gangplank, tearing off his white porter's jacket and cap and tossing them into the nearest trash receptacle.

"Why do I feel like we just enabled a gambling addict?" said Lola.

"Because we did. Sad, really." He scanned their tickets, and the gate before them popped open with a hiss, revealing the lush interior of the ship.

"I hope he's all right," Lola added as she, Phin, and their self-driving steamer stepped aboard.

As for Lucky, it's true he immediately boarded a shuttle for the casinos of Singularity City, where over the course of a week he gambled away the entire fortune Phin had tipped him. Broke again and miserable, he spent all but his last few nickels on a platter of franks and beans, which turned out to be the worst meal of his life. But we can't imagine that information will be relevant later.

PART 3

THE ARCHDUKE AND DUCHESS OF SAGITTARIUS RUN AMOK

19

BY LOLA'S COUNT IT was seven days since they'd left port, but it was difficult to say exactly, since there was no sun to count the days by, and all the clocks on board told Frillian time, where the weekends are twice as long and brunch has been known to last months.

"Ooh, they're doing Kardashev tango after dinner!" Phin said, showing her the itinerary on their suite's massive screens.

"Sounds fun!" said Lola.

In the time they'd been aboard, things couldn't have gone better. Lola had worried they'd be found out immediately, but Phin had quickly charmed the other guests, and even most of the staff, impressing them with his encyclopedic knowledge of the galaxy. At Kardashev tango he danced with all the ladies and a number of the men, and both of the sphinxes. Of course, no one knew who they *really* were. As far as the crew and guests were concerned, the boy with the impressive two-step was none other than the rarely photographed Archduke of Sagittarius, sporting a young new body. It turned out Phin did an excellent job of impersonating a rich and important person.

"Ooh, look!" Phin had said as they explored their suite on the first night. "They've got a Look-e-Me automatic outfit generator! What do you say we go to dinner dressed in full Krastle Bracken Peacekeeper armor?"

"Sure!" said Lola.

At first, Lola was having just as much, if not more, fun. Their suite was twice the size of Lola's apartment back home and featured an emperor-sized bed—two, in fact, which meant Lola could stretch out like a starfish on the million-thread-count sheets, toss and turn all she liked, and stay up all hours with no one telling her it was time for bed. In the morning, the Conveen-U-Munch downloaded her favorite breakfast—espresso and scrambled eggs—and no one asked her to do the dishes. The bathroom was a palace, and no one yelled at her to hurry up, or wipe down the sink, and there was always plenty of hot water.

"Lola!" said Phin, still sweaty from their match of Quark-Squash. "They're doing an interactive screening of *ShadowMancer Wars* with live musical accompaniment after dinner! I've always wanted to do one of those. You're up for it, right?"

"Of course," said Lola, chugging her ninth or twelfth bottle of complimentary Reconst-D. "Just . . . give me a minute to catch my breath."

The days stretched before Lola, each promising the most fun money could buy—from superstring yoga to levitation classes, space walks, and waterslides, and even a virtual game room offering something called Mega Conkers, where, if Lola understood the pamphlet correctly, one could smash together the planets of distant uninhabited star systems in cataclysmic one-on-one tournaments. It was the dream vacation she'd always wanted, and she was free to do whatever she pleased, unsupervised, with no responsibilities, and no one asking her to share, or slow down, or act her age.

But over the past few days the shine had started to come off. At first she thought she was just worn out from the million activities Phin wanted to try. But it was something else. She was starting to miss the familiar comforts—and even the inconveniences—of Earth. Yes, the food synthesizer made her breakfast, but the eggs didn't taste *quite* right. And it was hard to sleep without Gabby's snoring, or the hiss of Mary's baby monitor. And the other passengers were hardly welcoming. Some stared at Lola's questionable table manners (hardly her fault; the dining set featured no fewer than seventeen different spoons). She tried making friends, but once the usual topics of "Which waterslide is the most terrifying?" and "What's your score in Mega Conkers?" were exhausted, she simply had nothing in common with anyone.

"You're coming to the pool party," Phin said. He was standing at the foot of her bed, holding a cricket bat (which she hoped wasn't for her) and wearing a jumpsuit that blinked and shimmered and rearranged itself at will. It was sort of hard to look at.

Lola had spent the afternoon alone in their suite, scrolling through channels on her Ultrabox 3000, hoping that somewhere, somehow, an episode of *Dimension Y* might be playing. But nothing seemed to have survived from Earth as she knew it. All was lost or forgotten, and Lola felt forgotten and lost, too.

"It's okay, you go," she said.

"No, no more moping," said Phin, tapping the bedpost with his cricket bat or whatever it was. "I won't have you getting the ultra-sads on my watch. If there's one thing my family does well, it's vacation. And I'm not leaving anyone out of the fun." He batted a truffle off the room service cart, and it bonked her in the forehead. "Okay?"

"Okay," she said, considering the truffle. "I guess you're—"

"I'm always right!" said Phin, and he skipped to the Look-e-Me to get dressed for dinner.

A Frillian hour later Lola stood on the lido deck, watching the other guests mingling by the pool, laughing and chatting, and sipping sparkling mineral water from the ice moon Titan. Phin, or rather, the Archduke of Sagittarius, as they all called him, sat at an oversize grand piano, entertaining the party with some funny songs. "Where *did* you learn to dance?" they asked him. "And play the piano so well?"

"Online courses!" he said, and they all laughed, knowing a royal such as he simply must have an army of attendants to teach him everything he wished to learn.

The *SunStar* was drifting slowly through the frozen depths of space. Or at least, to Lola, it seemed to drift slowly. The stars moved in cloud-like wisps and the gentle rocking made everyone on board feel as if they were on a luxurious cruise ship chugging across the sea—rather than on a luxurious cruise ship hurtling at several hundred times the speed of light toward Alpha Centauri.

Lola leaned against the ship's rail and sighed. She had gone so far as to do up her hair in what the Look-e-Me device called a Bolesian twist, and even dialed up a set of Nectarian pearls for the occasion. But in the middle of getting ready she'd lost all enthusiasm for dress-up, and rather than donning the crimson gown the Personal Style User Interface had suggested, had settled on wearing her *Dimension Y* T-shirt and plain old battered jeans instead.

"I can't believe I'm saying this," she mumbled to herself as Phin started a sing-along rendition of "All My Loves Are Matrioshka Brains"—a song she didn't know and didn't like—"but I am sick of this ship."

"I know what you mean," said a young steward girl.

Lola started, jangling the pearls around her neck. She hadn't seen the girl standing there a moment ago.

She was young, maybe thirteen, with red hair and freckles, tall and slim in her stiff uniform. She wore a simple charm around her neck, and her eyes sparkled like someone much too smart for her job.

"At first this was great." Lola almost smiled. "But now, I don't know. I guess I'm not meant for this kind of party."

"No sane person is," said the girl. She stuck out a hand. "My name is Gallabulala." She smiled at the look on Lola's face. "But everyone just calls me Gabby."

"That's my sister's name!" said Lola.

"The Empress of Thraal?" the girl said, perplexed.

"What? Oh, I mean, yes." It was easy to forget they were here under assumed identities. "Well, we call her that sometimes." Lola made a lazy swirl in the air with her glass, the way a duchess might. "We royals."

"Ah." The girl nodded. "Are you going to see friends at Sirius Jinx?"

"No," said Lola, looking mistily at Phin, who had stopped playing the piano and was now tap-dancing with an eight-legged oguloid. "I'm headed home. At least I hope so."

"You sound a bit sad," said the girl. Until now she'd been standing at attention with hands behind her back, but she relaxed.

"Yeah?" said Lola. "I don't know. I guess I should be, and then I guess I shouldn't be, but then I am again." She frowned. "That probably doesn't make any sense."

"Sometimes," said Gabby, leaning in, "I think I should love this job. I get to see the galaxy, travel to distant stars, meet amazing, important people." Her smile was sad. "But sometimes you just feel . . ."

"Invisible," finished the presumed duchess of Sagittarius.

"Exactly. You know," she said, "I read about the royals. It's kind of a hobby of mine."

"Oh?" said Lola. "That's . . . interesting."

"You know the funny thing about the duke?" she said, and they both glanced at the pool, where Phin was showing everyone how to do the Frillian backstroke in a tux.

"What's that?"

"Well," said Gabby. "I just read on GossipX that he and his wife were arrested for crashing their limo into a fish tank," she said. "Yesterday. On Pluto."

"Oh," said Lola, panic clawing across her face. "That is . . . there must be some kind of mix-up. You know how those gossip columns—"

Gabby laughed. "Don't worry, I won't tell your secret. People always pretend to be someone they're not on these cruises. It's nice to get away from yourself for a while. Say," she added. "Would you like to see the engine room? That's another interest of mine. Engineering, I mean."

Lola hesitated, glancing toward Phin, who was complimenting his dance partner on her shiny pelt. "Sure," she said, setting her jaw. "You can call me Lola, by the way."

"Pleased to meet you," said Gabby. "Now let's get the heck out of here."

Together the pair made their way through the party, and just as they were about to duck through a Staff Only door, she heard Phin call to her. She looked up to see him waving, his tux dripping pool water.

"I just need to talk to the, uh, duke," Lola told Gabby. "I'll be right there."

Phin hobbled over, grinning and wild-eyed. Up close she could see that someone with a pair of lips far too large to be human had planted a massive kiss on his forehead.

"You have lipstick on your forehead," she told Phin.

"Where are you going? Why don't you come swimming? The water is lavender-scented!"

"I'm good, thanks." She tried to smile reassuringly.

Phin's grin remained fixed, but his eyes less so. "Are you all right?"

"I'm not really in the mood to party."

Phin waved this idea away, splashing her with droplets of pool water. "Why not?"

"This just . . . isn't really my thing."

"Your Highness!" a translucent jelly woman called from the bar. "Come back! You were going to show me how to do the no-armed backstroke!"

Fissures appeared in Phin's smile. He glanced between the party and Lola, and she could see him deciding whether to follow her or return to the fun.

"It's okay, enjoy yourself!" said Lola, and before he could reply she was off, following Gabby away from the lido deck and through one of the doors leading down into the ship's lower levels.

Phin stood there a moment, looking hesitant, until the Lizard King of Torus G bounced an olive off the back of his head.

20

"TRUST ME," SAID LOLA, "a lot farther than that."

"Hmm. Ursula Heptoid?"

"Farther."

"Nano 7?"

"You're way off. Ice cold."

"The ice cities of Trogdor B?"

"Nope."

The girls were playing a little game, wherein Gabby tried to guess where Lola was really from, and though they were both enjoying themselves, Gabby was losing terribly.

"Wait, wait, I've got it!" Gabby snapped her fingers. "The Rajak Colonies of the Horsehead Nebula . . ."

Lola waited.

"In the Isotope Swamps," Gabby continued, "on the left bank, in the clock tower, on the second floor, just above the falafel place."

"Close!" said Lola.

"Really?" said Gabby.

"No," said Lola.

They were descending together through the bowels of the SS *SunStar*, winding through cramped corridors, climbing through hatchways, sliding down long ladders into the very bottom of the ship.

"I give up," said Gabby.

"Hoboken," said Lola. "On Carol Street, in the Mercer Tower, on the second floor, above a sub shop."

Gabby snapped her fingers, then confusion pinched her neat, fair brow. "Hoboken? Never heard of it. Where's that?"

"A long way away from here," sighed Lola.

They'd come to another hatch, this one much larger than the others, and it was marked *Steerage*. This was where the superrich stored their toys and things for the seven-day voyage to Alpha Centauri. It was a huge, cold place, several stories high and filled to the ceiling with storage containers. Most of these were flat gray, with the words *Fragile* or *May Contain Peanuts* stamped in different languages. Rustling and the occasional growl emanated from a few. One bore the message *Warning: Contents May Have Mutated During Transport*. Ships, at least a hundred, were parked in bays stacked on top of one another like a parking garage—but instead of sedans and minivans, here were sleek planet hoppers and star racers, astrobikes and mini yachts, tandem sub-ether surfboards, and a handful of solar-sail boats, shining, brand-new, and to the one mind-numbingly expensive.

"Wow," said Lola, taking it all in.

"Which one's yours?" Gabby asked.

"What? Oh, none of them," said Lola.

"You don't have a ship here? How did you get to Luna?"

"Oh, we've got one," said Lola, her mind still boggling at the immense displays of wealth. "Just not here."

"Huh," said Gabby.

They'd come at last to a door marked *engine room*. Gabby turned the crank and they stepped through the hatch. It was hot. It was loud. It was enormous. This made Lola think of something profound about luxury, and wealth, and the systems and people that keep it all in place.

"You know . . . ," she started, "sometimes I thiiiiiiAAHHHHHH!!!!!"

This was not the profound thing Lola had intended to say.

The profound thing was completely forgotten in the wake of what she saw standing before her. It wore a soggy blue jumpsuit, waved a translucent green hand, and wobbled with the vibrations of the ship.

It said, "Hello, my name's Jeremy! What's yours?"

21

A DOZEN DECKS ABOVE, Phin kicked open the door of his royal suite and twirled through the first three entrance arches. He leaped over the megasofa, made a graceful bow to the hat rack, danced with it across the edge of the infinity pool, gave it a wink when it blushed at him, and skipped over to the massive spread of before-bed snacks he'd ordered up. It could have fed a small nation.

He was in a fantastic mood.

This, after all, was what he always wanted, what he always suspected space travel would be like. His parents had been on countless cruises, and now here he was, not only part of one, but positively being the best at it, ever. For the first time in his life, Phin was surrounded by people. He was actually interacting with real people—not just in digichats and on Mobius boards, but in real life. The smells were richer, the jokes were funnier. He was *dancing.*

And what was wrong with that? Nothing. He was in a fantastic mood, and no one better suggest otherwise.

The grandfather clock chimed twelve. When it was done, a hollow silence filled the room. Below it all was the thrum of the *SunStar*'s engines, but otherwise it was quiet. Too quiet. A certain sound he'd almost completely *not* gotten used to the past few nights was absent. It was the sound of Lola's snoring.

"Hello?" he said, knocking on the door to her half of the suite. "Lola, are you in there?"

Her room was dark. He sniffed the air. He listened. He said, "I'm turning on the lights now," and did. But she wasn't in bed. She wasn't in the bathroom either. She also apparently hadn't accidentally locked herself in the Look-e-Me automatic outfit generator again.

There was an ache in Phin's chest that had nothing to do with bumping into a massive table of before-bed snacks. It was concern. Concern for someone other than himself.

"Snuggling snuggle snugs," grumbled Phin, and went to find his friend.

"Hello," he said to the porter he met in the hall. "You haven't seen my w-wife . . ." It still felt funny to call her that. The word stuck in his throat like a walnut. "Have you?"

The porter scratched one his three noses and said, "I'm afraid I don't know, sir. Could you describe her?"

"About yea big." Phin measured a distance from the floor with his hand. "About yea smart." He measured a different distance between his two hands. "And about yea brave." He measured a third distance, much larger than the other two, which involved running from one end of the hall to the other.

"Human, sir?"

"Technically."

"Female?"

"Most definitely."

"Was she wearing a T-shirt and jeans with a string of Nectarian pearls, her hair in a Bolesian twist, and an expression at once awestruck and slightly dopey?"

"Yes!" said Phin. "That's her!"

"Then no, sir," said the porter. "I'm afraid I haven't seen her."

"Oh," said Phin.

"Perhaps she's on the holodeck?"

Lola definitely did not know how to use the holodeck.

"Let's hope not," said Phin, and tipped the man thrice his annual salary.

Above deck, the party had wound down and some of the more amphibious guests had passed out in the pool. Phin tapped his foot. It wasn't like Lola to wander off for so long.

"Have you seen . . . ?" he began to ask a drunk sluggoid, then, "Oh, never mind."

"The stars?" the sluggoid offered. "I have seen them. Have you?"

"Yes," said Phin. "I know, they're lovely."

"Mmm," said the sluggoid. "They appear to be . . . wobbling."

"You've been partying too hard," said Phin, annoyed and trying to extricate himself from the conversation.

"That's definitely true," said the sluggoid, and hiccuped. "But the stars are definitely wobbling. Won't you look at them?"

"I certainly will not," said Phin.

He left the sluggoid at the railing and decided to try the upper decks. A pair of amoeba-like creatures were canoodling there and told him to shoo. He searched the entire deck front to back, and finally found himself at the prow of the SS *Sun-Star*. The ache he'd been feeling had grown to a full-blown burn, and it wasn't due to the half dozen Sarkusian truffles he'd eaten earlier. He was profoundly, almost deliriously worried about Lola. He decided he needed to calm himself down. Relax a little bit. And so he did what all life-forms have done throughout the history of the universe when they need a little perspective. He took a deep breath and considered the stars.

They were wobbling.

Normally, when hurtling through hyperspace, stars appear as wispy contrails. They shimmer, they streak, but they do not wobble. These stars were most definitely wobbling. It was as if the entire universe was drunk.

Did Phin Fogg know what this meant? He did. And his considerable intellect began to fume.

They were all in terrible danger.

"I have to get to the captain, immediately," Phin said aloud.

"He's probably in the captain's quarters. He's usually there, for some reason," said the creature mopping the deck a few feet away. Phin whirled to face it.

"Oh, wait a minute," the creature said, pausing in its work to put a gooey finger to its gooey chin. "Captain. Captain's quarters. I just got that!" The creature smiled. "Hello," it said. "My name's Jeremy. What's yours?"

22

LOLA WAS SCREAMING. IT sounded like, "Ahhhh-hhhh!!!!"

The Bog Mutant was screaming. It sounded like, "Aagh-ghghghghgh!!!"

Some other Bog Mutants, who were standing nearby, felt a bit left out and wanted to be part of whatever was going on, so they started screaming too. It sounded like eleven Bog Mutants going, "Aaghghghghghghgh!!!"

Gabby was also screaming. But hers sounded like this: "Stop screaming! Everyone, stop! Why are you screaming?"

Lola had leaped behind a reactor column. This had been her third choice of hiding places. The first was behind Gabby (which would have been rude); the second was behind herself (which proved impossible).

"Get away from them!" she shouted at Gabby. "They'll liquefy you! They're evil!"

Gabby did not get away. Instead she stood with her hands on her hips, cocking a thin eyebrow in a way that perfectly expressed the phrase *Girl, what on Zibulon are you doing?*

The Bog Mutants kept screaming until Gabby shushed them. Now Lola was the only one screaming—at intervals, and with decreasing intensity.

"AHHH," she screamed. "Ahh . . . ah . . ." She cleared her throat. "Um . . . *ah?*"

"What have you got against Bog Mutants?" Gabby said. "They run the ship!"

"What?"

Lola stepped out from behind the reactor column. Getting a closer look, she saw their badges did not read *Temporal Transit Authority*, but rather, *Staff.*

"Oh," said Lola. "Oh!"

"This is Jeremy," said Gabby, making a sweeping motion to all the Bog Mutants in the room.

"Hello!" they said.

"I'm Jeremy!" said one near the back.

"H-hi," said Lola. "Sorry about that. It's just . . . I've had some bad experiences with Bog Mutants."

"So have I!" said one. "Jeremy stepped on my toe this morning."

"That wasn't me! That was you!" said another.

"Oh, that's right," said the first, and turned back to what he was doing, stepping on his own toe in the process. "Ow!"

They were running the ship. Or rather, they were running the engine. Or rather again, they were stoking the engine. It looked like a giant coal furnace, only much bigger, and outfitted with sensors, dials, and electronic readouts. The mouth of the furnace was simply a massive iron grate into which the Bog Mutants were shoveling piles of coal.

Or what looked like coal.

"Dark matter," said Gabby, kicking a few briquettes across the floor. Every surface was dusted with dark-matter residue. Some of it had even seeped into the bodies of the Bog Mutants themselves, making their slime cloudy.

"We like Gabby!" shouted one of the Bog Mutants.

"Yeah!" said another. "We don't know why. But she seems neat."

"We don't like most solids," said a third, shoving his shovel into a crate of black, chalky fuel. "But Gabby's great."

"We like Gabby!" said the first, who'd already lost track of the conversation.

Gabby shrugged and smiled.

Lola considered the conditions the Bog Mutants were working in. It was cramped and sweltering. Not only did the dark-matter dust choke everything, the heat seemed to be melting the Mutants slightly. They smiled whenever they looked at Gabby, but when they returned to work, their expressions were solemn, even pained. They grunted with the exertion of their constant labor.

"Do you have to do this for the whole trip?" Lola asked.

"Someone's gotta keep the engine going," said one.

"But," said Lola, "don't you get a break?"

"Oh yeah!" said another, nodding sloppily. "Sometimes, you die! Then you get to stop."

"Oh," said Lola.

"It's great," said the Bog Mutant with gusto.

Just then a great wrenching, tearing, grinding, screeching, shuddering sound ripped through the heart of the ship. The floor beneath them shunted violently to one side and Lola was thrown to the ground. A plume of toxic dark-matter exhaust erupted from the furnace, engulfing one of the Jeremys.

"What was that?" Lola shouted.

"I . . . I don't know!" said Gabby, who had been tossed against a pylon. She winced and brought her hand from behind her head. It was covered in green blood.

"Hey, look," one of the Bog Mutants shouted. "Jeremy's been poisoned!"

They were all pointing to the Bog Mutant who had taken the exhaust blast straight to the face. He clutched his throat with one hand and coughed violently. With the other he gave a thumbs-up. The Bog Mutants cheered.

"Hooray! Good for you, Jeremy!"

"Enjoy your break, buddy."

The Bog Mutant wheezed, extended his other hand so that he could give two big wobbly thumbs-up, and collapsed on the pile of dark-matter briquettes, dead.

"Good old Jeremy," said one Bog Mutant.

"Lucky son of a gun," said another.

The ship gave another violent heave.

"Did we hit an iceberg?" shouted Lola, then caught herself. "I mean, like a space . . . iceberg?"

"Those are called asteroids," said Gabby, wincing at a readout from one of the wall-mounted terminals. "And that's impossible . . . unless . . ."

"Unless what?" shouted Lola. The room around them had begun to tremble, the solid steel walls rippling like . . . well, like Bog Mutants.

"Something pulled us out of hyperspace," said Gabby, considering the blood seeping from her head wound. "Or someone."

And with that, she promptly passed out.

23

AN ENORMOUS STAR LINER flung out of hyperspace and smashing into an asteroid is a sight to behold. The tractor beam—for that's what it was—that had pulled the *SunStar* out of hyperspace had also decreased its speed and adjusted its position so that the ship merely grazed the asteroid. The collision obliterated the ship's thrusters. Intact but crippled, the vessel hurtled through the darkness toward a red dwarf known as Proxima Centauri. All things considered, it was an incredibly lucky break. Though to the passengers on board, it hardly felt that way.

The asteroid, by the way, was the very place from which the tractor beam had emanated.

Everything was transpiring according to a very precise and intricate plan.

On board the SS *SunStar*, the sirens were deafening. So deafening it was hard to hear all the screaming. And all the screaming and all the sirens made it almost impossible to hear the great cruiser rending and buckling under the massive g-force, which the ship's antigrav computer was working madly to combat.

The ship twisted and flipped, until at last the antigrav computer got a grip on which side was supposed to be down. Passengers, deck chairs, teacups, and complimentary bottles of shampoo, all of which had been tumbling through the air, fell at once to the floor. For now, at least, to everyone on board it *felt* as if the *SunStar* was right side up.

In fact, it was still tumbling willy-nilly into a star.

Lola moaned. She was covered in dark-matter dust, as well as regular dust, and a few chunks of piping and ductwork that had come loose from the machinery around her. She coughed and worked herself into a sitting position. Gabby lay a few feet away, unconscious but breathing. The Bog Mutants were scattered like debris from an exploded jelly doughnut. One by one they picked themselves up, brushed themselves off, and separated themselves from one another.

"I think you've got my nose, Jeremy."

"Hey, looks like I do! Can I keep it?"

"Sure! I always liked your nose better anyway."

"What happened?" said Lola. She hacked. "Are we sinking or . . . whatever the space equivalent is?"

"ATTENTION, PASSENGERS, ATTENTION, PASSENGERS," came a voice over the loudspeakers. Lola quivered. Voices on loudspeakers were almost never a good thing in her experience.

"THIS IS YOUR CAPTAIN SPEAKING. WELL, I'VE GOT SOME NEWS. FIRST, TONIGHT'S SCREENING OF *STARSHIP TITANIC* HAS BEEN CANCELED."

"Aww," said one of the Bog Mutants, who'd been looking forward to it.

"I KNOW THERE WAS A LOT OF ARGUMENT OVER WHETHER SHOWING A FILM ABOUT A HORRIBLE INTERSTELLAR CRUISE SHIP CATASTROPHE ON AN INTERSTELLAR CRUISE SHIP WAS INAPPROPRIATE. AND I KNOW THE DETRACTORS ARE STILL A BIT SORE. BUT I'M HERE TO TELL YOU, THE WHOLE THING HAS BECOME MOOT."

"Oh, for Pete's sake," Lola said, getting to her feet.

"THE SECOND BIT OF NEWS, WHICH I'LL GET TO IN A MOMENT, HAS REALLY THROWN THE WHOLE *SHOULD WE SHOW A MOVIE ABOUT A STAR SHIP CRASHING WHILE ON A STAR SHIP* DEBATE INTO RELIEF, LET ME TELL YOU. THE IRONY IS . . . WELL, IT'S JUST PRETTY ASTOUNDING."

There was a mumbling sound off mic.

"QUITE RIGHT, ENSIGN. ENSIGN SANDERS INFORMS ME, CORRECTLY, THAT THIS ISN'T AN EXAMPLE OF IRONY, PER SE. BUT RATHER MERE *COINCIDENCE*. AND I'M SURE WE'LL ALL

TAKE GREAT COMFORT IN THAT KNOWLEDGE. THANK YOU, ENSIGN SANDERS."

Lola took it upon herself to see if the hatch out of the engine room was jammed shut. It was.

"SO, TO THE SECOND BIT OF NEWS. WELL. IT SEEMS WE'VE STRUCK SOMETHING, AND NO, IT WASN'T AN ICEBERG, SMARTYPANTS. THAT WOULD BE ABSURD." The captain cleared his throat, a sound meant to be small and unassuming, which was loud and bone-rattling when transmitted through the loudspeakers. "WHAT WE'VE STRUCK IS AN ASTEROID, WHICH, YES, SOME MIGHT COMPARE TO AN ICEBERG IN SPACE. THOUGH THIS ONE, IT SEEMS, ISN'T MADE OF ICE, THE WAY SOME ASTEROIDS ARE—A FACT MANY OF YOU WILL RECALL FROM TUESDAY'S AFTER-DINNER SCIENCE LECTURE: SPACE JUNK AND YOU. ANYWAY."

"Come on!" Lola said, gesturing to the Bog Mutants. "You've got to help me get this open!"

The Mutants looked at one another. They glanced at the piles of dark-matter briquettes that needed to be cleaned up. They glanced at the engines, which weren't going to stoke themselves. They glanced at the floor, sheepishly, and had no idea what to do.

"I'm ordering you," Lola tried, feeling a bit bad about bossing them around but deciding she could live with it under the circumstances, "to help me get this hatch open."

"THE ASTEROID HAS DESTROYED OUR PROPULSION SYSTEM, AND WE'RE UNABLE TO CONTROL THE SHIP," the captain continued. "WHICH WOULDN'T BE SUCH A BIG DEAL IF WE WEREN'T ON A DIRECT COLLISION COURSE WITH A RED DWARF, WHICH WILL CONSUME THE SHIP IN A FIREY CATACLYSM IN—ENSIGN?"

There was a pause.

"ENSIGN SAYS WE'VE GOT ABOUT TWENTY MINUTES. SO WHAT YOU SHOULD DO," the captain continued, "IS GO AHEAD AND GET TO YOUR EMERGENCY TELEPORT RAFTS IMMEDIATELY. PLEASE PROCEED IN AN ORDERLY FASHION, BUT, YOU KNOW, DON'T WORRY ALL THAT MUCH ABOUT BEING ORDERLY. THE PRIORITY HERE IS GETTING OFF THE SHIP BEFORE IT FALLS INTO A STAR, IS WHAT I'M SAYING."

Lola had an idea. "Hey, Bog Mutants!" she called. "Congratulations, you've all been promoted! You've all been promoted to official, uh, door openers!"

Expressions of pure wonder and delight consumed their faces. Never, in all their peoples' history, had anyone *ever* been promoted.

"Hooray!" the cheered. They high-fived each other splashily.

"Can we have a party?" asked one.

"Yes!" said Lola. "And there will be cake and streamers and hot chocolate, but first you've got to help me get this door open!"

"Stand aside, miss," said the nearest Bog Mutant. "That's our job!"

"LET'S SEE," boomed the captain. "IS THERE ANYTHING I'M MISSING? WELL NO, I SUPPOSE THAT'S ALL. IT'S BEEN AN HONOR TO BE YOUR CAPTAIN. SHAME ABOUT THE SHIP, BUT THEN, I'M SURE SHE'S INSURED UP THE WAZOO, SO REALLY I'M NOT TOO BROKEN UP ABOUT HER FALLING INTO A STAR.

"OKAY, THANKS EVERYONE! YOU'VE BEEN GREAT! THIS MESSAGE WILL NOW REPEAT."

EVERYONE ON DECK WAS running to the emergency teleport bays and blinking away to safety. Everyone, that is, except Phin. He scrambled over upended deck furniture, leaped over a cello, and slid under a spindly table that was, against all common sense, still neatly set for cocktails.

The crash had tossed him several yards from the bridge, but at last he reached the steely double doors, which had been rent apart by the collision. The control room was a maelstrom of tangled wires, blinking lights, and screaming alarms.

He was alone. The captain and crew were either helping passengers to escape or, more likely, had simply escaped themselves. Putting a hand to the bridge's teleport bay, Phin found it was still warm. Yep, they'd bolted. The ship's PA was still replaying the captain's final message to the guests on repeat. Phin switched it off.

Just go! a little voice in his head shouted. *Lola will be fine. She'll get to a teleport. Just save yourself!*

The voice was being a bit generous to Lola, whom, Phin knew, couldn't operate a teleport to save her life—which was exactly what she would need to do in this situation.

Muttering a series of Venusian curses about the pitfalls of friendship, Phin rushed to the security console. He shut off the sirens localized to the bridge. Now he could hear himself think, at least. The console was a wreck. Every monitor save one was dark, smashed, or just a mess of snowy static. Using the single functioning monitor, Phin began to cycle through the ship's security camera feeds. One by one, images of the state rooms, corridors, and antechambers of the ship flashed by. Quite a lot of these places were on fire. Even the swimming pool.

"Come on," he hissed. "Where are you? Where are you?"

Picture after picture clicked by. A Martian man grabbing jewels from his private safe, a sluggoid stuffing itself with food from the buffet, the band playing atop the aft deck, refusing to stop until someone agreed to pay them.

Now he checked the underchambers of the ship—the engine room (destroyed), the coolant chambers (drained), the cargo hold—

"Oh," said Phin. "You have *got* to be kidding me."

He zoomed in, adjusted the image, and saw that what he'd thought he'd seen was in fact exactly what he saw.

There was Lola Ray, having what looked like a serious argument with about a dozen Bog Mutants.

"Escape pods!" Lola shouted. "Or . . . transport . . . rafts! Whatever!"

"What about them?" asked a Jeremy. He was carrying an unconscious Gabby over his shoulder while his brethren sealed the door to the smoldering engine room. They'd rushed out into the cargo hold, where Lola hoped there'd be some method of escape. That hope was dwindling rapidly.

The cargo hold was a disaster area. The crash had sent several of the crates sliding into each other, and about thirty or so of the guests' sleek personal ships were piled against each other in a wildly expensive heap.

"Where," she said slowly, "are the transport rafts?"

"Oh, I know this one!" said one of the Jeremys not currently carrying Gabby. "All transport rafts are located on the luxury decks fourteen through nineteen, recreation decks eleven through twelve, service decks five through eight, and engineering deck seven."

"Wow," said Lola, impressed with his recall. "And we're on . . . ?"

"Engineering deck one!" said another Jeremy in triumph.

"Right," said Lola. She looked the way she and Gabby had come, which was now buried under an avalanche of expensive junk two stories high. The service hatch they'd used was now somewhere under two tons of leisure gear.

"Right," said Lola, with considerably less enthusiasm. "Super."

Lola scanned the room. The hatch they'd come through was person-sized, but these crates and ships had to get in here somehow. She stepped back, examining the hold's floor. A seam ran the length of the room, bordered by stripy yellow caution paint. Of course, there were the cargo bay doors! But opening them would suck everything and everyone in the hold out into the cold vacuum of space. Which, if the rumors were true, was not a super-fun place to be.

Thinking fast, Lola hurried to the mountain of wreckage. Her gaze settled on one of the less-badly damaged ships. This one was a sleek red space limo, about the size of a small truck.

"That one!" said Lola, pointing.

"It's red!" said a Jeremy.

"And it's in the corner!" said another, excited to be participating.

"It's going to be our life raft!" said Lola, trying and failing to yank open the passenger side door. Back home, the most she'd ever stolen was some gum (and she was still sick about it), and now here she was, a stowaway traveling under an assumed name, attempting to break into someone's limo. Life was funny.

But not hilarious.

The ship shuddered beneath their feet, just in case anyone had forgotten what kind of danger they were in.

"Jeremys, congratulations!" said Lola. "You've just been

promoted to official spaceship stealers. Now get into this thing, and get it started!"

"I'm excited by this new challenge!" shouted the Jeremy carrying Gabby. The young steward was beginning to regain consciousness. She swayed on her feet as the Jeremy set her down.

"Easy there, I've got you," said Lola, wrapping the other girl's arm around her shoulders. "Gabby, how do we open the bay doors?"

Gabby blinked at her thickly and gestured toward one of the wall-mounted control panels. Together the pair hobbled to the panel. Lola tried a few buttons.

"Like this?" she said, but Gabby's head lolled onto Lola's shoulder.

"It looks like you're trying to open Main Cargo Door One," said the panel in a chipper computerized voice. *"If this is correct, press one!"*

Lola pressed one.

"Please enter your twenty-seven-digit pass code, followed by the pound sign."

"Argh!" said Lola, and smashed her fist into the control panel.

"It looks like you're trying to smash Main Cargo Door One Control Panel Alpha. If this is correct, press two."

Over Lola's shoulder, something went *pop* and *hiss*. The

Jeremys had managed to open the limo's aft hatch.

"Great news!" said one, peering inside. "There are eleven seats!"

"There are twelve of us!" Lola growled. She thought of Phin, where he was, and whether he'd found a transport raft. "I could really use your help right now, Phin Fogg," she mumbled to herself.

"AHEM," came a familiar voice over the loudspeaker. "SORRY, I DON'T MEAN TO INTERRUPT. IT LOOKS LIKE YOU'VE GOT THINGS PRETTY COVERED DOWN THERE. BUT, IF YOU NEED SOMEONE TO OPEN THE BAY DOORS, I CAN DO THAT."

"Phin!" said Lola. "I am so glad to hear your stupid voice!"

"*Initiating Hold Evacuation*," chirped the little control panel, "*Main Cargo Door One will open in thirty seconds. If you would like to take a short customer satisfaction survey, press three now.*"

"You did it!" shouted Lola, looking up toward the ceiling and the upper decks where she imagined her friend to be. "Also hi! Also where are you? Also what's happening?"

"HOLD ON, LET ME COME DOWN THERE," came Phin's booming voice. "ACTUALLY, WHAT AM I SAYING? YOU COME UP HERE. LET ME JUST WARM UP THE SHORT-RANGE TELEPORT."

Lola felt her limbs go tingly. It was the same feeling she'd experienced when she and Phin had teleported to the ticket kiosk back on Luna, but where that had been a sudden, instantaneous yank, it felt instead as if she were being gently tugged away from where she stood.

"Jeremys!" she shouted at the Bog Mutants. "Go! Get in the limo!"

The Bog Mutants hesitated. "And do what?"

"Escape!" said Lola.

"That doesn't sound like a job," said one.

"It sounds like quitting a job, actually," said another.

"Bog Mutants don't quit," said a third, with a kind of resolve Lola hadn't heard from a Bog Mutant before.

The tingling sensation increased. Beads of ionic energy began to sparkle and lift from Lola's skin. Gabby moaned in her ear, barely able to support her own weight.

"Bog Mutants of the SS *SunStar*," said Lola as the teleport took its hold. "I am giving you your final promotion, the task you will perform for the rest of your days."

The Jeremys blinked. They listened in hushed wonder as the walls crumbled around them.

"Your job is to go out into the galaxy and live. Go to museums. Read good books. Go to the movies on rainy afternoons. From this moment forward you are professional life-livers. You will find your passions. You will fall in love. You will try new things and see as much of this universe as possible in whatever time you have left. You will be happy. Now"—Lola pointed at the limo with all the gravitas of a space wizard—"I command you: *go!*"

The Bog Mutants didn't budge.

"Um," said one. "That's a bit vague."

"Yeah, there's a lot of room for interpretation there," said another.

"Are we supposed to fall in love with each other, or . . . ?"

"What if the afternoon isn't rainy?"

"*Drab droof* it all," said Lola. "Fine. Go open a taco stand."

"Done!" said the Bog Mutants, and they all hurried joyfully aboard and closed the hatch behind them.

The tingling magnified, the air around Lola zapped and sparkled, and then with a soft *zzt* she felt herself whip through the blackness and rematerialize in a large room with a big steering wheel and lots of electronic panels flashing alarmingly.

"Welcome to the bridge!" said Phin. "Who's she?"

The teleport had picked up both Lola and Gabby, who was still leaning on Lola's shoulder. The other girl burped, held a fist to her lips, then stumbled to the nearest trash bin to be sick.

A series of clunking, grinding sounds reverberated through the hold. A fissure appeared from aft to stern, and the floor beneath the ships and luggage opened and fell away. And all of it, every last piece of absurdly expensive hardware, drifted out, like seeds released into the blackness of space. There was a long, interstellar silence.

And then a single ion thruster came to life in the darkness, and a small red space limo piloted by a ragtag crew of Bog Mutants shot away into the void, off to find a nearby planet in need of a taco stand.

25

ON THE DILAPIDATED BRIDGE of the SS *SunStar*, there was a lot of hugging going on.

"You're not dead!" Lola was saying, hugging Phin so tightly she lifted him off his feet.

"I'm not dead. I'm definitely not dead," he said. "But I will be if you don't let me *breathe*!"

"Sorry!" said Lola, and released him.

"Where have you been?" Phin asked, hugging Lola now. "I was going to teleport away and then I thought, no, Lola needs my help, but it looks like you totally didn't need my help. Well, you did *a bit* toward the end, but the point is *I stayed to find you*! Aren't you proud of me?"

"We're alive!" shouted Lola.

"We're alive!" shouted Phin. "And we're going to die any second!"

"I'm feeling a lot of very conflicting feelings right now!" said Lola, a smile and a grimace fighting to gain control of her face. "What's going on?"

"We were yanked out of hyperspace," said Phin, "and I think I know why." He pulled something out of his tux and tossed it to Lola. It was the lavender invitation. "I'm pretty sure that asteroid we struck is Satellite B."

"The Triumvirate of Pong!" said Lola.

"Precisely," said Phin. "But more pressingly, the ship is out of control," he added, reeling toward the guidance system. "The asteroid did a number on it, and I'm pretty sure someone's spilled egg salad on the navigation system."

"Can you get control again?" Lola asked. "Oh, Phin, you should have seen it," she rushed on, "I met some Bog Mutants, but they weren't evil—"

"Who said all Bog Mutants were evil?" said Phin, then waved this silly thought away. "And yes, I think I can regain control, but I'll have to reroute power from the—"

"Excuse me," said a voice behind them.

It was Gabby.

She was leaning woozily against one of the command terminals, wiping her mouth with the back of her hand.

"Hi," said Phin. "Who are you?"

"Uh," said Lola, her smile utterly and completely losing the battle for her face. "This is . . . Gabby," she said.

"Great," said Phin. "Why is she pointing a gun at us?"

Gabby straightened to her full height, leveling the molecular destabilizer she was holding on Phin and Lola simultaneously—which may sound odd, if you've never seen a molecular destabilizer before. They are very nasty weapons with bifurcated barrels, allowing the wielder to kill two people at once in very nasty ways. Gabby's destabilizer was set to *obliterate.*

"Gabby?" said Lola. "What are you doing?"

"Step away from the guidance system," she told Phin, and pressed her free hand to her throbbing head. "And tell me immediately if you have any aspirin."

"No," said Phin, not moving.

"To which part?" said Gabby.

"Either?" said Phin. "Listen, whoever you are—"

"Her name's Gabby," said Lola.

"It isn't," said Gabby.

"It doesn't matter," said Phin. "If I don't get control of this ship in the next three minutes, we're all going to be toast. And not metaphorically."

"Correction," said Gabby, who was not really a Gabby or a Gallabulala at all. "*You* will be toast. She and I will be miles away."

Phin swallowed. "Could we vote on this?"

"Gabby!" said Lola. "Or whatever your name is, why are you doing this?"

Phin, suddenly remembering their cover, straightened. "Don't you know who you're dealing with? I am the Archduke of—"

"You are the Archduke of Ninnies," said Gabby, and

flinched. This had sounded better in her head. "That is to say, I know exactly who you are, Phineas T. Fogg. And you"—she angled herself slightly toward Lola—"are none other than the infamous time traveler known as *Passport*."

"Why does everyone keep calling you that?" Phin asked.

"Oh," said Lola. "Yeah, about that . . . when I arrived—"

"It doesn't matter," said Gabby, reaching behind her back for what—Phin and Lola hoped—was something harmless, like a party hat or a chocolate bar.

It wasn't either of these things.

"Put these on," she said to Phin, and tossed him a pair of cellular handcuffs. To the eye, the "handcuffs" looked like a bottle of tiny blue pills. "Do it!" Gabby shouted. "Or I'll blast you to kingdom come."

Not wishing to be blasted there or anywhere else, Phin popped open the bottle and swallowed one of the little blue pills inside. Instantly his wrists snapped together, bound at the cellular level by the powerful mutagen in the pill he'd just taken. It also bound his wrists to the nearest object, which happened to be the navigation system control panel.

"Phin, what are you doing?" Lola shrieked.

"Don't worry," said Phin, looking much braver than he felt. "You'll be safe. They need you alive."

"What's going on?" said Lola, whirling to face Gabby, who was not Gabby at all. "Who are you?"

"I'll be happy to answer that," said Gabby, "after this."

And with a powerful kick she sent Lola reeling backward into the emergency teleport. Lola vanished with a *zap*.

Gabby sighed the sigh of a job well done, stretched, and lowered her weapon.

"I'm sorry about this, you know," she said, programming the teleport to follow Lola's trajectory through space. "I don't have anything against you, or your family."

"He's insane," said Phin. "Bolus. He'll destroy us all."

The girl who'd called herself Gabby seemed to consider this, then she shrugged.

"It doesn't matter to me. I have a job to do, and," she said, stepping into the teleport, "Bog Mutants don't quit."

There was a *zap*, and Phin was alone.

26

TWO TELEPORTS IN LESS than ten minutes is a bit rough on the system, and Lola lurched behind a boulder and was sick. She straightened and found that she was standing in the soft, sandy loam of a barren planet. For miles around all was rock and dust, and above her, the open void of black space.

She was standing on the asteroid.

And one thing Lola knew about asteroids—thanks to Tuesday evening's after-dinner lecture, Space Junk and You—was that they did not have atmospheres.

She collapsed, gagging, hands at her throat. Her vision tunneled. Her life flashed before her eyes—all the boring and lovely and sad bits followed by a quick flash of utter craziness toward the end. This was it. She was doomed. After all those near misses, her number was up. She could not breathe in a vacuum.

"What are you doing?" someone asked.

Lola opened her eyes. She looked up. Standing silhouetted

against the stars and the distant glow of a red dwarf was Gabby. She was still holding the molecular destabilizer, but it was lowered at her side. With her free hand she was fiddling with the gunmetal charm around her neck.

"I'm . . . dying?" tried Lola. And then she tried breathing and found she could.

"Don't be ridiculous," said Gabby. "There's plenty of air. Can't you smell the synthetic atmosphere?"

"Oh," said Lola, and stood up. "Where are we?"

There were a lot of questions she wanted to ask at this moment, but this one seemed the most pressing.

"The teleport would have sent us to the nearest safe place. In this case, I guess it's the asteroid that struck the ship."

Both girls looked up into the sky, toward the red dwarf known as Proxima Centauri.

Against its glare was a tiny speck. If you squinted, you could just see it hurtling and tumbling, end over end, through space. It was the SS *SunStar*.

"Phin!" Lola shouted, and ran, ridiculously, toward the ship, only getting a few paces across the barren wastes before the futility of what she was doing occurred to her, and she stopped.

"Sorry. I'm afraid his death was necessary," said Gabby. "Darn this thing."

Lola turned to see Gabby continuing to fiddle with the charm at her neck. Whatever she was trying to do clearly required two hands, and one of hers was still holding the destabilizer.

"Do you need some help?" Lola asked.

Gabby glared at her and sighed. "Yes."

Lola tromped over, her sneakers and jeans caked in meteorite dust.

"Don't try anything funny," Gabby said as Lola reached for the charm. She pointed the double barrel of the destabilizer at Lola's chest.

"I thought you needed me alive."

"I can do a lot of damage without killing you," Gabby snarled.

The charm had little clasps, or rather, switches, on both sides. Lola pressed them, and when she did, the girl standing before her shimmered like a mirage and was replaced by a very similar-looking person, except slightly taller, with skin the texture—and hue—of lime Jell-O.

"Who—" Lola started.

"My name is Gretta," said Gretta, "director of the Temporal Transit Authority. And you, time traveler, are my prisoner."

The green woman standing before Lola fished in the pocket of her now too-tight *SunStar* uniform and produced a pair of very stylish glasses. She put them on. Then she fished in another pocket and produced a small handheld communicator.

"Mr. Bolus," she said into the receiver, "I have the target."

"Well done, Gretta!" came a spidery little voice through the device's speaker. "Identify your location and we'll come pick you up."

Gretta tapped some buttons on the surface of the communicator with her thumb. A readout appeared on the screen.

"We are located in the Alpha Centauri System," Gretta said into the communicator, "near Proxima Centauri space, on an asteroid called Satellite B. We're near something called the, uh . . . it says we're near something called the North Entrance."

"Excellent," said the voice of Goro Bolus. "A transport will be there to collect you shortly."

"And that," said Gretta with a smug little smile, "is that."

Back on the SS *SunStar*, Phin was almost—but not quite—totally panicking.

"This is mission control, we have received your automated distress signal," a voice over the radio was saying. "Please confirm your Vessel ID number so we may dispatch a rescue team."

"Yeah, thanks," shouted Phin, struggling to free his hands from the guidance controls. "I don't actually know my Vessel ID number?" There was a small communicator button on his cuff link, if he could just get his face close enough . . .

"Vessel, you must confirm your Vessel ID number," the voice continued. "Would you like to speak to someone in customer assistance?"

"Wow, I super wouldn't," said Phin, trying to activate his cuff-link communicator with his nose, which would have looked very strange to anyone watching, which no one was.

"Vessel, this channel is for command communication only," the radio demanded. "If you are not a rank of captain or higher, you must clear this channel."

"Look, just forget it," said Phin, bracing one foot against the console and trying to yank himself free. "I'm kind of busy dying right now."

With one final yank, Phin's cuffs broke free from the panel. Or rather, a bit of the panel broke free from the rest of the panel, sending Phin hurtling backward into the captain's chair. Gasping, with not a moment to lose, Phin pressed his nose to the communicator node on his pearled right cuff link.

Somewhere in the ship, many decks below, something began to rumble.

"Sir," the radio said with a note of impatience, "if you are not the captain of the SS *SunStar*, you are in violation of Galactic Telecom Code SH-420 and will be prosecuted to the fullest extent of the law."

"Welp," said Phin, "just, you know, add that to the list."

The rumbling was getting louder. Not, it should be noted,

the rumbling of the crashing ship itself, which was also getting louder, but something else. Something was rumbling and smashing, and it was getting closer.

"Vessel, Sun-Liner security forces are converging on your position," said the radio.

"Excellent!" said Phin. "They'll probably find a lot of panicky passengers standing on an asteroid called Satellite B, very near my position. Could you pick those guys up? Thanks a million!"

Phin got to his feet. He listened. It was hard to isolate one kind of rumbling from all the rest, but he did it. And not a second too soon. Phin looked left, then jumped right, just as an enormous steamer trunk with leather siding and the letters *VRW* stamped on the side in a repeating pattern smashed through the floor. For a moment the trunk hung in the air like a breaching whale, before crashing to the deck, turning in a circle, and popping open its lid.

"About time!" Phin shouted, and dived headfirst into his luggage.

What happened next is difficult to put into words.

The trunk began to shimmer. It began to vibrate. Its surface seemed to ripple and bend. It wobbled, pulsed, and changed in a manner that can only be described as a large steamer trunk transforming into a significantly larger and less-expensive-looking Volvo Rescue Wagon.

Decloaking, the Rescue Wagon smashed its way through what remained of the bridge. Its roof clonked off the ceiling, its wheels skidded over the deck. Fishtailing through one wall and reversing through another, the vessel righted itself, unrighted itself, picked a direction at random, and blasted off through the hull of the *SunStar* and out into the black of space.

Through the windshield, Phin saw a tumbling kaleidoscope of stars as the Wagon spun through the void. He flailed, hands still bound together, now with a bit of the *SunStar*'s control panel stuck to them, as the steering wheel spun freely.

"Hooo boy!" called Bucky. "All that bouncing around seems to have damaged our rear thrusters. We're flying blinder than a one-eyed rattler with an eye patch. We're spinning faster than a bobcat in a tumble dryer. We're—"

"Out of control, I get it," said Phin. "Bucky, reroute all power to automated guidance."

"Ten-four, good buddy!" said Bucky.

Phin turned to greet the stuffed bear in the back seat. "Hey, Teddy. No need to say anything. It's good to see you too."

"Let's play a game!" said Teddy.

"Let's save the day first," said Phin.

His hands still bound, Phin cleared his throat.

"Turn us around, Bucky. We're headed to the asteroid

known as Satellite B. North Entrance."

"Can do, little doggies!"

And with that, the small Wagon did an elegant back-flip, peeled away from the doomed star liner as it erupted in flames, and rocketed, spectacularly, to the rescue.

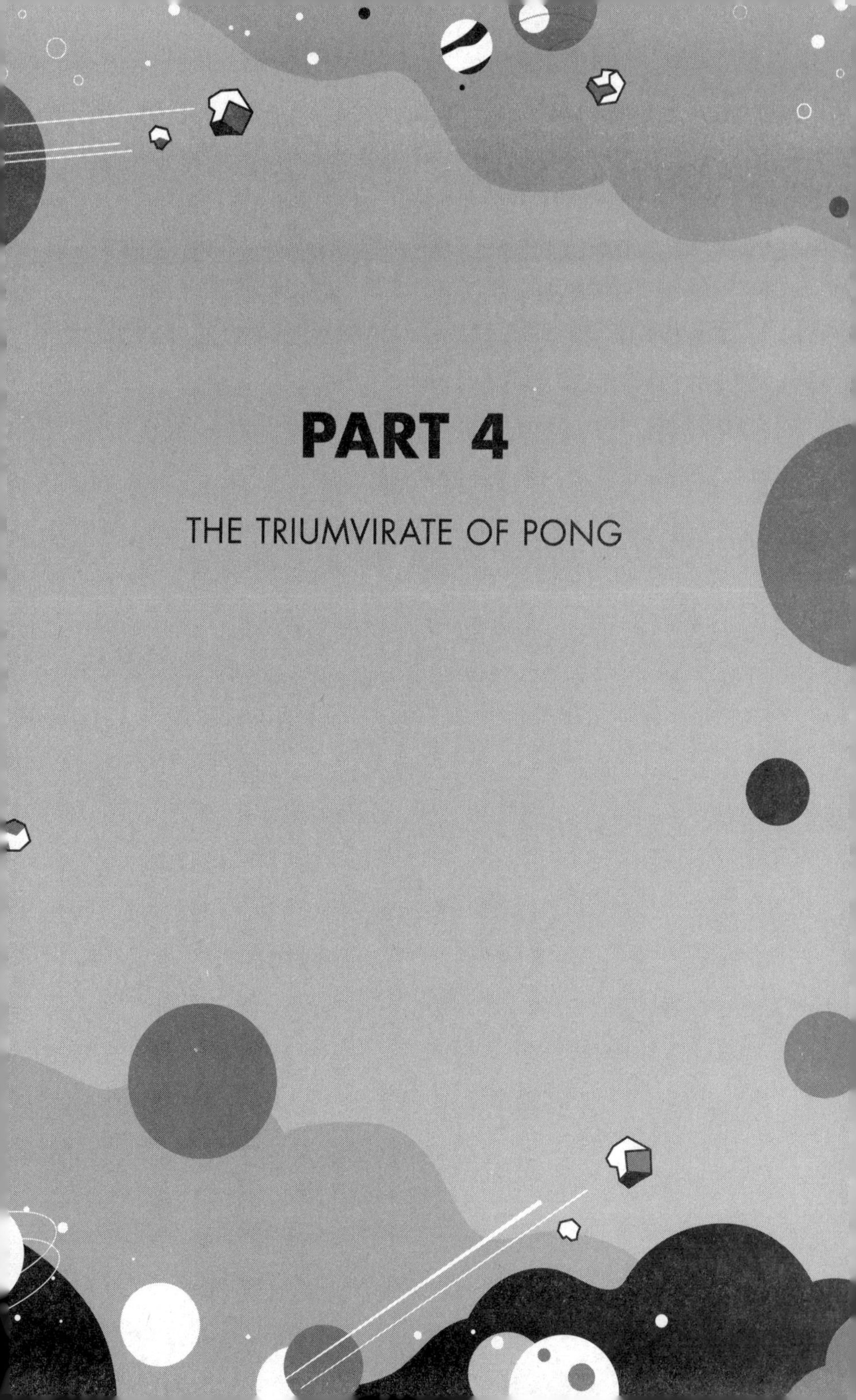

PART 4

THE TRIUMVIRATE OF PONG

27

IT WAS A VERY large, very dark, and very damp space. The air was hot and thick, and to stand within it was to know you were not alone.

Something immense lived here. Something as ancient as it was intelligent.

It was a creature born from pure energy, the agitation of particles slowly manipulated and gathered together over centuries. It was a being created by entities from another world, and it had been waiting with inhuman patience for this day.

With a voice that echoed through one's temporal lobes, the enormous creature, which spoke without lips, without a face, without a voice at all, said:

"The wizard draws near, as does the Child of Space and the Child of Time. The hour will soon be upon us, my wise companion. The time of the Great Unraveling, when the Triumvirate of Pong will make its final sacrifice, and the question that has

echoed across the dimensions will finally be asked."

"Excellent," said the much smaller entity in the large, dark, damp space. It patted its little paws together in eager anticipation. "Then I shall put the kettle on."

28

"DO YOU EVER GET the feeling," said Lola, "that you're being watched?"

"You are being watched," said Gretta, "by me."

They were seated on a pair of rocky outcroppings, facing each other. Lola sat with her head in her hands, elbows on her knees. She kicked at a pebble and watched it tumble through the dust. Gretta was more upright, keeping the destabilizer trained on her prisoner. She seemed a bit jumpy. This was in part due to where they were sitting—the spooky, dead wastes of an asteroid.

"You're shaking," said Lola.

Gretta had been squinting at Lola's T-shirt and trying to make out the design underneath the layers of dust and space grime, but at this comment her head snapped up.

"No, I'm not," Gretta snarled. "I mean, my hand's just tired."

She switched the destabilizer to her other hand. It did not shake. Gretta smirked. "See?"

"Anyway," sighed Lola, looking for another pebble to kick. "Do you know what I mean? About being watched? I feel," said Lola, "like someone . . . or something . . . is watching us."

Gretta growled. She actually growled. "Stop it. You're just trying to distract me."

Lola put her hands up in defense. "Really, I'm not. It's just . . . don't you feel it? It's like we're not alone here. That's all."

"Hmph," said Gretta. Then, after a long pause, "Yes, it does feel that way."

The pair lapsed into a tense silence. Wind howled across the plains. It dipped and tumbled through the craggy mountains to the west. It skittered in the dust around them.

Then, something else skittered.

"What was that?" said Gretta, whirling her gun on a group of boulders to the west.

"It was the wind," said Lola. "Like, skittering."

Gretta was on her feet. "That wasn't the wind."

In truth, Lola had been mostly trying to unnerve her captor, but now, ears straining, she heard it too. It was a sound like the scuffle of feet, or the twitching of tiny, inhuman jaws. A clackity, clinkity, altogether hair-raising sound.

"Do you see something over there?" Gretta asked, her voice thick.

The asteroid had begun to turn away from its neighboring

star, and in the devilish twilight, the shadows grew longer, stretching at mad angles from the cliffs and rocky spires. And in those shadows, specifically in the shadows near the boulders off to the west, it looked like something was moving.

Or lots of little somethings.

"It's, uh, your imagination," said Lola. Then added, "So would you please ask it to stop?"

"There's something behind those boulders," hissed Gretta. Keeping the destabilizer trained on the shadows, she looked around with a kind of twitchy franticness. With her free hand she wiped her brow. "I don't like it here," she said, almost to herself. "There's something—"

The skittering suddenly stopped. And like a refrigerator fan or a neighbor's television, the moment the sound was gone was the moment both girls knew with absolute certainty it *had* been there a moment ago. Its absence filled their ears like cotton. And then, just in case the goose bumps on their necks and arms were thinking about calling it a day, something new appeared in the shadows.

It was eight sets of tiny glowing eyes.

"Very slowly," said Gretta. "Let's back away very sl—"

She turned and saw Lola had already bolted halfway to the next canyon.

"*Oh, a black hole ain't no place for a cowboy!*" Bucky was singing. "*His spurs won't jingle-jangle in the void! When his best girl*

Betty turns to superstring spaghetti, you bet that all the cows'll be annoyed!"

"That's great, Bucky," said Phin. It didn't take a highly sophisticated user interface to detect his sarcasm. Bucky, however, seemed unfazed.

"Verse fourteen!" sang the computer. "*Oh, a black hole ain't no place for a rustler! A feller's got to stay home on the range! And did I forget to mention, when you're stuck in another dimension, all yer chaps and boots fit kinda strange!*"

"Stop," said Phin, as clearly as he could, "singing."

"Verse fifteen!" called Bucky.

The Rescue Wagon was making its way toward the asteroid. Though the immediate threat of immolation had passed, the little vessel's escape from the hull of the *SunStar* had left it badly damaged, and it hobbled its way across the expanses like a wounded bird, flopping and dipping and weaving toward the planetoid below. There was also something seriously wrong with Bucky. Battering around the *SunStar*'s bridge had knocked something loose in his mainframe, Phin figured, hence the more-annoying-than-usual behavior. Hence the *singing*. Under normal circumstances Phin would have simply covered his ears, but currently his wrists were bound together at the cellular level.

"And now a brief interlude in the music," said Bucky between verses fifteen and sixteen of "A Black Hole Ain't No Place for a Cowboy"—"to let you know we'll be touching down on the asteroid's surface in three point two minutes, which is just enough time to run through the chorus again!"

"Bucky," said Phin, "I'm going to delete you when this is over."

"Black hooooole! Black hooooole! You ate my hat but you won't eat my soul! Black hooooole! Black hooooole! Please give me back my cow, she is my frieeeend!"

29

LOLA DID NOT BOTHER to check if Gretta was following, on the off chance she might see the things with the glowing eyes—whatever they were—following them. Lola's sight was locked firmly on the terrain ahead, unwavering to the left or right, laser-focused. As long as she kept looking forward at the mile-or-so stretch of open plain, nothing, she assumed, would get the better of her.

Which is why she was so surprised when she ran face-first into the cathedral.

Lola toppled back, arms flailing, and came down hard in the dust. She sputtered. Her nose throbbed. Her brain did a double take. Slowly, with aching joints and wincing synapses, she raised her head to look at what she had bumped into, which had, she was certain, been completely invisible until the moment she'd bumped into it. Lola was certain it had been invisible, because an enormous gothic cathedral in the middle of a barren asteroid plain is a tricky thing to miss.

It was enormous.

The structure that loomed before her, casting its now visible shadow across the plain, was easily twice the size of Saint Patrick's in New York, three times the size of the Great Temple of Rock on the Planet Heavy Metal, and larger still than the MegaChurch of Thron's gift shop and cafeteria—rumored to be the largest emporium of affordable spiritual artifacts and ecclesiastical snacks in the galaxy.

The cathedral jutted from the earth like a fang. Its tower came to a sharp point hundreds of feet above where Lola now sprawled. It was stone, polished smooth by alien hands and lovingly—or at least exhaustively—hewn with carvings and gothic embellishments. Gargoyles peered from the eaves, their frozen features snarling or slobbering at the world below. And in places, figures one could only assume were angels reached up into the sky above Satellite B, their wings unfolded, their uniforms bunchy and ill fitting.

Lola sat up and made a fish face at it.

"Where did that come from?" she said. "And also, *ow*." She rubbed her aching nose.

Gretta had come to a hobbling, stuttering halt a few paces away, and now craned her neck back and back to take in the alarming structure.

"It's . . . it's . . . ," she said, very much as if she knew how to finish her sentence, which she didn't.

"It's a cathedral," said Lola, getting to her feet and dusting herself off—the little glowing-eyed creatures, at least for the moment, forgotten. "I mean, it looks like a church. What's that say over the door?"

There was a massive arch, housing double doors of stone. Above it were words in a language Lola didn't recognize or understand.

"It says," said Gretta, her voice soft with wonder, "*North Entrance.*"

A thrill of recognition rushed up Lola's spine. This could only be the North Entrance from their invitation to tea. But she certainly wasn't going to mention that, or the Triumvirate of Pong, to Gretta.

Gretta meanwhile peered hazily at some of the detail higher up on the central spire. "Those . . . angels," she said. "They almost look like . . ."

"Look!" said Lola, and pointed not at the cathedral, but at the way from which they'd come. There, at the edge of the plain, dust was beginning to billow. Something like a thundercloud was rolling toward them at a high speed, and whether it was a kind of sandstorm or the result of thousands of little alien feet beating after them in pursuit, Lola didn't care to find out.

"Come on," she said, grabbing Gretta's sleeve. The presence of danger and the appearance of the cathedral had brought them into a kind of uneasy truce. She ought to just leave Gretta to fend for herself, Lola thought. Instead, she used this moment of distraction to grab Gretta's destabilizer and hurl it into a gloomy crevasse.

"Hey!" said Gretta.

"Is for horses!" Lola shouted back, one of those annoying little sayings she'd picked up from her mother and couldn't seem to avoid saying no matter what the circumstance. "Come on!"

She yanked Gretta up the stone steps, under the archway, and to the stone doors, which refused to budge when Lola threw herself against them. Both girls now shoved the mighty barrier, but to no avail.

"Frizhadellus-Corpoilius," said Gretta.

"Is that some kind of password?"

"No. It's a very rude word."

"Oh," said Lola.

They looked out across the plain to where the dust cloud was rapidly approaching.

"Let's try again," said Gretta. "Put your shoulder into it."

"I did," said Lola, rubbing her sore arm. They tried again. They tried a fourth and fifth time, until both were panting and sore.

"What's crunching?" panted Gretta.

"What?"

"Something in your pocket," said Gretta, "made a crunching sound."

Before she could stop her, Gretta slipped her long green fingers into Lola's pocket and pulled out the small lavender invitation.

"Hey, that's mine!"

"*You are cordially invited to tea*," Gretta read aloud. "*North Entrance*. But that's where we are," said Gretta. "You *knew*?"

"No!" said Lola. "Well, yes, but I wasn't *sure* sure."

"What's the Triumvirate of Pong?"

"I don't know!" said Lola.

"Oh, so I guess you just get invited to tea across the galaxy by people you've never heard of, do you?"

"Yes," said Lola, eyes agog. "I guess I do."

"Well, we're here!" said Gretta. "Hello!" she called, and pounded on the doors. "We're here! Let us in!"

Unsure what else to do, Lola joined in. "We have an invitation! Triumvirate of Pong? Hello!"

Nothing happened, save for the approach of the sandstorm and whatever it presaged.

"Well, that's a bust," said Gretta.

"No, no, there's got to be something else," said Lola, panic beginning to clamber up her spine. "Something we're missing."

Gretta sighed and sat down on one of the steps. "Well, you know what they say."

"Hello!" Lola was banging on the doors now. "No, what do they say?"

"You know," Gretta said, and chuckled despite herself. "About tea and all."

"I don't," said Lola. She banged on the door again. "Open up! There are things chasing us!"

"How can you not know that saying?" said Gretta. "You know, it's one of those annoying little sayings you pick up from your parents that you can't help but say no matter how silly it is." Gretta blinked, a memory flickering past her eyes and not quite resolving itself there. "I think my dad used to say it . . ."

"This is Lola Ray!" Lola shouted at the door. "And Phineas Fogg is my friend, even though he's not here right now. You invited us to tea!" Lola was nearly breathless with shouting. "Maybe that's it? Maybe Phin needs to be here for the doors to open?"

"They say," said Gretta, as if trying desperately to remember something that was just at the edge of her awareness. "They say, *If someone offers you tea, always think twice before saying yes.*"

Lola slowly turned. She looked at Gretta.

"What was that?"

"Hmm?" said Gretta, coming back to the present. "Oh, you know. *If someone offers you tea,*" she repeated in a kind of annoyed singsong, "*best think twice before saying yes.*"

Lola turned to the doors.

"Yes?" she said.

"Yeah—" Gretta started, and then gaped as the ground began to shake. Dust sifted from the crags and crevices of the cathedral's towers. And then, with a great grinding wail, the doors swung open.

Gretta leaped to her feet and rushed to Lola's side. "What did you do?"

Lola looked at her, blinked, and smiled a dazed, daffy smile.

"I thought *twice*," she said with a little laugh. "And said *yes*."

"Oh," said Gretta. "Oh . . ."

"Yeah," said Lola.

"That is . . . that is just *so* . . ."

"Yeah," said Lola. She turned to the now-open doors and the stairs descending beyond. "Come on," she said. "Let's go."

A CIRCUS TENT PLUMMETED through the artificial atmosphere of Satellite B. Its flaps rippled in the wind, the little triangular flag jutting from its peak bent back by the g-force. Then the tent shimmered, throbbed, and transformed into a Sarkusian Long-Range Exploration Shuttle, before throbbing again and turning into a Sarkusian truffle, and then a crate of avocados, then a small escape pod for a moment, before at last settling on the form of a 1998 red Volvo station wagon.

The ship was crashing.

Phin was screaming.

Whether Bucky was screaming or going for the high C in the second sub-bridge of "A Black Hole Ain't No Place for a Cowboy" was unclear.

The Rescue Wagon swung in low over the mountains, clipped a peak, buzzed the camp of recently teleported and marooned *SunStar* passengers and crew awaiting rescue, hurtled up again, tumbled over another mountain, and then skipped across a plain before coming to a rest, smoldering, front fender half buried in the dust.

The emergency impact rescue foam—a bit late but still trying its best—exploded through the interior of the ship, encasing everything in a protective sponge. The foam then retreated back into its evacuation jets, satisfied it had done its job well, if a bit after the fact.

Phin coughed and gagged.

He was alive. He was impossibly, excruciatingly alive.

Something had saved his life, and it sure as Sally wasn't the emergency impact rescue foam. Something soft was between him and the dashboard, which would have certainly smashed his brains out otherwise.

The soft thing was big, fuzzy, and slightly mildewed. It was Teddy.

"Oh, buddy," Phin said, resting his head on the bear's familiar old tum. "Thank you thank you thank you thank you."

"Let's play a game!" said Teddy.

Phin glowered, or tried to glower—he was so relieved to be alive it was hard to affect a good scowl. "So, I suppose you'd have me believe that you were just tossed up here and that you saving my life is a lucky coincidence."

"Let's play a game!" said Teddy.

"And that you're really just a toy bear with nothing special about you at all."

"Let's play a game!" said Teddy.

"Fine," said Phin. "Have it your way."

Unfortunately, the crash had cracked the Wagon's aft window, or rather, shattered it in a spiderweb pattern, making it impossible to see through. Which simply meant Phin couldn't *see* the things approaching his Wagon from the rear.

He heard them though.

It was a strange sound. An eerie sound. A skittering, clicking, clacking sound. Images of asteroid crabs and deep-space vampire spiders flooded Phin's mind.

"Bucky? Bucky, you there?"

The dashboard was dark. The ship's computer was offline. Phin swallowed.

The skittering sound was getting closer. They—whatever they were—had reached the ship. He heard their little feet (claws? talons?) clattering across the roof. Coming for him.

Phin decided to shut his eyes.

He kept them shut as the things began to surround his vessel. He heard them on the windshield, on the hood now. He heard them clicking against the side paneling, clacking against the windows. Phin's breath came in ragged gasps. His pulse raced, it rocketed, it skipped several beats, did a somersault, jumped on a motorbike and sped away without him.

On the window just inches from Phin's left ear, something went *click-click.*

It was different from the other clicks. Deliberate. It had a purpose. It was a message.

Then again. *Click-click.*

Something was knocking on his front window.

"Nope," said Phin. "No thank you. No."

Click-click.

"I'd really rather not, thanks," said Phin. "Please go away."

Click-click . . . CLICK.

"All right, fine!"

With fearsome, mad force, Phin wrenched his eyes open and turned to look at whatever it was that had been doing the clicking.

It was a mushroom. And it was adorable.

It was the size of a footstool, with big, curious, blinking eyes that glowed slightly beneath its large, bell-shaped head. It had a tiny slit of a mouth, and little feet in what looked like tiny steel-toed work boots. It had little arms with little hands, one of which it was using to hold itself to the side of the Wagon. In its other hand it held a cute little wrench, which it had used to tap on the window. And around what could be called its waist was . . . well, a tool belt.

Phin glanced around. His ship was covered in mushrooms. Cute little mushrooms with cute little faces, all of them wearing cute little tool belts that clicked and clacked as they moved, their tiny tools clinking together. The clattering he'd heard on the roof was the sound of their steel-toed boots on their tiny little feet. There were smaller, rounder mushrooms, taller willowy ones, brown ones, red ones, ones with flat wavy heads like chanterelles, and others rounded and umbrella-like, like shiitake.

"Fungi," said Phin.

"Boop," said the mushroom at his window. "Boop moop boop?"

"Sorry?" said Phin. "You're a bit muffled. Through the glass I mean."

"Boop boop," said the little mushroom. It tapped again on the window with its wrench. "Moop?"

"I can't roll it down," said Phin. "It's jammed."

The little guy nodded, tucked the wrench into a pocket on his tool belt, and pulled from another a small flat piece of metal. In a moment, he'd jimmied the door open. Phin felt a flash of panic as the asteroid's cold atmosphere rushed into the Wagon, but he found the air was breathable and actually, quite refreshing.

The little mushroom climbed up onto Phin's lap, the pressure of its little feet pressing into his knees, but then his new friend produced a third tool—this one a small electronic device—and waved it over Phin's hands. There was a feeling like pins and needles all up and down his arms, and then, poof, Phin's wrists were no longer stuck together.

"Thank you," he said, rubbing the feeling back into his wrists.

The mushroom held out his little hand.

"Oh," said Phin. "Uh." He reached into his pocket, found it empty, reached between the seat cushions, found about seventy-five cents there, and dropped it in the little mushroom's hand.

"Boop," said the mushroom, and nodded, then hopped down off Phin's lap and joined his brethren outside the ship.

Phin wrapped one arm around Teddy and stepped out onto the dusty, musty surface of Satellite B—home, he guessed, of the mushroom people. Or mushroom mechanics, anyway.

"Do any of you speak . . . well, anything other than what you're speaking?" Phin said, talking loudly in that annoying way people do when speaking to someone who doesn't speak their language. "I speak a bunch of languages, actually. But I don't speak, um, Moop."

"Moop," a few of the mushrooms on the roof said in chorus. "Moop boop!"

Their words had a note of apology to them, so Phin waved and said, "That's okay. Could you just point me in the direction of the North Entrance? I'm looking for the Triumvirate of Pong."

"Boop. Boop-a-loop," said the little mushroom who'd freed him, and took Phin by the hand. Together, the family of mushroom mechanics led Phin, with Teddy under his arm, away from his ship and across the barren wastes. Except for a few, who stayed behind to repair the Rescue Wagon—a job for which they would overcharge him exorbitantly.

31

LOLA AND GRETTA DESCENDED into the catacombs beneath the cathedral. The staircase was not steep, but it was slippery, and wound in lazy curves, corkscrewing away from the surface, the air within growing closer and damper. The torches along the walls seemed to dim the lower they went, as if the flames were working all the harder to burn and sputter in the thickening humidity.

Gradually the gentle slope of the staircase leveled itself until they were walking on nothing but a winding ramp. Rivulets of moisture trickled freely past them, dribbling down the hollows. Here the stone had been worn away by centuries of exposure to these slow, steady streams. Images of slipping pried at Lola's mind. If you started sliding, how far would you go? The bottom could be miles away. An endless tumble to nowhere. She shivered despite the heat.

The ramp came to an abrupt end at the start of a long, wide, torchlit corridor. The open space only reinforced Lola's claustrophobia, the knowledge that she was somewhere underneath a mile of rock and stone. A little voice in her head was telling her to scream, but she told the little voice to go off and play with its friends for a while; she would listen to what it had to say later.

"Do you hear that?" said Gretta.

"This is scary enough," replied Lola. "You don't have to add to the atmosphere."

"No, really!" said Gretta. "It sounds like music!"

Lola listened. And it did sound like music. Soft, warbling, echoing music. Old music played on a gramophone, the kind that might accompany a silent film.

And it was coming from the end of the hallway.

The music grew louder as they approached. At the end of the corridor was another archway. It opened onto a larger chamber from which a gentle hot breeze pressed itself.

Together they stepped into the darkened vault. It was impossible to tell how large it was, but a small area just through the entrance was lit from above as if by a spotlight. In the center of the circle of light were a few objects of note.

Firstly, there was a medium-sized Victorian tea table, set with five places. There were five little tea saucers, five bone china teacups, a teapot, and little bowls for sugar and cream. There was also a tower of cucumber sandwiches and scones.

Beside the table, on a spindly platform of its own, was a large, old-fashioned gramophone, a record turning on its table, music issuing from its large, bell-shaped mouth.

And finally there was a sign set in an iron stand, the way one might find a menu displayed outside a fancy restaurant. It said:

Welcome!
Please seat yourself.
We suggest you take a moment to relax
Before
Looking
Up

The effect of the sign had the opposite of its intention, for immediately upon reading it Lola felt the intense urge to look up in the darkness of the cavern and was only able to stop herself by sheer force of will.

"I suppose we better seat ourselves," she said.

"No," said Gretta.

"What?"

"I said *no*."

It was a clear, quiet, firm refusal. It was a *no* that said *You do what you want. I won't make a fuss. But I am not moving from this spot, and I won't feel the least bit bad if you go ahead without me. This is my life and my choice, and what you make of it is your business.*

She stood on the threshold of the chamber, folded her hands behind her back, and did not budge.

Lola shrugged. She'd come this far, and she certainly wasn't going to stop now. Feeling nestled in the hands—or perhaps trapped in the jaws—of incontrovertible fate, Lola sat herself down to tea.

She took a moment to relax.

She looked up.

She couldn't see anything. The chamber stretched far above her head into an impenetrable darkness behind the spotlight. She could sense . . . *something* large in the gloom. Or perhaps it was only her imagination.

Again, Lola shrugged.

She helped herself to a cucumber sandwich. It was disgusting and flavorless, which is to say, it was a perfectly normal cucumber sandwich. She tried a scone instead.

"Excuse me! Excuse me!" a tiny voice called from somewhere in the chamber. "Please wait for the others! Please! Don't be rude now. Others are coming. Let's wait for them, please! I've put the kettle on. Sorry to ask you to seat yourself, but please if you would, please hold off on the scones and things. They're nearly here."

Lola, mouth full, replaced the half-eaten scone and sat straight in the uncomfortably fancy chair, feeling chastened.

"Sorrah," she said, a few crumbs leaping from her mouth and landing on the floor.

She was about to swallow and try this again, when a new sound filled the chamber. It was a scuttling, tinkling, clacking sound, identical to the one she and Gretta had heard on the surface. Lola nearly choked. She looked around at Gretta, who was staring off in the direction of the noise, frozen in terror.

Then, a new voice echoed around them.

"So I was standing right there," the voice said, halfway through some long and rambling story, "and I was like, you know, just take the teleport! But then I thought, no, she needs my help. So I *stayed*. I mean, I think that's pretty heroic."

The tinkling clanging sound drew closer, as did this new voice.

"And like, yeah, she was basically doing all right for herself by that point. She was helping a bunch of Bog Mutants escape the crashing ship, but I mean, come on. *I* didn't know that. She could have been captured! Or trapped under a bed somewhere! All I'm saying is, you know, it was a moment of personal growth for me. Oh, hey, Lola. I met some mushrooms."

32

IT WAS PHIN. HE emerged from the dark surrounded by half a dozen little mushroom people wearing tool belts. None of them seemed particularly interested in his story.

"Phin!" said Lola, blinking so hard she nearly bruised her eyelids. "How did you get here?"

"Service elevator," he said, jerking a thumb in the direction he had come. "Did I mention I met some mushrooms? Say hello, guys."

"Moop," said one of the mushrooms, and waved. "Boop boop."

"I call this guy Bertram," he said, referring to one of the smaller, round-headed ones.

In a flash she was on her feet and hugging him. "I thought you might be dead," she said.

"So did I. Still not completely sure I'm not. Hello." And he hugged her back.

"Oh good," mumbled Gretta. "More hugging."

"You!" said Phin and picked up a mushroom to throw at

her. "Stay back! I'll shroom you!"

"No, no, it's okay," said Lola. "She's lost her weapon, and besides, I think she's sort of okay."

"I am *not,*" hissed Gretta, crossing her arms, "in any way *okay.*"

"Moop!" shrieked the mushroom Phin was holding. He gently put it back on the ground.

"Oh, relax, Bertram. I wasn't really going to throw you." He straightened and grinned at Lola. "So, pretty awesome right? You thought I was dead, then, bam, here I am, totally alive and hanging out with some awesome fungi."

"Don't gloat," said Lola.

"I see you found the tea," he said, nodding toward the place setting. "And you've got crumbs on your chin, by the way."

"Do you have any idea what's going on?" Lola said.

"I'm not sure exactly," said Phin. "But I'm hoping the three-legged cat can explain."

He was looking over Lola's shoulder. She turned. Waiting very patiently a few feet away, not wanting to interrupt, was a three-legged cat. It wasn't a very peculiar cat, perhaps a little overlarge, with orange fluffy fur, long whiskers, and a tail that twitched. It was, as Phin pointed out, three-legged. The only unusual thing about this particular cat was that it stood upright and leaned on a small sleek cane, on account of its left rear leg, which was a metallic prosthesis. It also wore glasses and a nice tweed suit.

"Welcome, welcome," it said. It was the owner of the voice who had spoken to Lola a moment before. "We're so glad you're here. I've just put the kettle on. Everything's nearly ready. Thank you ever so much for coming. My name is Professor Donut, and on behalf of the Triumvirate of Pong, I welcome you."

This, thought Lola, would have been the perfect moment for a commercial break. But since this was real life and not a television show, things just went right on happening.

"Please," said the cat, "have a seat."

"The cat," Lola said, who would have thought herself used to this sort of thing by now, "is talking."

Phin made a face. "And wearing tweed."

"Ah yes, the suit," said the cat who called himself Professor Donut. "It is a bit academic I suppose, but then I do have tenure. It so happens I am the preeminent authority on cute fusion and subatomic fur straightening. I still teach a class at Flighty Shiny Thing University. You've heard of it, of course."

"Of course," said Phin and Lola in unison, though one of them was merely being polite.

Not sure what else to do, they sat. Phin cast a glance at Gretta, then arched an eyebrow at Lola as if to say, *Isn't she going to join us?* Lola shook her head as if to say, *Just let it go.*

"Are you comfortable?" asked Professor Donut. He was eager and anxious to please—two qualities Lola did not normally associate with cats. "We have a selection of herbal and black teas to choose from. No Darjeeling, I'm afraid. You wouldn't believe the troubles I've had with deliveries out here."

"So," said Phin, clearing his throat. "*Triumvirate* implies three. Where's the rest of the, um, Pongs?"

"Oh, that," said Professor Donut. "One of them is directly above us."

Together, all of them, Gretta included, looked up. Helpfully, the spotlight switched off. There was lots of blinking and eye rubbing, and then, with a collective gasp, they saw it.

Suspended above them, nearly the size of the asteroid itself, was a great spherical green orb. It was attached to the walls of the cavern by thousands—millions—of stringy green filaments. The sphere, whatever it was, pulsed with life. A strange phosphorescent glow seemed to emanate from its core. It was massive, ancient, and alive.

And then it spoke.

It spoke without words, without voice; it spoke directly into their minds. It was itself a mind so huge and fibrous its synapses were the size of telephone poles, and its neurons discharged with the force of small electromagnetic bombs. It was the only one of its kind in the universe, and it had been created by beings from another dimension. This thing, this impossible thing, spoke to them. It said . . .

"I—"

And then the kettle went off.

"Oh dear! Sorry, just a moment," said Professor Donut, and hurried off to fetch it.

"*Ah,*" sighed the thing above them. "*Hmm. I guess . . . I'll just wait . . .*"

The whistling subsided into a gentle hoot, and the professor reappeared carrying the kettle. Lola stood to help him, but he waved his paw.

"No no, please sit. I'm quite all right."

Lola sat.

With painstaking ceremony, Professor Donut set down the kettle, opened the teapot, poured the water, closed the teapot, hobbled away with the now-empty kettle, and returned a moment later now carrying a fresh plate of scones. He helped himself to one of the spindly chairs, sat, and folded his paws together in satisfaction.

"There now," he said at last. "Please, continue."

"*All right,*" said the voice, its power resonating through their skulls. "*Are you sure?*"

Phin and Lola exchanged a glance.

"Yes, everything's set," said the professor. "Go right ahead."

"*Ahem, okay, then,*" said the voice. "*I . . . ,*" it said, "*am Mr. Jeremy.*"

33

"THOUSANDS OF YEARS AGO, some interdimensional beings known as the Phan became aware of our universe. For a very long time they knew our reality existed, but we knew nothing of them.

"One day a question began to beat in the heart of the Phan, a question so persistent and important it drove them half mad with wondering. And the Phan with their near-infinite intelligence came to believe that the answer to this question lay not in their own universe, but in ours. And so they formulated a plan. A plan to cross between worlds, to traverse the irrational space that separates dimensions, and enter our own.

"But they could not break through without aid from our side. And so the Phan made small holes. Tears, if you will, in the fabric of space, too small for them to travel through, but just large enough to influence things here. Little things. Like particles.

"Their first task was to create an army to do their bidding in our world, a species of mutants to act as their slaves and prepare our galaxy for their coming. And so, after hundreds upon

hundreds of years, they succeeded in coaxing, prodding, and influencing billions upon billions of tiny atoms into acids, and acids into cells, and then cells into mitochondria, mitochondria into complex synapses . . . and after a long, long time, I *was formed.*

"I was to be the source of a mutant army for their nefarious Temporal Transit Authority, and so I am, the father of every Bog Mutant, every Jeremy, in the galaxy."

Lola suddenly remembered something. "When I first arrived," she said, "a Bog Mutant tried to arrest me. I called him Mr. Jeremy and he said Mr. Jeremy was his father."

"Correct, child. I am the same."

"So if the Phan made you," said Phin, "and you make Bog Mutants—who occasionally try to kill us, by the way—does that mean you're going to, you know, try to kill us?"

Mr. Jeremy sighed again. This time it was not a sigh of patience, but a sigh of immense sorrow, the sigh of a parent who loves his children.

"The Phan have made slaves of my offspring. Here in my subterranean home there is little I can do to stop them, but I wish my children to be free," Mr. Jeremy rumbled with righteous and ancient anger. *"I have vowed to stop the Phan's evil at any cost. And so, I sent a message into the universe, a request for help. It was a complex message, decipherable only by the greatest minds in the galaxy. It was answered by only two."*

Professor Donut gave a small wave. "The pleasure was all mine."

"Together, we formed the Triumvirate of Pong, dedicated to combating the Phan, ensuring they never breach the gulf between dimensions and find the answer to the Question of the End."

"Ah," said Phin. "I see," he added. "I'm not . . . totally getting it."

"I have a question," said Lola, raising her hand politely.

"Just one?" said Phin.

"Sorry," said Lola. "But why is it so terrible if they get an answer to this . . . what was it? The Question of the End?"

"A brain as large as Mr. Jeremy's," said Professor Donut, "is capable of a certain degree of foresight. He has foreseen a possible future in which our enemy triumphs."

"*In this future,*" Mr. Jeremy continued, "*the Phan will ask the Question of the End. And when it is answered, the whole of creation will unravel itself. I have foreseen this.*"

Everyone took a moment to take this in.

"What's the question?" said Phin.

"*The question is not important,*" said Mr. Jeremy.

"Sure sounds like it is," Phin mumbled.

"*What's important is* who *may answer it, for only one person in the universe can. And it is this person the Phan have labored so long and so hard to find.*

"*The only person who may answer the Question of the End*

is a time traveler . . . ," said Mr. Jeremy. "*It is you, Lola Ray.*"

"*Frizhadellus-Corpoilius,*" mumbled Lola.

Professor Donut gasped. "My dear! Language!"

"*This is why you must leave this space-time, Lola,*" said Mr. Jeremy. "*Not only for your own sake, but for the sake of the universe.*"

"You can send me home?" said Lola.

"Wait," said Phin, eyes twitching between the cat and the enormous sentient fungus, "*Triumvirate* implies three—"

"Teddy!" said Lola, cheered to see the mushroom people had propped the old mildewed bear on the seat between her and Phin.

"*Ah,*" said Mr. Jeremy. "*I see our third member has arrived at last.*"

On the far side of the red dwarf our heroes now orbited, the Alpha Centauri hypergate turned slowly in space. It wasn't a very active hypergate, as Alpha Centauri wasn't a popular destination. At most it was a stopover between other, larger ports. A ratty-looking space station, the galactic equivalent of a truck stop, orbited nearby, its beacons advertising cheap food, hot coffee, and restrooms.

All at once, the hypergate's portal began to shimmer. Its quantum sauce pulsated and bubbled. Then, with a terrific flash, several hundred heavily armed ships emerged from its depths.

They were Sun-Liner security drones—sleek, silver, and deadly, heeding the supposed distress call of a vessel that had refused to confirm its Vessel ID number. The fleet emerged from the hypergate in tight formation. It flew in a deadly arc, buzzing the space station, and firing a few shots across its surface just for the sheer bullying fun of it.

Then, like birds in a flock, the drones swerved as one and turned toward the small, unremarkable asteroid floating nearby, the planetoid classified as Satellite B.

A distress signal was emanating from the sunnier side of the asteroid, and as the drones drew closer, the space castaways who had teleported there hours before cheered to see their rescue boats approaching. The drones, soulless automata tasked with obliterating anyone foolish enough to steal from Sun-Liner Space Cruises Limited, grumbled to each other. They'd hoped there'd be something here to kill, but this looked like a boring old rescue and recover job.

"ATTENTION, PASSENGERS AND CREW OF THE VESSEL SS *SUNSTAR*," the drones broadcast in their cold, robotic voices. "PLEASE CONFIRM YOUR VESSEL ID NUMBER OR BE OBLITERATED."

The people on the surface of Satellite B radioed back that if the drones would just hold on a minute, they'd find the captain and go ahead and confirm that number.

"YOU HAVE TEN SECONDS TO COMPLY," the drones added helpfully. "WE CAN ALSO CONNECT

YOU TO THE CUSTOMER SERVICE SECURITY DRONE ARMADA, WHICH WILL BE HAPPY TO HELP YOU RESET YOUR ACCOUNT AND/OR YOUR MOLECULES." As one, they powered up their weapons systems, taking aim at the crowd of three hundred or so rich folk huddled together around their pop-up emergency tents and lanterns. "TEN. NINE. EIGHT . . ."

The surface radioed back. They had the captain, who mercifully remembered their Vessel ID number. It was sixteen-oh-seven-nine-two-B, for the love of God.

"OH, FINE," the drones spat. "HAVE IT YOUR WAY. VESSEL ID NUMBER CONFIRMED. WE NEVER GET TO HAVE ANY FUN."

While all this was going on, another ship had slipped unnoticed through the hypergate. It had hidden itself in the security drones' slipstream and now peeled away, following its own course around the dark side of the asteroid. It descended through the upper atmosphere, gray and unassuming, and landed by some nasty-looking boulders at the exact coordinates its automatic pilot had been given.

The little ship settled, its exhaust stirring the dust around its landing gear. A hatchway opened, casting light out into the night. A ladder descended.

A figure lowered itself carefully, gingerly, onto the planetoid's surface.

It looked around.

It took a few hesitant steps out from under the canopy of the ship's hull. It looked around again.

It checked its personal tracking device. The coordinates were correct.

It scratched its head.

The figure, just trying to be thorough, jogged all the way around the ship, peered behind some boulders, peeked under some rocks, then climbed to the top of a stony outcropping to gaze out over the barren wastes of Satellite B.

It called out, "Hello!"

There was no answer. The person it had come to collect, and her prisoner, were gone.

"Oh, come on!" it called, its voice echoing into the spooky distance.

The figure glanced over its shoulder at its shuttle, and then, with a heavy sigh, it began to jog across the tundra, just a small wobbly creature in a Temporal Transit Authority uniform that was a size too big.

34

TEDDY, THE THIRD AND final member of the Triumvirate of Pong, did not suddenly look around at them and say hello.

He did not light up his bubble pipe, wink at Phin, and say something jolly, like, "Well, my boy, we've certainly come a long way, haven't we?"

He did not move at all, but everyone waited in hushed silence as if he might.

"It's good to see you," Professor Donut said at last, patting Teddy on the leg. He smiled at the rest of them as if to say, *Well, isn't this nice? All of us here together?*

"Um," said Phin, "are you all . . . *crazy*? He's just a stuffed bear!"

Lola shifted uneasily in her seat. She was fond of Teddy, but he was, as Phin said, just a stuffed bear. She'd been taking all of this very seriously and now wondered if their hosts were barking mad.

"*Sadly*," intoned Mr. Jeremy, "*no, we are not insane. Would that it were so. It would make everything much simpler.*"

"I'm afraid our friend here," said Professor Donut, indicating Teddy, "is under what you might call a spell."

"A spell?" said Lola.

"You might call it that, but you'd be wrong."

"Oh."

"What he's under would more accurately be described as a transformative hyperstasis transfiguration. It's a very fascinating branch of the cute sciences." The professor patted his paws together, hoping someone would ask him to explain it.

"Someone turned him into a bear?" Lola tried.

"Not quite," said the professor. "He's always been a bear. Someone transformed him into a *stuffed* bear, and that someone was me."

"But why?" said Lola.

"It was necessary to keep an eye on dear Phineas here," said the professor. "The three of us knew the day would come when Eliza and Barnabus Fogg would have an offspring, and that offspring would be crucial to the fate of the universe. And so, one of us volunteered to stay close to the boy, to watch over him while safely disguised so as not to arouse the attention of the enemy . . . to be nearby when the moment was right to tell Phin all he needed to know."

"But he *didn't*," said Phin, standing in a fury. "He didn't tell me all I need to know! I mean, *clearly*! He hasn't done anything! He's just been sitting there!"

The professor shook his head. "Though his outward appearance may appear inert, I assure you Theodore has maintained a psychic link with you for years."

"Phin," said Lola, reaching for his hand. "Are you okay?"

Phin was scowling. He was visibly shaking.

He felt lied to, manipulated, and used. He felt swept up in something he had no control over and he felt that the universe had unfairly put him in this position. His favorite bear was not at all the person he'd imagined him to be but was rather a total stranger. And so were these people, this Triumvirate of Pong. And so, after all, were his parents. All of them benevolent strangers. Who did not trust him with the truth, with his own life, with anything.

He felt as if the world had just patted him on the head and said, *There, there, be a good boy and do what we say*. And he had had quite enough.

"I'm out!" he said, and threw up his hands and walked away into the gloom of the cavern. Whether he was *out* in the sense of *out of the conversation* or *out of the room*, or whether he was out of this *interdimensional-save-the-universe* situation, was unclear. But they all watched him go in stunned silence—except for Teddy, who just stared at nothing at all.

And except, of course, for Lola.

"Phin, wait!" she said, getting to her feet. She felt a tender paw on her hand.

"I think Mr. Fogg would prefer to be alone just now," said

Professor Donut. "This is a lot to take in."

"*Mmm,*" said Mr. Jeremy. "*Perhaps Ms. Ray would like to see how she will return home.*"

Lola's universe grew very still. Part of her yearned to chase after Phin. But *home.* She'd come a long way to go back where she started. Her family. Her mother. Her father. Her sisters. McDonald's and Netflix and chocolate-covered espresso beans. Everything perfect and imperfect about her normal, long-lost life.

"Show me," she said.

With quiet compassion, Professor Donut took Lola by the hand and gently led her away from the table, the end of his cane clicking against the stone.

Then it was quiet.

The walls dripped. The warm breeze rustled in the corners. The planets turned.

Then Gretta, whom everyone seemed to have forgotten about, cleared her throat.

"So," she said, gazing up through her glasses at the planet-sized fungal core suspended above her. "Hi Dad."

35

EVERYONE KNOWS ABOUT THE power of cuteness. What you may not know is that cuteness is one of the five fundamental forces of the universe—in fact, it is the most powerful.

For centuries, scientists have harvested the power of cuteness to fuel spacecrafts, solve complex calculations, and even create pocket universes so small they literally fit in your pocket. It is said that a hundred baby chicks, a newborn bunny, and an infant dressed as a pumpkin can, with the proper equipment, create a bomb so powerful it would destroy the entire galaxy. Thankfully, this theory has never been proven, as in every experiment, researchers became so distracted by the cuddliness of their subjects that nothing ever got done.

(There is also a theory that very cute spaceships, especially adorably tiny ones, can, under the right conditions, travel at speeds faster even than those provided by hypergates. But this theory has also yet to be conclusively proven.)

Professor Donut was one of the leading experts in the cute sciences and had the laboratory to prove it. Lola found herself in a large cylindrical room, much like the base of a silo. The walls were polished aluminum, lined with storage bins labeled *googly eyes*, *pom-poms*, and *neutrinos*. The floor was cluttered with large machinery. Cannon-like ray guns on heavy bases, blinking computer bays, and everywhere a hopeless tangle of wires, ductwork, copper piping, and clumps of orange fur.

In the center was a large dais, ringed with lights that illuminated in a circular pulse, suggesting great, thrumming energy. This platform was clearly meant to power and elevate whatever stood upon it. The entire room, in fact, seemed designed to draw one's eyes to a single revered object, the object Lola knew without asking was the crowning achievement of Professor Donut's career.

On the dais, connected to a series of wires and intricate sensors, was the cutest set of fuzzy pajamas Lola had ever seen. It was a onesie, complete with footies and a butt flap, and a little hood with round teddy bear ears sewn on. The fabric was a warm and cuddly cotton, pink and decorated in smiling moons and stars. Over the belly was a cozy kangaroo pocket, perfect for keeping your hands warm while you snuggled in front of the television or drifted off to sleep in an equally cozy bed.

"Am I supposed to get in that?" said Lola. If one were going to travel back in time, doing so in a comfy, cute onesie didn't seem so bad. Assuming no one saw you in it.

"Not precisely," said Professor Donut. "You're going to get in the *pocket*."

"I don't understand," said Lola. "I thought you said you were sending me home?"

"I most certainly am," said Professor Donut, beaming with pride. "Lola, these machines harness the power of cuteness. With them, I have created my own tiny universe. A *pocket* universe, identical to our own in every way." He took her hand and led her closer to the dais and its pulsing lights. Lola could feel its power, like a buzz in her back teeth. "I have grown my pocket universe, nurtured it from its adorable little big bang through to what you would call the present day. And there I have held it for you, on a September afternoon in the year 2018. Now, with this ray," Professor Donut said, indicating a cannon-sized machine with a tapering barrel and blinking node at one end, "I will shrink you down and transport you inside this pocket universe, where you may resume your life just as it was the moment you left it. Your parents will be there. Your family." Professor Donut beamed with pride and wise compassion. "Everything will be just as it was."

"But," said Lola. "But it's not my actual home, then. I mean"—she stared at the strange fuzzy suit and its network of cabling—"it's just a . . . pretend version."

"It is a bit," said Professor Donut. He hesitated.

"However . . . pretend has its benefits. If you like I can make . . . *adjustments*."

"Adjustments?"

Professor Donut swept his paw over the room. "This pocket universe is yours, Lola. It was made for you. And if you wish, I can change it. You could look different. You could be a superhero. If you choose, I can bend the very laws of physics to fit your needs. You can go home, and you can go to any version of home you desire."

Lola let this sink in. Any life she wished. She pictured a world where her father never left. Where her mother was more certain, her sisters more appreciative, where there were no late-night phone calls heard through bedroom walls, no tears and trembling voices. Maybe even a world without war, or sickness, or fear. Her imagination pushed further than she wished it to: a world where maybe, just maybe, it was just her and her parents. Where there were no sisters at all. No, that was a terrible thought. But still . . . if it was all pretend . . .

"Once you enter the pocket universe, the Phan will never find you. You will be beyond their reach, indeed beyond the reach of any danger at all." Professor Donut tried a sad smile. He was proud of his work and surprised at the Earth girl's reluctance. "Aren't you pleased?"

"I . . . ," said Lola. "Are you . . . are you certain there's no way for me to get back to my real home?"

"I . . . cannot say," said Professor Donut, trying to hide

his disappointment. "But I do know that no one has yet perfected time travel. This," he said, placing a paw on the control panel, "is the closest thing you will ever find."

Lola considered the choice before her, the opportunity to have everything she ever wanted, tucked safely forever in the pocket of a onesie. Safe. So insanely safe.

"I need a moment to think," she said, and before the professor could answer, she left the room.

The tunnels and chambers winding through the shell of Satellite B were complex and ancient, filled with blind falls and dead ends. Phin had stomped aggressively through most of them, not caring where he went, cursing when he nearly fell into a bottomless pit or smashed his nose on one of the many hard, wet walls that seemed to jump out at him in the low light. He didn't care that he was lost or that the way was dangerous. He was throwing an epic tantrum, and it felt good. He barked and screamed in his solitude, raged and cried and laughed madly to himself. A stranger coming upon him in this state would have certainly thought he was a raving lunatic, and that was all right with Phin. He wanted the world to cower. He wanted everyone to see just how mad he was.

But there was no one around to see it.

He came at last to a set of doors. These were steel rather than stone, and large enough for heavy equipment and machinery to pass through. There was even a steel track running along the ceiling, suggesting to Phin these doors led to some kind of workshop or garage. A closer examination revealed a sign that read *Workshop/Garage: Keep Out!*

"We'll see about that," Phin growled, and went right the heck in.

Every kid of every species needs a place to be alone. A special place, whether it be their room, a tree house, or a hidden corner of the attic. Every kid needs a place to go and think and be away from the maddening world of adults. You can usually tell when you've found such a place. They tend to be exquisitely messy and filled with half-finished bags of potato chips. The walls tend to be covered in posters or drawings, and always, in such secret places, a special, private project will be lying half complete. Such rooms, clubhouses, and hideaways have their own kind of magic, and Phin knew he'd just found one.

"Moop," said one of the mushroom people gathered in the center of the workshop, and it waved.

"Moop," said all the rest, and they waved as well.

"Hey," said Phin. "Mind if I come in?"

The shop, much like Phin's bedroom back home, was a mess. A food replicator lay in pieces in one corner (the mushrooms had disassembled and reassembled it so many times it wasn't fun anymore), a vortex manipulator had been painted a startling violet (splashes of paint stained almost every surface in the shop), and several semismashed computer terminals lay in a haphazard pile across the floor, clearly the result of a recent game of "How High Can We Stack These Before They Fall Over?"

For the first time in a long while, Phin felt at home.

"Hey," he said when saw what the mushrooms were working on. "That's my ship."

"Boop," said a familiar mushroom with a roundish head—the one Phin called Bertram. He made a series of swirling motions in the air with his arms, then stuck them out straight and ran around in small circles going, "Brrrooop! Vrrrooop! Grrrrroooop!"

"You're fixing it," said Phin, marveling. "Making it fly again."

"Boop!"

The Majulook SuperFake cloaking device had been disabled, and the Rescue Wagon looked only like itself—a lumpy, squarish escape pod with thrusters in the back, headlights up front, and a little Extraweb radial on top. Phin thought that something so plainly wonderful shouldn't spend so much time hiding itself.

"How is the old girl?" he asked, approaching the mushrooms gathered around the hood. They'd repaired the guidance system and rotated the cooling vents. The quantum intake had been outfitted with a new carburetor, and they'd even replaced the radio. A few other modifications had been made to the ship's inner workings that Phin couldn't quite identify—various mushroom-made thingamajigs and doodads that had been affixed to the inside and undercarriage of the Wagon. They had even, just for fun and much to Phin's delight, painted a pair of wicked racing stripes down the sides.

They had also hot-glued what looked like a pair of teddy bear ears to the roof, rendering the ship 45 percent cuter.

"This is amazing!" Phin said. He glanced around the shop. "This is where you guys come to be alone, huh?"

"Moop moop," said Bertram.

"Ba-ba-boop," said a chanterelle.

Something else he'd been wondering resolved itself in his mind. "And that Mr. Jeremy is your dad, huh?"

The mushrooms went back to work, tinkering with the Wagon, tightening bolts, focusing subatomic lasers. They seemed uninterested in this topic of conversation.

"And the Bog Mutants, they're like your big brothers. Except they don't get to stay here. They get shipped off to work, whether they want to or not." No wonder Mr. Jeremy hated the Phan so much, thought Phin.

"He's basically a good guy, your dad," he said.

Bertram shrugged. "Boo-boop."

Phin sat down on a nearby bench. A big, rough, truffle-looking mushroom handed him a tiny cup of strong, milky tea, and a doughnut. Phin sipped, nibbled, and thought. He watched the mushrooms work.

“We’re going to change things,” he said to himself, but a few of the mushrooms looked his way, paused in their work to hear what he was saying. “We’re going to free your big brothers. And Lola will get to go home. And we’ll save the universe. And everything is going to be okay.”

He didn’t half believe it himself.

He wasn’t even sure if they could understand him.

But it didn’t matter.

One of the rounder-headed little mushrooms took his empty mug and patted him on the knee.

“All right, break’s over,” Phin said, slapping his thighs and standing. “Let’s get to work.”

36

LOLA DIDN'T WANDER FAR but soon became lost. The tunnels of Satellite B seemed grown, rather than designed, and soon she'd followed their twisting hollows to a dimly lit storage room. Metallic shelving loomed out of the darkness, heavy with unrecognizable equipment and boxes overflowing with mechanical paraphernalia.

Lola hoisted herself up on a crate. She didn't care that it was dusty and damp, or that the close, humid air was making her sweat. She curled her knees to her chest, closed her eyes, and tried to think. Her brain was a hurricane of activity, but no answers revealed themselves. She breathed in and sighed.

"I miss you guys so much," she said.

The dust irritated her sinuses. She was going to sneeze. The quiet of the moment vanished as panic gripped her. After all, the last time she had sneezed she'd been thrown forward several centuries, and a thing like that tends to stick with a person. She swallowed. She tilted her head back—which her mother once told her helped nose tickles. She blinked away the water in her eyes. She breathed deep and slow. The sneeze passed.

"ACHOO!" said someone else.

"Bless you," said Lola.

"Thank you," said the voice.

"Ahhh!" said Lola, and nearly tumbled off her crate.

She clambered back, pressing herself to the wall. Her eyes searched madly for the owner of the voice, but the room was dark and hazy. But something was *there.*

She waited. She listened. It was quiet.

"ACHOO!"

"Um, bless you again?" Lola tried.

"Thanks," said the voice, and sniffed.

There was nowhere to run. The thing, whatever it was, was between her and the way she'd come.

Lola swallowed and forced her eyes to focus. She couldn't see much, just the barest outline of a lumpy shape in the corner. No, strike that—not a lumpy shape, but a *person,* with its knees pulled to its chin just like hers. No, strike that again. It was a *lumpy person* huddled in the corner, its knees pulled to its chin just like hers.

Lola cleared her throat. "Hello?"

"Hi," said the thing in the corner.

The thing didn't move. It spoke no more. Lola, mustering her courage, inched forward.

"Are you . . . okay?" she asked.

The thing cleared its throat. Its voice was thick, syrupy, like it had a nasty cold. Or maybe hay fever.

"I think I'm lost," it said. There was a quaver there that wasn't just phlegm, Lola realized. It was fear.

"Oh. Well, me too."

"I was supposed to be on an asteroid," the thing said. "But I wandered away from my ship and now . . ." It sounded like it was going to cry.

Lola scooted forward, trying to get a better look at whatever it was she was speaking to. Now she could make out a head and arms, and a peculiar sheen to the skin. There was also the glint of something . . . like a name badge.

Lola swallowed.

"My name is Lola," she said.

"Hello," said the thing. "I'm Jeremy."

She shuddered.

"Have we . . . met?"

"Sure!" said the Jeremy. "Just now! Oh . . . wait. You mean before? Maybe? You solids all look alike to me."

Lola and the Bog Mutant sat in the dark, facing each other. Lola was trembling, though she wasn't sure why. It wasn't fear, not quite, though she felt certain this was the Jeremy from the Temporal Transit Authority she'd met when she first arrived in the future, and while she'd met some nice

Bog Mutants since, this was undoubtedly one who worked for the Phan. But he was different, somehow.

Something about this place made him different.

He'd come home, Lola realized.

"I think . . . ," she said, and hesitated. "Does this place seem familiar to you?"

"The room?"

"No," said Lola. "The asteroid."

Again there was a pause, all the more unnerving here in the dark, as Lola couldn't see what Jeremy was doing, whether he was thinking or reaching for his weapon.

Though she didn't quite feel afraid.

"I think I was here a long time ago," he said. "Yeah," he said, remembering. "Yeah, I remember! I was here with all my brothers. And there were ships. Ships from all different places, but mostly ships from the TTA. They made me get on one of those ships. And I had to say goodbye to all my brothers. And all my other brothers . . . the little ones."

He must mean the mushroom people, Lola thought. All of them Mr. Jeremy's offspring, with all the smarts given to the mushrooms, and all the nasty, unpleasant jobs given to the Bog Mutants.

"That sounds terrible," said Lola.

"It wasn't too bad," said Jeremy. "I got a job! It's good to have jobs."

Lola inched a little closer. "Do you like your job now?"

"Mmm . . . there used to be a lot more pinochle and waiting around. Less getting lost in asteroids."

Lola chuckled.

"But the job's always the same. We're looking for a girl."

Lola stopped laughing. She cleared her throat. "Why?"

"Because she has the answer."

Lola felt her breath catch in her throat. "The answer to what?"

Jeremy sniffed, and sneezed again. "Some big question."

Lola's pulse quickened. When she spoke, her throat felt dry. "Do you know what the question is?"

"Oh, everyone knows that," said Jeremy.

"I don't know the question," said Lola.

Jeremy considered this. "Well, then maybe you know the answer," he said.

Somewhere in another room a machine chugged and rumbled. Dust sifted from the ceiling.

"Could you at least tell me what the question is?" Lola said. "Please?"

"Sure!" said Jeremy.

And he told her.

"Oh," said Lola.

She asked him to repeat it, and he did.

"Oh," she said again.

"So. Do you know the answer?"

The universe seemed to hold its breath, as if ready to unravel itself when she spoke. It waited and tensed.

"No," said Lola at last. "I have absolutely no idea."

37

SOMETHING VERY BIG AND alarming was going to happen, and it was going to happen soon. But most of them didn't know it.

Back in Mr. Jeremy's main chamber, Gretta had been spending some quality time with her father.

It wasn't going well.

"*It's not that I don't approve of your choices,*" Mr. Jeremy was saying. "*You're a capable young Bog Mutant with a mind of her own.*"

"And here comes the guilt trip," said Gretta, picking at what was left of their tea snacks. She rather liked the cucumber sandwiches and was curious why no one had touched them.

"It's just, you're my only daughter, and I want the best for you."

Gretta rolled her eyes. "Dad."

"I'm sure there are plenty of great careers out there. I'm just

not sure being evil is right for you."

"Oh, *now* he shows some concern," said Gretta. "Not one phone call! Or a card on Child Appreciation Day!" She pointed at him, which was easy to do since he was so massive you could point pretty much anywhere in the room and be more or less on the money. "No wonder I'm maladjusted."

"*Well . . . um . . . ,*" said Mr. Jeremy awkwardly. "*Do you have a boyfriend?*"

"Oh, seriously, don't start."

Mr. Jeremy, without a voice, and indeed without a throat, cleared his throat.

"Sweetheart, it's just I've been so busy trying to save the universe. And, you know, it's not easy for a planet-sized fungal core to be a father figure."

Gretta shook her head. "Whatever, Dad. I'm over it."

She stood and checked her tablet. "Something very alarming is about to happen, you know," she said.

"*I am aware,*" said Mr. Jeremy, whose extrasensory perception was much more acute than his paternal sensitivities.

"So," said Gretta. She wasn't sure what else there was to say. "So," she said again.

"*I am sorry I wasn't there for you, my child,*" said Mr. Jeremy, his words rolling like waves through her mind, crashing on the hard, jagged rocks of her soul. "*And I am proud of you.*"

"Well," said Gretta. "It's not enough."

"It could not possibly be," said Mr. Jeremy.

And with that, several hundred quivering tendrils of mucus shot out from his body—disgustingly, lovingly—and wrapped Gretta in their embrace, shielding her from the massive explosion that brought down the walls around them.

"HEY!" shouted the Sun-Liner security drones as several dozen sleeker, smaller ships appeared over the horizon of Satellite B. "LOOK, FELLAS! SOMETHING TO DESTROY!"

The ships ignored the drones completely and opened fire on the planetoid below. The last of the refugees yet to board their evacuation drones ran screaming helplessly from the inferno. Mountains were upended, valleys rippled like bedsheets, and the planetoid's surface began to splinter and crack.

"WHOA," said the drones, uncertain what they ought to do in this situation. These new arrivals were awesome and destructive, and frankly the drones felt a bit inferior.

Dozens of sleek landing ships emerged from the holds of the larger vessels. In balletic formation they spread across the asteroid, alighting like fleas on the mange of an unlucky dog. These were troop ships, and soon their hatches opened, and an invading army began to march into the night.

The drones, feeling their pride threatened and refusing to be shown up, turned their weapons on Satellite B. "COME ON, BOYS," they radioed to one another. "LET'S SHOW 'EM HOW IT'S DONE."

As one, the drones pummeled the bejesus out of the asteroid below, just to prove they were better at destroying things than these other ships, which had the words *Temporal Transit Authority* stenciled on their sides in nasty slanted lettering.

"What was that?" said Jeremy. Another quake shook the strange room, sending chunks of stone tumbling from the ceiling.

"Something's wrong," said Lola somewhat redundantly as the world fell down around them. Suddenly filled with a clear sense of purpose, she hopped down from the crate and took Jeremy by his squishy hand. "Come on."

Close enough to see her face now, he gasped. "Passport!"

"That's not my name!" said Lola. "Now hurry, we've got to get out of here! I'm pretty sure we're under attack."

The rumbling and quaking was worse in the tunnels.

"Which way?" Lola hissed, and just then saw Professor Donut hobbling toward them, paws waving in adorable panic.

"We've been discovered! We're under attack! The Temporal Transit Authority has found us! Bog Mutant troops are invading the catacombs! We must get you out of here, Lola! Oh," he said, coming up short just before them. "Hello, Jeremy."

"Hello," said Jeremy, and waved.

"Where's Phin?" said Lola.

Professor Donut pressed a few keys on a wall-mounted control panel. "That's what I'm trying to establish now. He was last seen in the workshop, which is exactly where we need to be going."

"What about the others?" said Lola.

The professor's whiskers twitched with heartbreaking resignation.

"I fear the main chamber has collapsed, with Mr. Jeremy and your green friend inside. They're sealed off."

"We have to try and get them out," Lola said. The professor clutched her hand before she could run off.

"I'm afraid we can't, my dear. But Mr. Jeremy is resourceful. And we can't let you fall into the Phan's clutches."

Together the three of them ran, hobbled, and wobbled through the catacombs. Blast after blast rocked the asteroid, and Lola tried desperately not to think about the tons of rock above her head. She tried thinking about kitties, but now she associated kitties with interstellar warfare and destruction. Same problem with lime Jell-O. And teddy bears. And scones. All of her go-to happy thoughts seemed to be associated with something nasty now.

Purple, thought Lola. She would think of the color purple. It was her favorite color. Her favorite T-shirt was purple. The walls of her room back home were painted purple. And so far in her galactic travels nothing bad had happened with the color purple. That would be her happy thought.

Ahh, thought Lola.

"Ahh!" shouted Phin, blasting them with a high-pressure cannon full of purple paint as they came through the doors.

38

IN PHIN'S DEFENSE, HE had grabbed the nearest thing at hand when it appeared a Bog Mutant had burst through the doors of the workshop—albeit a Bog Mutant in the company of two other Bog Mutants cleverly disguised as Lola and the professor. Now all three and most of the wall were cleverly disguised as purple pond monsters.

"Sorry!" he said, realizing his mistake. "Sorry, sorry. It washes right off, I promise."

It didn't.

"Phin!" said Lola in a swirl of relief and fear and supreme annoyance. "What is going *on*?"

"Lots!"

In the center of the workshop was some sort of spacecraft, looking like a station wagon and a ham radio had a baby, but spliced some Formula 1 DNA in there just for fun. Whatever the ship was, it looked to be half finished or under repair. Tubing snaked from its exposed engine, and bits of paneling hung open, spilling their wire guts onto the floor. Frantic mushrooms swarmed everywhere.

"Is that the Rescue Wagon?" said Lola. "And are those teddy bear ears glued to the top?"

"It is, and they are." Phin hauled a length of tubing out from under the ship's chassis. "The mushrooms fixed it. And they've also done a bunch of other stuff to it. But right now it's our only way out of here, and by the way feel free to help at any time."

Lola looked around for something to help with. Bertram was trying to clamber onto the roof. Lola gave him a boost.

"I assume all that shaking and all those explosiony noises," Phin said, frantically twisting a bolt while frantically looking at Professor Donut, "are something bad?"

"We've been breached!" said the professor. "Temporal Transit Authority troops are now swarming the asteroid."

Bertram gestured for Lola to help him down into the interior of the Wagon. She lowered him through the open rear window and saw that Teddy had been propped up in the back seat. Lola had no idea how he'd gotten there, and decided not to ask Phin about it, as this seemed like exactly the sort of mystical nonsense that really cheesed him off.

"The mushrooms and I will finish the ship," Phin was saying. "Professor, why don't you get the bay doors open so we can get to the surface."

“I’m afraid you’re not going to the surface, my boy,” the professor said with an air of grim calm.

It was exactly the sort of tone someone uses just before you turn around to see they’ve pulled a gun on you.

Slowly, Phin and Lola turned around.

In his little paw Professor Donut held a small tin can with a familiar label.

“You’re going in the beans.”

“In the . . . *what?*” said Lola. She wasn’t sure whether or not she was being threatened or rescued. She’d experienced quite a bit of both lately and they were beginning to blend together.

“It’s the only way,” said the professor. “We have to get you both out of here.”

Lola looked at Phin, who was usually the source of this kind of crazy talk, but at the moment he looked as confused as she was. He wiped his forehead, which only smudged more grease onto it, and shrugged.

“Apparently,” he said to her, “we’re going in the beans.”

“Prepare the shrink ray!” the professor shouted to one of the mushroom people.

A pair of shiitakes rushed to a large piece of equipment, identical to the one Lola had seen in the laboratory. Like everything else in the shop, it was half finished and lightly speckled with purple paint. Otherwise, it looked more or less like what you'd expect a shrink ray to look like—a large cannon mounted on a turret with lots of glowing green rings along the barrel and a big flashing node at one end.

The rest of the mushrooms were making the last of their adjustments to the Wagon. Cables were unhooked, the tendrils of tubing were removed from the undercarriage. Phin slammed down the hood.

Lola went to his side.

"Phin, I have a feeling."

"Just one?"

"I think something is very wrong here."

"Oh really. Glad you finally caught up."

"No! Phin, look at me!" She grabbed him by the shoulders and forced him to meet her eye. "I think there's something wrong about this whole setup. With the Phan and the Question and all that big gobbledygook. I think we've got all of this terribly, terribly wrong."

Phin was breathing hard. His face was smeared in grease and sweat, and his expression was pained. She could practically see the gears turning in his head. He believed her but didn't understand her, and was desperately trying, in his silly boy way, to sync up their brains.

Then he said something Lola never thought she'd hear him say.

"So what do we do?"

Lola glanced at the professor, who had nearly finished powering up the shrink ray.

"Just . . . whatever happens," she said, and this really was the moment to say something profound, at the last second before what might be their final journey, as the world crumbled around them. "Just, whatever happens . . . ," she started again, hoping with a good run-up the sentence would finish itself under its own momentum. "Whatever happens . . ."

And then it came to her, clear and true and honest and pure.

"Don't swallow your gum."

"My . . . what?" said Phin.

It was, Lola wanted to explain, a catchphrase from her favorite television show, *Dimension Y.* It was what Professor Rivulon said to his plucky assistant, June, whenever they were in serious trouble. It was a recurring joke, in a way, a bit of nonsense that would always make June smile even when things were at their worst, and among die-hard *Dimension Y* enthusiasts, it was a kind of mantra, a symbol for bravery and humor in the face of stupidity and evil. In fact, Lola's favorite T-shirt, the purple one, had the words *Don't Swallow Your Gum* written on it in spangly letters. She'd bedazzled it herself and wore it on alternate days during Comic-Con and Y-Fest (along with her Bog Mutant T-shirt, which she was wearing now).

But there was no time to explain all of this.

Unbelievably, Phin felt strangely reassured by this piece of wisdom. No matter what happened, no matter how impossible and difficult their situation now seemed, he felt fairly confident he would *not* swallow his gum. He didn't even have any gum. He didn't even like gum. So how could he possibly swallow it? It was the one thing he had control over, and this comforted him immensely.

The asteroid jolted. Disintegrator blasts began to pummel the bay doors.

"They've found us!" Professor Donut cried. "Quick! Get into the ship!"

Lola and Phin scrambled into the Wagon.

"Shrink ray activating!" Professor Donut called to the mushrooms.

"Wait!" said Lola, leaning out the window. "Aren't you coming with us?"

"Don't worry about us! Just get as far away as you can!"

The can of beans had been opened and was waiting on a nearby pedestal, strange cables and sensors attached to its base. The shrink ray hummed. The bay doors were beginning to crack, and would soon crumble, releasing a horde of Temporal Transit Authority Bog Mutants. The little mushrooms were waving goodbye, and a few of them were blowing kisses.

"Phin!" shouted Lola.

"Hold on!" shouted Phin.

There was a terrific *bzzzzzzt*.

And everything went black.

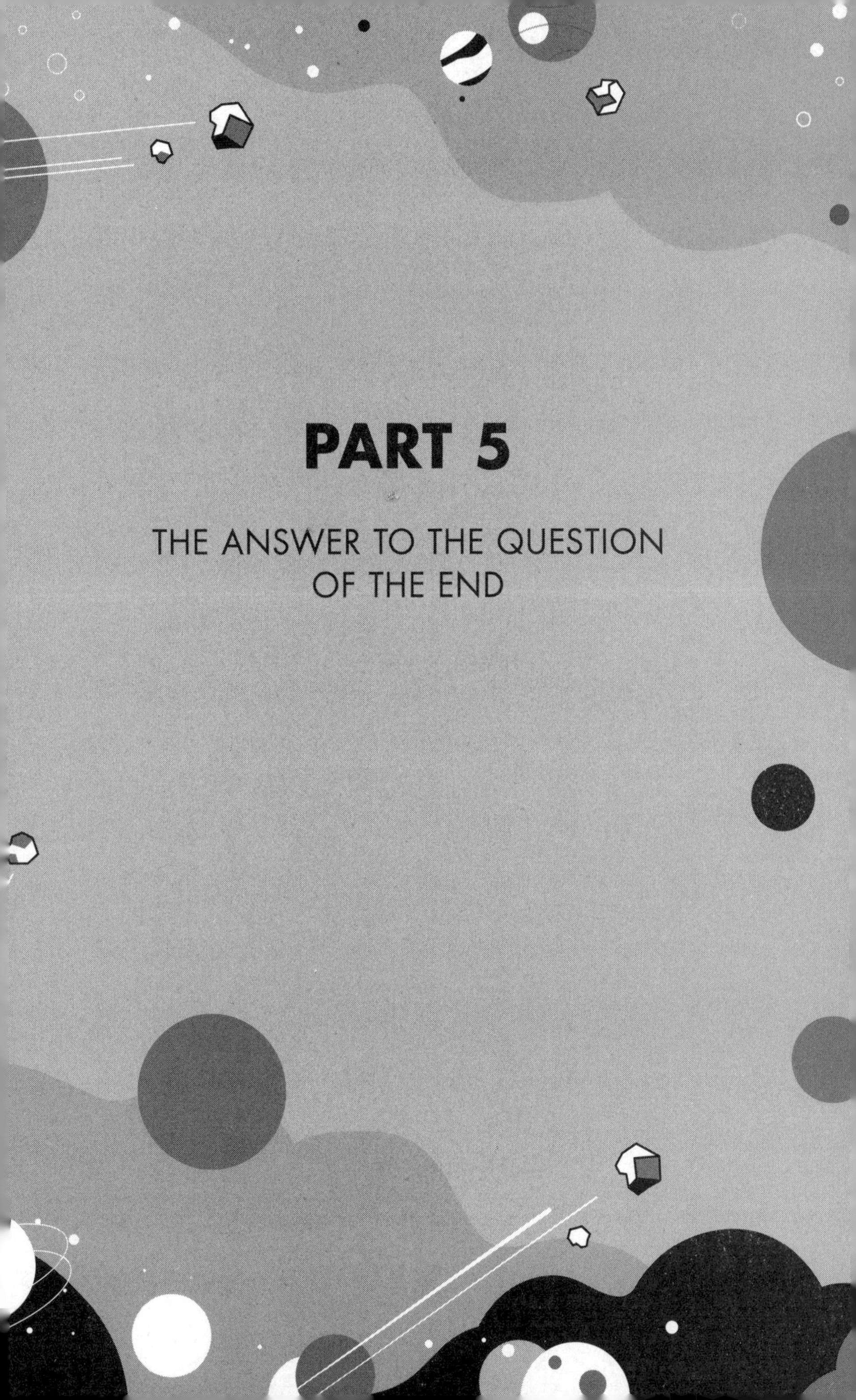

PART 5

THE ANSWER TO THE QUESTION OF THE END

39

THE BIGGEST AND MOST popular attraction in the Milky Way is, without question, the Singularity.

Located at the center of the galactic core, the Singularity is a supermassive black hole, a gravitational well four million times larger than our sun. In fact, it is the biggest *thing* in the Milky Way. To look upon it, say some, is to gaze into the eye of creation itself. A swirling vortex of gases and redshift twisted into a spiral whose center is a single black dot—a point so dense not even light can escape.

Not only is the Singularity the largest black hole in the galaxy, it is also the most overdeveloped.

Orbiting just beyond the event horizon at unreal speeds are thousands upon thousands of fancy hotels, midpriced resorts, restaurants, bars, observation ships, theme parks, and gift shops, all selling their own stock of Singularity-themed merchandise. Singularity dining sets. Singularity 3D Magic Eye™ posters. Singularity toothbrushes and beard trimmers. And of course, Singularity apparel, with slogans like *I Saw the*

Biggest Black Hole in the Galaxy and All I Got Was This Stupid T-Shirt, and *The Singularity: Take it from me, it SUCKS!*

In all of their travels, Eliza and Barnabus Fogg had never visited the Singularity. If asked, the Foggs would have told you they thought black holes were tacky, giving new meaning to the phrase "tourist trap," and that a respectable and sophisticated space explorer wouldn't be caught dead near one.

In truth, they both had always wanted to see it, and were saving it for their last stop. Which it now very much looked like it would be.

Phin's parents stood—or rather, teetered—on the deck of a ship overlooking the Singularity at a distance of several million miles. Like the SS *SunStar*, this ship's deck was open to the stars, protected by a transparent force field, which afforded them a smashing view of the anomaly below. At this distance, the hotels and theme parks at the edge of the swirling halo seemed to twinkle like a ring of jewels. You could almost hear the classic rock emanating from all the tiki bars down there, the laughter of people enjoying themselves, and the *ca-ching* of a billion cash registers gobbling up their cash.

"It's . . . beautiful," said Barnabus. His voice was hoarse and thin, but full of genuine wonder at the majesty of the universe.

"Silence the prisoner!" spat Goro Bolus.

Barnabus received a hard whack on the back of his head.

"Sorry about that," said the Bog Mutant who had struck Barnabus. "That sounded like it hurt."

The Foggs were shackled together, their clothes tattered and damp after days of torture and imprisonment. Their eyes were sunken and bloodshot, and they looked ready to collapse on the spot. Not just ready, but quite eager to, in fact. They were surrounded by Bog Mutants, each armed with his own disintegrator. The Mutants were supposed to be guarding the Foggs, but even they weren't immune to the beauty of the Singularity. They stared at it in mute wonder—though, to be honest, they would have stared at a hoagie in mute wonder, so easily blown were their minds. One of them took a selfie with the Singularity over his shoulder.

"Stop that," growled Bolus from his position behind the control board. "You're supposed to be *menacing them*, not taking pictures!"

The Bog Mutant he was addressing sheepishly tucked away his camera and shifted his weight.

The ship on which they now stood was Goro Bolus's personal yacht, the *Tin Can*. It was parked in space just a few hundred miles from a hypergate—the largest the Fogg-Bolus Corporation had ever built, big enough to accommodate the titanic amount of tourist traffic the Singularity received. Even now, cruise ships and budget star liners streamed through its portal, flying in long neat lines toward the hotels, spaceports, and parking garages below.

"I wanted you to be here when it happens," Bolus said, drumming his fingers. "I felt it only right you should witness the coming of our new overlords, seeing as you built the gates that will allow them to enter our world."

The plan, in its essence, was simple, and had been planted in Bolus's mind all those years ago, during the short phone call with the Phan. With the Foggs' access codes, Bolus had control over the mainframe connecting every hypergate in the galaxy. By inputting computations the Phan had embedded in his brain, Bolus could link the hypergates together. Their combined power would then resonate with the Singularity, creating a tear in the fabric of the universe—one big enough to allow the Phan *in*.

And then . . . *something* would happen. Bolus wasn't actually sure what. It had something to do with the half-articulated question that echoed in his skull, that infuriating *How . . . ? How . . . ? How . . . ?* But the Phan had promised him a reward. Wealth and power everlasting. And that was all that really mattered.

"You used to be so kind," moaned Eliza Fogg to their captor. "They've *changed* you somehow. Can't you see that?"

"I was never kind," spat Bolus. "I was *polite*, at best. Too polite to tell you how much I despised the pair of you. I mean, honestly, always gallivanting around the galaxy. Leaving me to run things by myself. *I* did all the work while *you* had fun."

"You could have taken a vacation!" said Barnabus. "Heck, take one now! We can recommend some great places!"

"Nice, out-of-the-way places," Eliza insisted. "With wine lists miles long. It'd do you good!"

"Really," said Barnabus. "You could get a tan! Or, er . . . does your species get tanned?"

"Silence!" growled Bolus, rapping his fist on the control panel. The Foggs, and the Bog Mutants guarding them, quavered. "I brought you here to witness your doom, not talk!"

The Foggs fell silent. Eliza leaned her head against her husband's shoulder, and together, wrists bound, they fumbled for one another's hands.

"I almost wish . . . ," she said softly, the light of collapsing reality shining in her eyes.

"I know," said Barnabus. "I wish Phin were here to see it."

LOLA OPENED HER EYES. She felt that something had happened, but she didn't know what. Her breathing was hard. She could still smell the smoke and ash of the crumbling Satellite B. But her limbs vibrated with a sense of having just traveled at unbelievable speed. Her fingertips trembled, her teeth chattered, her brain was still going *whoooo!*

She was sitting in the passenger seat of the Wagon, same as before.

But no, not the same as before: the Wagon was sitting on a plate of franks and beans in a kitschy little theme restaurant.

Which was all well and good, except the shrink ray had worn off immediately upon arrival, and so the station-wagon-sized ship was not only sitting on the plate of franks and beans, but also on what used to be a table, in what used to be the nicest corner of a small restaurant.

To everyone else in the restaurant, it appeared as if a spaceship had just exploded itself out of the special of the day and smashed everything in its path.

Lola took all of this in—the windows were badly smeared in baked bean sauce, so it was difficult—and pieced it together as best she could. The next thing she noticed was that Phin was not in the driver's seat, which is where he had been a moment ago. Frantic, she turned to check the back seat. Teddy was also gone.

But she wasn't alone.

"Moop," said Bertram, still sitting in the back seat where she'd left him. "Boop?" he added in a sheepish tone, as if to say *Whoops?*

Whoops was right. For where the ship had landed after its random flight through space was none other than a Big Tom's Earth-Style Home-Cooked Food Products, located on the mezzanine level of the Hotel Maximus in the Double Platinum Gold Quadrant of the orbiting entertainment metropolis known as Singularity City, a mere four billion miles above the Singularity itself.

The goal had been to get away, to get *anywhere* . . . but *here.*

Phin couldn't see. Wherever he was, it was dark. And ow-y. Every part of him ached, especially his nose. He felt for his legs. Still there. He felt for his arms. Definitely still there. The hurting nose suggested his face and probably his head were still there too, so that was all good news, at least. He was learning to look on the bright side.

Something had gone wrong. Or perhaps something had failed to go right. Predictably, something unpredicted had happened.

Some very interesting noises were happening now. Noises that sounded a bit like voices, and other noises that sounded a bit like music. There were smells too, the smell of fried food and salt. So perhaps he wasn't lost in some uncomfortable void but had actually materialized *somewhere.*

And *perhaps*, thought Phin, *perhaps the fact I can't see and the fact my nose hurts are somehow related.*

He took a moment to ponder this, then lifted up his head, which had been pressed facedown into a sack of rice. Phin sat up.

He was seated on a counter. A steel countertop, in fact. It was evening on the boardwalk of some unknown planet. He could hear the ocean, he could hear the distant hoot and rattle of a fairground. He could smell beans. In fact, he was covered in sauce.

What he saw were eight wobbly green faces, gaping back at him in total shock.

They were Bog Mutants. They wore jumpsuits from the SS *SunStar*. And over these jumpsuits, aprons.

"Wow!" said one. "I never seen beans do that before!"

"I have!" said another. "Just once though."

"When?" said a third.

"Today!" said the other. "Don't you remember? We were

making the tacos, and a kid and his bear just exploded right out of them."

"That was just now!" said the first.

"I know!" said the second, and they all gave each other high fives for successfully completing a conversation without anyone getting hurt or burning themselves on the griddle.

Phin looked around. There was indeed a griddle. There were also little bins of lettuce, diced tomatoes, and, of course, beans. There were also eight Bog Mutants who, until a moment ago, had been desperately trying to figure out how to fold a tortilla in half.

There was no ship. There was no Lola. There was only Phin and Teddy, who had landed, apparently, in a taco stand.

About a light-year away, in Big Tom's Earth-Style Home-Cooked Food Products, people were screaming—at least, the sorts of people who were new to galactic travel and hadn't gotten used to this sort of thing yet.

The gentleman who'd ordered the platter of franks and beans into which the Rescue Wagon had violently materialized had, by sheer luck, just gone to the buffet a moment before and now returned to what was left of his table and gaped at what had become of his dinner.

By amazing coincidence, this man's name was Lucky.

The ship lay smoldering in the wreckage of cheap plastic restaurant furniture amid a growing circle of gawkers. A hatch opened and a girl in very strange clothing emerged. She shook herself and looked around.

"Hi," she said. "Where am I?"

"Oh! Oh! Oh!" said the man whose dinner had just been obliterated. "Oh, this is really too much. Waiter! Waiter!"

The waiter, a pimply-faced Gropuloid in an unflattering uniform, looked up from his terminal.

"Huh?"

"Waiter! There is a *ship* in my *beans*," said Lucky.

The waiter blinked three sets of eyelids slowly. "A ship?"

"Yes! A ship! In my beans! Destroyed half the restaurant! Look at it, man!"

"That's . . . ," the waiter said, trying to think of the response that required the least effort on his part. "That's supposed to be like that."

Lucky sputtered. *"What?"*

"It comes with that," said the waiter.

"You're saying my *beans*," Lucky replied with fearsome slowness, "my *beans and franks* comes with a *ship* in it?"

"It's the special," said the waiter, returning his attention to the terminal before him. "It's the Franks and Beans Surprise."

"Well," Lucky said through gritted teeth, "I am surprised!"

"I'm glad," said the waiter, and he went on break.

Lucky, who through his seething fury figured he must be having some very strange luck today indeed, decided to go play the slots, and the matter was effectively resolved.

"Come on," Lola was saying to Bertram. "We've got to find Phin."

"Boop."

"Climb up," she said, offering Bertram her shoulder. Lola turned to the crowd of onlookers, a few of which had overheard the conversation between the customer and the waiter and were now looking warily at their own orders of franks and beans, wondering if it might suddenly surprise them in a similar way.

"Sorry, everybody," Lola said. "Really sorry about the mess."

She wondered what Phin would do in this situation, and then realized that she knew. Lola puffed out her chest, threw her head back haughtily, and said, "Well, we've got to save the universe now, so we're just going to leave this ship here. If you've got any complaints, call someone less important."

And then she hurried out of the restaurant, feeling wickedly smug.

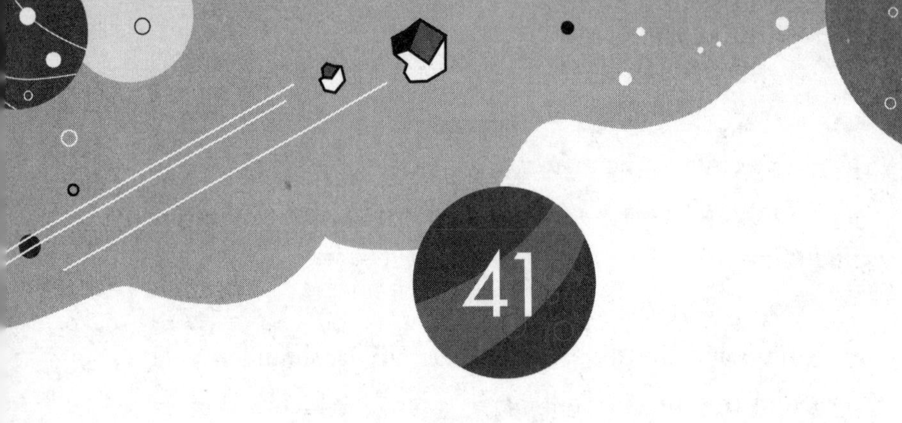

THE STREETS OF SINGULARITY City were not so much streets as flashing, jangling, pulsing causeways of strobe lights, neon signs, and glowing marquees. If the concourse on Luna had been a feast for the eyes, Singularity City gorged them.

"It's like Atlantic City on steroids," Lola said.

"Froop," agreed Bertram, and buried his face in her hair.

Ambling, hovering, and slurping along the sidewalks was every variety of alien. Sluggoids and Squid People, humans and Farquoids. Families of Driplions chattered at each other about which attraction they should visit next. A pair of life-bonded Thwoks argued over whether their quickie marriage had been a good idea, or whether they should try getting married again at the chapel across the street, just to see if that one had better hors d'oeuvres. And giggling Chambloons knocked their five heads together in giddy revelry.

They came to a small square with a fountain in the middle, the gap in the glimmering spacescrapers affording a slivered view of the swirling sky above. To one side was a large terminal, above which a complex hologram slowly rotated, a flashing arrow indicating *You Are Here.*

"We've got to find Phin," Lola said. "Do you know how to work this terminal thing?"

"Shoop," said Bertram, and trotted down her arm to the controls. His little fingers whirled across the keys. A pale-green halo began to pass back and forth through the hologram, scanning, Lola guessed, for Phin. At last it flashed red. *Subject Not Found.*

"We were supposed to arrive together; maybe he's somewhere nearby?"

"Groop," said Bertram, and pointed.

Across the square was an identical terminal, and it was doing the same green-flashy-scanny thing. Lola peered through the crowd, hope catching in her throat. Perhaps it was Phin scanning for *them.* A gap appeared in the pedestrian traffic, clearing her view—and she gasped.

Huddled around the terminal were three Temporal Transit Authority Bog Mutants, and Lola had a sinking feeling they were scanning for *her.*

"Oh no."

She could see a red dot appear on the Mutant's holographic map, and with that the trio turned . . . and looked right at her.

"Boop!" said Bertram.

"Good idea," said Lola, and ran.

The Bog Mutants took slimy, wobbly pursuit.

"Stop right there!" they shouted. "Or there! Or there is fine!"

"Nope!" Lola shouted back, leaping over a bench, ducking under a pair of flying Grograks.

"Broop!" said Bertram, impressed.

"Well, I get chased a lot," said Lola.

Suddenly she had an idea. Or at least, the beginning of an idea.

Skidding around a corner, she paused for just an instant to scan the avenue. There, under a gleaming marquee, was a door.

"Aha!" she said, and ducked inside.

The Bog Mutants rounded the corner just as the door swung shut.

"She went in the *thing*!" said one, so excited to have spotted her he'd forgotten the word for *gift shop*.

The Bog Mutants formed up ranks. They had her now. Disintegrators at the ready, they marched into the store.

The little bell above the door went *ding-ding*.

"Hi!" said the clerk. "Can I interest you in a Singularity mug? See, it's got a little programmed gravity well inside so any coffee within a ten-foot radius automatically gets sucked right in! Only five ninety-five! A steal at twice the price!"

"Yes!" said the lead Bog Mutant with determination. "But

not right now." It was a small shop. The walls were lined with Singularity trinkets. In the center were several circular racks of T-shirts with dumb slogans, and along one wall hung three-wheeled star-trikes for rent. A fan turned slowly on the ceiling. Apart from the clerk, it was vacant. No sign of their prey.

"Find her!" ordered the Bog Mutant commander, who was, by an almost imperceptible degree, smarter than the other two. "She's got to be in this shop!"

"Maybe she's in disguise!" said his lieutenant.

"As what?"

"Um, a mug?"

"Get her!" shouted the third, and blasted the mug the clerk was holding to smithereens.

"You idiot! We need her alive!" snapped their leader. "Don't shoot any more mugs."

"Right, sorry."

They made their way grimly through the shop. They peered behind mirrors. They checked under hats. The girl, it seemed, had vanished.

"You might try," the clerk said, waggling his hand, which still smarted, "the dressing room."

"She's disguised as a dressing room!" shouted the Bog Mutant lieutenant, and raised his weapon. The commander snapped at him to lower it at once.

Together they entered the changing area.

There were three stalls. They opened the first.

Empty.

They opened the second.

And found her.

"Dang it," said Lola. "I thought you'd just skip right to the third one. Don't you know they're always hiding in the third one?"

"You're coming with us," said the Bog Mutant commander.

"Wait, wait," Lola pleaded. "Can't I just . . . could I just . . ."

"No last requests," growled the Bog Mutant commander.

"I just want to buy a T-shirt!" Lola hollered as they dragged her, struggling, into the night.

42

BACK AT THE TAQUERIA of the Bog Mutants, things were not going well. It was cramped. The front panel had not yet been opened for business and though the evening was cool, the unventilated tin box in which Phin and the Bog Mutants stood was hot and sticky. Phin was the stickiest of all, covered in sauce. And to be the stickiest, grossest person in a small room full of Bog Mutants was quite an accomplishment.

"What planet is this?" Phin asked.

"We're not . . . sure? We just landed on the first planet we came to."

"Well," said Phin, "how long did you fly? What was your trajectory? What did your ship's computer tell you?"

There was a long pause in which ten Bog Mutants' mouths opened with excruciating slowness.

"No, stop it, don't even try to answer," said Phin.

Without another word he turned and marched through the door and out into the night.

It really was a beautiful night on Garboling-Lang, the

planet Phin now found himself on. He recognized it immediately by the twin crescent moons and third, heart-shaped moon that had been carved that way by a lovesick terraforming drone a few years back. (It had been all over the news, one of those "This Terraforming Drone Falls in Love, and You Won't Believe What Happens Next: Click Here to Find Out" articles.) The taco stand, Phin now saw, had been fashioned from the airlock of a large, sleekly red space limo, the very ship the Bog Mutants had used to escape the SS *SunStar*. They'd simply parked it and opened up shop.

In all, the Bog Mutants hadn't chosen a bad place for a taco stand, positioned on the boardwalk near the Lang-o-Lin Sea. It was a beautiful and romantic spot, and just the kind of place where you'd want to grab a taco after a long walk up the beach.

Several people had this same thought, apparently, as there was a long line of customers waiting for the taco stand to open—or, to be more accurate, waiting for the Bog Mutants to figure out how to make tacos. Phin found himself standing at the front of this line.

The front panel of the taco stand opened up behind Phin, spilling halogen light and the smell of frying beans out onto the boardwalk.

"Hello!" said one of the Bog Mutants. "I think we've got it figured out now! Step right up!"

"Hey!" someone at the back of the line shouted. "That guy cut the line!"

"I'm not cutting!" Phin shouted. He tried to back out of the way. "Go right ahead, I don't even want a . . ."

"Here you go!" said a Bog Mutant, placing a very poorly assembled taco in Phin's hand.

Phin looked at it. He looked at the line of angry customers. "Oh," he said wearily. "Fantastic."

"Get the line cutter!" someone shouted.

They rushed him. Phin was grabbed by several powerful tentacles and hoisted into the air. The plan, it seemed, was to chuck him into the alkaline sea, which was perfectly fine for the jellyfish people of Garboling-Lang but would sear his skin off in seconds.

"Throw him in!" the crowd chanted. "Throw him in!"

"Stop!" Phin hollered, struggling the best he could. "Here, just take the taco! It's not even a good taco. You can have it!"

"Throw him in! Throw him in!"

"Unhand that boy!" said a voice.

It was a deep and burly voice, a voice of wisdom and compassion. It was the kind of voice that could stop an angry mob in its tracks, which is exactly what it did.

Together they turned to see who had spoken. Standing on the counter, sticky with bean sauce and powdered here and there with cornmeal, was a bear. A teddy bear.

"Teddy!" said Phin, or rather, *thought* Phin. His mouth merely hung slack.

"I said, unhand that boy!" Teddy stretched out his paws

like an angry deity, seeming massive and imposing despite his small size.

"*Space wizard*," someone whispered.

Slowly, slowly, the crowd lowered Phin to the ground.

"Good. Now, Phineas," said Teddy, pulling a pair of roundish spectacles from the folds of his fur and putting them on. "Apologize to these good people."

"What?" said Phin. "I mean . . . what! You! I . . . !" Phin fumed. "I didn't do anything wrong!"

"I believe you owe them," said Teddy with infinite patience, "an apology."

Everyone was silent. Phin felt several dozen eyes fall to him. He cleared his throat.

"I, uh . . ." He coughed into his fist. "Sorry, everybody."

"Now give them the taco."

"Here's your taco," said Phin, handing the nearest jellyfish the now-mangled remains of tortilla, lettuce, and undercooked rice.

"And as for the rest of you," said Teddy, climbing down from his perch and dusting himself off. "Your evening snack will have to wait. This lad and I have a universe to save."

"That's true," said Phin.

"And I'm afraid we will need to commandeer," finished Teddy, "this taco stand."

43

WE ARE COMING VERY close to the end now. Can you feel it?

In a way, every creature in the universe felt it. It was a tickle at the back of the neck, or necks, or gills, or misty-plasma-ventricles, depending on the species. It was the phantom vibration in your pocket, just before your phone rings, the sense that something is about to *happen*.

A question rumbled through the walls of the universe, and its askers were approaching. It pulsed, it throbbed, it burned to be answered.

How . . . ?

How . . . ?

How . . . ?

A small transport shuttle buzzed quietly away from the lights of Singularity City. It carried its occupants from the hubbub into the great nothingness above, where the largest hypergate in existence was no longer turning slowly, and where a small private space yacht, the *Tin Can*, waited.

The hypergate system, as everyone across the galaxy was discovering right about then, was offline. *Temporarily Unavailable Due to Heavy Traffic* was the message winging its way across the Extraweb. Millions of ships hovered in immense traffic jams in hundreds of millions of star systems.

We Apologize for the Inconvenience, the message continued, appearing on screens and tablets, whispered through radios and sub-ether sensors. *Service Will Resume Momentarily—Sincerely, The Fogg-Bolus Hypergate and Baked Beans Corporation.*

If you enjoyed this message, please like and subscribe for more updates.

The tiny shuttle docked with the *Tin Can*. Air locks pressurized, doors slid open with a cold hiss, and the prisoner was brought to the bridge.

The bridge itself was on the top deck, open to the stars, protected by a transparent force field. There was a steering wheel and ship's nav computer, and all the other accoutrements one would expect to find. There was also—and the prisoner's eyes fixed on this almost immediately—a very peculiar-looking chair.

The captain stood over a control panel, uninterested in the breathtaking view. With the space traffic stalled, the view was almost placid, like a lake before someone sets off some dynamite in it.

"We have the girl," said the Bog Mutant commander.

The captain turned in his little chair.

"You look like a bean," said Lola.

Goro Bolus chuckled. "Well, my dear, you look like an ape."

Lola supposed that was fair.

"Put her in the machine," Bolus commanded. The Bog Mutants picked Lola up and took her to the peculiar-looking chair.

It was unmistakably a device of evil. Black and garish, no thought had been given to the subject's comfort or aesthetic sense. Lola felt the blood drain from her face as the Bog Mutants strapped her in. Nodes were attached to the backs of her hands, to her temples.

"You're fortunate," he said, turning back to his control panel. "It was delightful to torture the Foggs, but the information you contain cannot be extracted by such . . . indelicate methods."

"If you're talking about the answer to the Question of the End," said Lola, "I really don't know it. Someone already told me what the question is, and I mean it, I really don't know the answer at all."

"Oh, but my dear," said Bolus with a smile, "you do know the answer. Perhaps you do not know that you know it, but you do. And that is why you are sitting in that machine. Shall I tell you what it is?"

"No," said Lola immediately. "It's fine. I don't need to know."

Bolus grunted. "Well, I'm going to tell you anyway."

He stood at her side and drew his fingers along the cabling in a way that made Lola's skin crawl. "It's a Truth Machine. A simple name for a complicated device. Once switched on . . ." Bolus leaned across Lola and flicked a switch. The chair began to hum. Lola's spine tingled. ". . . the subject can speak only the truth and will answer any question given to her. The process is painless, which is good news for you, I suppose. But when the Phan arrive and ask you the Question of the End, you will answer it," said Bolus, a grin slithering across his features like something alive trying to escape his face. "The Phan will be appeased. Now . . ." He leaned in. She could smell his breath, earthy and stomach turning. "Let's test it out, shall we?"

"We shall," Lola heard herself say, and gasped. She hadn't meant to speak. What she thought was translated instantly into words, without filter. "This is how Phin must feel all the time," she said out loud, and gasped again. "And I don't even feel bad about saying that!" She gasped a third time.

Bolus looked pleased.

"Tell me," he said, steepling his fingers, "what is your name?"

"Lola Ray."

"What did you have for breakfast the day after your second birthday?"

"Peach baby food and mashed green beans in a baby-blue bowl."

"What do you want more than anything in the world?"

"To own a reasonably priced scooter that gets great mileage."

Goro Bolus frowned. That last answer wasn't quite what he'd expected, but the readouts confirmed the subject had spoken the unequivocal truth.

"Very well," he said. Bolus rose and strode to the door. "Make yourself comfortable, Ms. Ray. It won't be long now. The end is inevitable."

"It is," Lola said. "It's already happened."

Bolus paused at the door. He turned slowly toward her, narrowing his beady eyes. Then, with a sneer, he left her strapped to the Truth Machine, in the company of the Bog Mutants and her own frantic thoughts.

44

THE SLEEKLY RED SHIP hurtled through space at several times the speed of light, a crimson streak of mind-blistering speed. And still it was too slow.

"We're never going to make it in time," Teddy said, studying the controls. He and Phin were seated in the cockpit. It was a luxurious cockpit, outfitted with leather seats and crystal tumblers, one of which Phin held in his hand. His glass was filled with NectaPop, the most expensive soft drink in the galaxy. *This*, Phin thought, *is the way to travel.*

"You don't look very alarmed," Teddy grumbled.

"Hey, I'm in a limo that's been converted into a taco stand by Bog Mutants," said Phin. "And my stuffed bear is at the controls. Things are just pretty wacky right now. We're headed into almost certain death. I'm going to take a moment to enjoy myself."

Teddy shook his head. He scanned the latest readout from the ship's computer. "The hypergates have been put on lockdown. That means Bolus has almost certainly gained control. Look at this . . ."

He turned the screen so Phin could see. A set of angry red digits were ticking down.

"What's that?"

"It's a countdown, Phineas," snapped Teddy. "It's a countdown that's pulsing through the hypergate mainframe. And what do you think it's counting down to?"

Phineas swallowed and took his feet off the dashboard. "Um."

"It's counting down to the arrival of the Phan. They're on their way. Even now the hypergates are linking. Bolus has done it. He's going to bring them through."

"Well, look," said Phin, sitting up. "What are we supposed to do about it?"

"We've got to stop Bolus, of course. There's something else you might want to see."

A few keystrokes and the image on the screen changed. It was a security feed. The view was of a ship's bridge, a very nice-looking ship's bridge, though not as nice as the ship they were now piloting. A few Bog Mutants were standing at attention, disintegrators at the ready. Otherwise the bridge was vacant, save for a peculiar-looking chair and a girl strapped to it.

"Lola!" said Phin. "Where is she?"

"On Bolus's ship," said Teddy. "And if I'm not mistaken that's a Truth Machine she's strapped to."

Phin put down his glass and swallowed. "This is bad."

"It is bad," said Teddy.

"We've got to rescue her," said Phin.

"Indeed we do."

Phin sank into his seat. It made a lush, squeaking sound underneath him. They flew in silence for a while, the ship's engines humming, the stars streaming past the view screen in a hyperspace blur.

"I'm sorry," said Phin.

"Hmm?" said Teddy, focused on the controls.

"I said I'm sorry." He shook his head. "You told me to save her. You told me only I could do it. And I've completely flarxed it up."

This word, *flarxed*, wasn't even a rude word. It was a word Phin had made up, since none in existence could express just how badly he'd flarxed.

Teddy sighed. "Phineas T. Fogg, you have a part to play in all this yet." He turned to face Phin and smiled sadly. "You're a good boy, Phin. No one knows you better than I do. I've been with you your whole life, and I see who you are when no one is watching." He turned back to his controls. "You are my best friend."

Phin looked away, out the window, and blinked a few

times. Then he blinked a few more times and wiped at his face.

"How long until we reach the Singularity?" he said after a moment.

"Another twenty-five minutes, I believe," said Teddy.

They flew on in silence, and then Phin cleared his throat, sat up straight, and said, "Well, we've got some time to kill. Let's play a game."

One short, very distracted game of Apples to Gravleks later, the limo materialized a few thousand miles from the Singularity hypergate. Wrapped in a cloaking device, it slowly, stealthily approached the *Tin Can*, floating nearby. Unseen, it hovered just beneath the larger ship's aft docking port, and there it waited.

The limo's airlock hissed, oxygen vented into space, and a hatch opened. To an onlooker it would have appeared as if a glowing doorway had opened in space itself. Debris began to float out, turning against the stars—bags of beans, loosely chopped lettuce, and cornmeal tumbled like stardust through the void. And then, a young boy in a space suit appeared, floating after it. The door closed behind him.

"The yacht's aft docking port is just above you," Teddy's voice buzzed in Phin's helmet radio. "There is a maintenance hatch just to port."

"Ten-four, Tederino," said Phin.

"Don't call me that," said Teddy.

With a small burst from the suit's onboard jets, Phin maneuvered himself along the underside of the massive yacht. To his left the docking port flashed red, its edges rimmed with yellow-and-black safety paint. The maintenance hatch was considerably smaller and unmarked. Phin positioned himself beneath it. It was tricky to get the override panel open with the clumsy space suit gloves, but he soon got it. The hatch opened, and silently he slipped inside.

Meanwhile, the Bog Mutants who had accompanied Phin and Teddy in the limo were staring out a rear porthole in wonder. They'd never seen such an incredible sight, a beautiful ballet of weightlessness.

"Look at that!" said one, pointing.

Amazed, they watched as a single tortilla wafted past the double-pane glass, catching, as it did, some beans and a bit of lettuce that happened to be floating in its path, and folding itself around them, neatly in half, to form a brilliant half-moon.

"Amazing!" said another of the Bog Mutants. "So *that's* how you do it!"

"But," said the third, "but then, how do we *reach* it?"

They watched as the taco floated farther and farther into space and were stumped.

45

THE INTERIOR OF THE *Tin Can* was dark. Wood-paneled corridors stretched in two directions, studded with portholes. Phin, having shed his space suit and stowed it in a nearby hamper, crept down the hall.

He could hear Bog Mutants arguing over a hand of pinochle. He backtracked and eventually came to a less comfortable section of the ship. Here were the engine room, the ventilation chambers, and the coolant tanks. Piping snaked along the ceiling, and the way was lit by halogen security lights that cast strange shadows as the ship teetered in space.

Phin turned a corner and found himself facing another long corridor, this one lined with windows opening onto an interior chamber. He pressed himself to the wall and peered through the glass.

His jaw fell so hard and fast, it nearly sprained.

In a flash Phin had the security panel open and pulled the release valve. A door slid aside and he rushed through. The occupants of the tiny brig were nearly unrecognizable, huddled and broken, filthy and shivering.

"Mom! Dad!"

Wincing in the light, the prisoners looked up.

"Buddy?" croaked Barnabus Fogg.

". . . Phinny?" rasped Eliza.

What followed was one of the longest, tightest, stinkiest hugs in all of galactic history.

"You guys you guys you guys," said Phin, pressing his face into his parents' tattered clothing. "Oh it's so good to see you, I love you, I love you. You smell terrible." He pulled back. "I just realized I've never smelled you guys before. Is this the way you always smell?"

"Oh baby, my baby," Eliza said, stroking her son's hair and pressing him to her. "My precious boy."

"We're so sorry we didn't believe you, Phineas," said Barnabus. "You were right about Bolus. He captured us."

"Evidently," said Phin.

"Where have you *been*?" Eliza said, taking in his appearance. "How on Earth did you get here?"

"Oh, guys, I saw just like . . . so much cool stuff," Phin babbled. "It was amazing. I wish you could have been there. I was on a cruise ship, and I met a superintelligent fungus core and his mushroom children, and did you know they have a ball pit on Luna?" Phin was unable to keep the grin from his face. "Anyway, it's a long story. I'll tell it to you as soon as I finish saving the universe."

"Phin, Bolus has rigged the hypergates together," said his father. "We think he may be using them to open a hole in the universe."

"Yeah, yeah, I know all this," said Phin.

"He's bringing something through," said Eliza. "We heard him talking. It's some sort of alien consciousness from—"

"Another dimension," said Phin. "Yeah I know!"

"We think he's got that girlfriend of yours locked on the bridge," said Barnabus.

"Oh, for Pete's sake!" said Phin. "I love you guys but yes, I know all of this! It's under control. Also, gross, she's not my girlfriend."

The Foggs fell silent.

"Do you trust me now? Can you believe, for a microsecond, that I know what's going on and I just might know what I'm doing?"

They hesitated. This was clearly difficult for them. At last, Barnabus said, "Yes, we trust you."

"We believe in you, baby," said his mother.

"Awesome," said Phin, and clapped his hands. "Please say that more often. Now, is there any way to stop the hypergate countdown?"

"Now that Bolus has access to the mainframe, he has control," said Barnabus.

"But there's an autodestruct," said Eliza, quietly, almost to herself.

The boys turned to her.

"What?" said Phin.

"Honey, no," said Barnabus.

"Phin," said Eliza, "in the event of an emergency, a sequence can be initiated that will destroy all the hypergates. But the only one who can activate it is you."

"What?" said Phin again. "Why me?"

"For this exact scenario," said Eliza. "If we were ever to be kidnapped, we couldn't activate the sequence ourselves, even under torture. It has to be you."

Phin's face went slack. "That's why you guys kept me locked away all these years. That's why you wouldn't let me out. Because if I were ever kidnapped, I could destroy the hypergates!"

There was an awkward pause.

"No, baby, we kept you at home because we're overprotective," said Eliza.

Barnabus nodded.

"Oh," said Phin.

"But now there's no other way," Eliza rushed on. "You have to get to Bolus's control panel, Phin. The sequence is linked to your exact DNA. Only you can initiate it."

"But, Mom," said Phin. "Destroying all the hypergates, I mean . . . that's the family business! Wham-pow, no more company!"

"Phineas, buddy," said Barnabus, and put his hand on

Phin's shoulder. "You're thinking of putting the business before the fate of the entire universe. My God, you are a Fogg."

"*Drab droof* the company, sweetheart," said Eliza.

Phin set his jaw. He looked at his parents. Then, he kissed his mother on the cheek and ran for the door. "Okay. You guys follow this hallway to the end and take a right. There's a maintenance hatch I used to sneak aboard. You can hide there until Teddy can work out a way to get you off the ship."

"Who?" said Eliza.

"Just trust me!" said Phin, and bolted out the door.

"Wait! Where are you going?" called Barnabus.

Phin reappeared in the door, a wild look in his eyes. "I'm going to save my girlfriend!"

He dashed down the hall and only got a few paces before rushing back and adding, "I mean, my friend who's a girl, not my girlfriend. Okay, see you later!"

And with that, he was gone.

46

BOLUS HAD RETURNED TO the bridge of the *Tin Can*. He'd spent the last half hour sprucing himself up for the arrival of the Phan. His skin shone, his little beard was freshly waxed, and he'd dressed in a dapper waistcoat that would have been cute if its occupant weren't so evil.

"You're going to get away with this," Lola spat, meaning to say something else but unable to speak anything but the truth. "You're going to get everything you ever wanted!"

"Glad to hear it." Bolus chuckled, and took his seat in the captain's chair.

"I totally don't think we're going to win," Lola added with as much grit and determination as she could muster. "But I hope we will."

"Save your voice," said Bolus. "You'll need it in a moment."

There was a small hissing sound as a hatch at the back of the bridge opened. No one, including the Bog Mutant guards, heard the patter of feet as the intruder hurried along the wall and hid behind a terminal. No one noticed the snapping sound as the intruder opened a panel, nor did they hear the scuttle of the intruder's fingers across the keypad there.

"Only two more minutes," Bolus said, grinning so hard his teeth threatened to crack. "Watch closely, boys."

The guards approached the railing to get a better view of the hypergate and Singularity below. This was just what the intruder needed.

He entered the final keystroke and the bands securing Lola to the Truth Machine popped open.

Lola gasped and quickly covered her mouth.

Bolus and the guards had their backs to her. Slowly, slowly, she inched out of the chair and moved toward the door. But something caught her attention, a frantic movement in the corner of her eye. And there, crouching behind a terminal, was the intruder.

It was, of course, Phin.

"Let's get out of here," Lola whispered.

"One second, I've got to do something first," said Phin. "There's an autodestruct function programmed into the hypergates. If I can just access it . . ."

"Sir! The girl has escaped!" one of the Bog Mutants shouted.

"What?" growled Bolus.

"Hurry," Lola hissed.

Phin's fingers sped across the keys. He'd accessed the

deepest recesses of the hypergate mainframe. A pad extended itself from the wall, a pad just large enough for a thumbprint.

"Search the bridge!" Bolus commanded his guards.

"This is it," said Phin. "No more hypergates."

"There they are!"

The Bog Mutant guards rounded on them and raised their weapons.

"It's the Fogg boy!" Bolus howled. "He's in the mainframe. Shoot him!"

"No!" said Lola.

Zap zap zap! went the Bog Mutant guns.

There was a hush, a sizzle, and the scent of ionized air.

"What?" said Phin. "Wait, what?"

Lola slumped into his arms, her chest smoldering from three direct hits to the heart.

47

SHE'D JUMPED IN FRONT of him.

She'd saved his life.

She was shot.

"No!" said Phin.

"You idiots!" Bolus railed. "You absolute morons! Don't you know how important she is?"

"No!" Phin said again, and pressed his face to Lola's. "No no . . ." His voice grew hoarse, quiet. "Don't you know how important she is?"

Lola looked up at Phin, barely clinging to life. Her eyes found him, and lost him, and found him again.

"Hang on, hang on, it's going to be all right," he said.

"I know," said Lola, and managed a small smile. "Hey, look at that. I can lie again."

"Get her into the chair!" Bolus was howling at his guards. "Get her into the chair before she expires!" Bolus reeled at the Bog Mutants, who had lowered their weapons and were scratching their heads, bewildered. "What are you waiting for, you idiots?"

"Please don't go," Phin pleaded. "Please don't leave me."

Lola, somehow, for some reason, was smiling. Smiling up at him, as if she'd just gotten the punch line of a really dumb, really great joke.

"You know what I think?" she said.

"What?" said Phin, certain he was hearing her last words. "What do you think?"

"I think," said Lola, "you should really buy a new tuxedo."

Phin blinked. "What?"

"This one's getting really ratty. It's all stained and scorch-marked. You should buy a new tux." She coughed. "And shoes. And a new hat. I just really think"—her eyelids fluttered—"you would look great in a fresh new pair of sunglasses . . . on sale now . . ." Her eyes opened widely one last time, and she winked at him. "Don't you agree?"

And with that, she vanished in a poof of smoke.

Phin was left holding nothing but air.

"Consumercation!" thundered the voice of Lola Ray through the ship's public address system.

"Look, sir!" One of the Bog Mutants pointed off the port bow, where a pair of ships had just materialized—a very nice star yacht and small rental space scooter, in fact. Seated on the handlebars of the latter, protected by the scooter's mini force field and holding a short-range broadcasting radio, was Lola Ray.

"Microscopic nanobots," Lola radioed through the entirety of Bolus's ship, "replicate consumers. You find them in places like bookstores, malls, and in the gift shops of Singularity City!"

"Lola!" shouted Phin, leaping to his feet, relief shooting through every capillary of his body.

"They stick around as long as you're thinking about buying something, and hey," Lola went on. "I've been debating buying this space scooter all afternoon, and I've just made my purchasing decision. I used your card, Phin. Knew you wouldn't mind."

Seated at the scooter's controls was Bertram, who waved.

"Bertram wanted to drive," said Lola.

"Take the ship!" Bolus shouted to his guards. "Capture her! We need her!"

"Sir, look," one of the Bog Mutants shouted. He was pointing to the countdown clock, which had reached zero.

"Oh," came Lola's voice through the loudspeakers, slightly less giddy now. "Right."

"Darn," said Phin.

"Yes!" said Bolus and turned on Phin where he stood. "You're too late, Phineas Fogg. The Phan are arriving!"

✶✶✶

The hypergates were live. Their power cells thrummed at double capacity, their enormous rings turning at quadruple speed. And above the Singularity at the center of the galaxy, a portal opened.

It was a sight beyond comprehension, an experience beyond comparison. It was indescribable.

From this hole in space a million miles across, two beings emerged. The creatures were not visible; they were not detectable in any way by senses born of this universe. What the onlookers aboard the ships below witnessed was instead but a footprint, a shadow of a shadow, of the truth of the entities now hanging in space like supermassive planets. They were, or appeared to be, spherical, and glowed from within with a radiance brighter than any star. And yet the onlookers were not blinded, their bodies were not incinerated. And this was because the Phan wished it to be so.

They also appeared to be wearing T-shirts.

Then, with a voice like the eruption of a billion supernovas, one of them spoke.

"Wobble-dobble-dibble-dibble-dooble," it said.

The galaxy waited in hushed confusion.

"Fibble-fobble-dibble-dabble!" it continued.

Across the vastness of space, there was a confused silence.

"Frabble-fribble-frickle . . ."

"Oh, stop it, Garth," said the other. "It's not funny."

The first being giggled.

"Sorry, sorry," it said. "Wouldn't that be funny though? If beings from another dimension showed up and then you're all . . . *oh no, we can't understand them!*"

"They don't think it's funny," said the other. "Just let it go."

"Maybe they *don't get it*, Becca," said the first.

"There's nothing to get," said the second.

"You're no fun," said the first. "You haven't been fun in millennia. What happened to you?"

Garth and Becca were of course not their real names. Their real names would have taken centuries to pronounce and melted the brains of every living creature within a light-year's radius. These were merely reflections, shadows of shadows of the Phan's true names.

"Right, where were we," said the one who seemed to be called Garth. "We are the Phan."

"What he said," added Becca.

"We have journeyed far, and our question must be answered."

"It is the Question of the End!" said the other, in a tone that could melt stars, but didn't.

"Should we just ask it, then?" said Garth.

"Well, what do you want to do, have a snack first?" replied Becca.

"Might be nice. You're not hungry?"

"I told you to eat before we left!"

"I did! That was a thousand years ago!"

"And you're hungry already?"

"I'm talking about a snack! Not, like, a whole meal. Just something to tide us over. I don't want to hear the answer on an empty stomach, do you?"

Of course, they didn't have stomachs. They did not experience hunger. This was all merely the comprehendible afterimage of the truth of these wise and infinite beings.

"You can wait," said Becca.

"Fine," said Garth. "Do you hear something?"

"I do," said Becca. "I think that little bean person is shouting something at us."

"That's not a bean person, that's our guy."

"Oh," said Becca. "You're right, that *is* our guy! The guy from the phone call!"

"Should we listen to what he has to say?" said Garth.

"Let's," said Becca. And they did.

With their attention turned to the tiny form of Goro Bolus, who was jumping up and down and waving his arms on the deck of the *Tin Can*, the little bean's voice was suddenly magnified so that every living thing in the galaxy could hear him.

"My lords!" screeched Bolus. "Oh! Goodness, that's loud. Ahem," he spoke again, without shouting this time, and was still the loudest thing in existence. "My lords, welcome! Welcome to our universe! I have worked so long and hard to make the world ready for your arrival. I've found the girl, my lords. The time traveler, the one with the Answer! And I secured the hypergates so that the doorway could open for you."

"Good for you," said Garth. "What a great guy."

"Seriously, we owe you one," said Becca.

"Yes, well, um, my lords . . ." Bolus cleared his throat. "I'd like to ah, well . . . You did promise me wealth and power beyond my wildest dreams."

"Did we?" said Garth. "I don't remember that."

"Oh, actually," said Becca, "I think I recall you saying something about that, Garth."

"Oh, fine," said Garth. "What is it they value here?"

"Love, isn't it?"

"Is that right?" Garth said, addressing himself to the speck of a person on the speck of a ship in this speck of a galaxy. "Love? How about some love?"

"Well, my lords," said Bolus. "I was actually hoping for, uh, well . . . something more monetary."

"Monetary?" said Becca.

"Yeah. Um, yes."

"Well, what's the most monetary thing you got around here?" asked Garth.

Bolus had to think about this.

"Gold, I suppose?"

"Done," said Garth, and zapped Bolus to the lost treasure

planet of Frankta D'Or, where he lived out his days utterly alone and in possession of the most valuable piece of real estate in the galaxy.

"Now," said Becca. "Was there anyone else we owed something to?"

"Hey, where are our little buddies?" said Garth. "We got any Bog Mutants in the house tonight?"

With that, every Bog Mutant across the galaxy was summoned, blipped through space almost as an afterthought, and materialized safely suspended in a bubble of space-time just above the decks of the ships below.

"Hello!" said ten thousand Jeremys in unison.

"Look at 'em!" said Becca. "They look great! Like real Bog Mutants!"

"Oh, that is awesome," said Garth. "Should we take them out of the bubble?"

"No, they lose their value if you remove them from the packaging," said Becca. "Wait, is it value? Or is it their lives? I forget."

"Whatever," said Garth. "Hi guys!"

"Hello!" said the Jeremys.

With another flick of the Phan's infinite power, a second bubble in space-time appeared, this one containing what looked like a smaller, greener version of the Phan. Standing on its surface were several people, almost too small to see at a distance. This green sphere was none other than Mr. Jeremy, free of the cavernous confines of Satellite B. And the persons on his surface were none other than Professor Donut, Gretta, and the mushroom people.

"Hey there," said Garth. "Way to go, making all these Bog Mutants. Just a super-good job, dude."

"*DEMONS!*" bellowed Mr. Jeremy. "*Bringers of destruction! Go back to the hell whence you came! You shall not have this universe! I am no longer your slave, and my children shall be free!*"

"What's he saying?" said Becca.

"Hey, what's your deal, little dude?" asked Garth.

"*You shall never prevail in your dastardly plan! The Question shall not be answered! The Question—*"

"Let's put him on mute," said Becca.

"Sorry, dude," said Garth. And instantly Mr. Jeremy was silenced.

While all of this was going on, Lola sat perched on the handlebars of her new star-trike and stared up at the Phan.

"Boop," said Bertram worriedly.

"I know," said Lola. "I'm . . . thinking."

Lola was thinking, and she was thinking hard. The tickle of a thought that had begun back on Satellite B had transformed into a full-blown tickle attack. Her brain was in spasms. It jittered and rolled. It was desperately trying to work out the thing it had been trying to work out for what felt like ages.

The radio receiver Lola was holding squawked. It's tiny vis-screen flickered, and an image resolved itself—an incoming transmission from Phin, who, with the Bog Mutants transported to the space bubble above, and Bolus whisked away to Frankta D'Or, was now alone on the bridge of the *Tin Can.*

"Lola!" said the tiny picture of Phin.

"Phin!"

"I'm so glad you're alive! I thought . . ."

"I know," said Lola.

"What are we going to do?" he said. "I don't think we can sneak away from them. They seem pretty all-powerful."

"I have no idea. But I'm just . . . something's weird about all of this."

"Just one thing?" said Phin.

"No, I mean . . ." Lola thought. "Have you ever seen that show *Dimension Y*?"

"Lola," said Phin, sighing. "No one has seen that show. You need to stop talking about it."

"My T-shirt," said Lola.

"Yes," said Phin. "It's hideous. What else is new?"

"*Do you see what's on it?*" Lola lowered the radio's camera eye so Phin could get a better look.

"Um," said Phin, "that looks like maybe a coffee stain? And, uh—"

"Bog Mutants!" said Lola. "There are Bog Mutants on my shirt! From *Dimension Y*! But also . . . from like . . . here! And now!"

"I'm not sure I follow," said Phin. "I'm not sure I even saw where you went."

"It's the Question . . . ," said Lola. "It's got to be something to do with where I'm from," said Lola, speaking rapidly now. "Something to do with Earth. Something to do with something that's no longer here in the future. How else could I be the only one who knows the answer?"

"*Lola Ray*," the Phan suddenly said, and Lola felt the hot, glowing beam of their attention fall to her.

"Boop!" said Bertram, and hid behind her back.

"Lola!" said Phin on the vis-screen. "Just don't answer it. Just refuse. Whatever happens, whatever they ask, just don't say anything!"

"I don't think—" said Lola and came up short. Her voice boomed from her tiny frame, the way Bolus's had done, magnified by the Phan.

"It'll be okay," said Phin, and then a thought seemed to flicker past his worried eyes. His eyes told her he wanted to do something, to save her, he would take her place if he could. His eyes told her he was powerless, but he would have given anything to change things. And failing all this, his eyes said he wanted to say something, anything, that might reassure her.

"Lola," he said, pressing his palm to the view screen as if he could reach through and touch her. "Don't swallow your gum."

Lola's eyes went wide.

"Lola Ray," said the Phan. "Come on up here."

Lola felt herself lifting off the handlebars. Up, up she went, through the scooter's protective force field into cold space. She was enveloped in a bubble of space-time, just as Mr. Jeremy and the Bog Mutants were. Protected . . . and prisoner.

Up, up she flew, at a thousand miles an hour, until she was at eye level with the two Phan.

From this new angle, high above the ships, high above the hypergate, high above the swirling cataclysm of the Singularity, she felt terribly small, and terribly alone.

She faced the gods before her.

From here they seemed even more enormous. Their cores radiated like white-hot stars, penumbras like double-helixing rainbows. They were incredible. And their T-shirts were super cool.

Now, from this angle, Lola could see what was on them. Garth's appeared to be an image of Bog Mutants climbing out of the bath. On Becca's, in letters a mile high, were words in a language Lola could not decipher, but somehow she knew what they meant. And they were silly, and bold, and immensely reassuring.

And all of a sudden, Lola got it.

"Now," said Garth, his tone commanding. "Now it is time. In the name of the Phandom, we ask you, Lola Ray, the Question."

"The Question!" echoed Becca.

Together they asked, "*How . . . ?*

"How . . . ?

"How does it end?"

Lola took a deep breath, and without hesitation or fear, she told them.

48

THE VOICE OF LOLA Ray echoed through the cosmos. Magnified by the Phan, it reached every ear in the galaxy. Her words played like music through the stars, they strummed the nebula and played bongos of moons and planets. And as she spoke, the tension, the worry, the painful not-knowing at the heart of the universe slowly, slowly released. For the story that had made its way across the universe, on electromagnetic waves, through the space between spaces to the home of the Phan, the tale that had begun and was cut off by an unforeseen disaster, could now be completed. The question of *How does it end?* was being answered.

"So," Lola said, "then, in part two, Professor Rivulon and June are still trapped in the space whale's belly. And that's when June tells the professor she's always been in love with him!"

"No!" said Becca.

"Shush," said Garth. "Let her talk. Do they kiss?"

"I was just getting to that," said Lola. "June leans in, and it looks like they're going to kiss, and then *wham!* Space quake!"

Garth and Becca gasped.

"What happened then?" Becca said in a kind of titanic whisper.

"The professor is hurtled through time!" said Lola, waving her arms to illustrate the tumult. "And he travels all the way back to Mars."

"That's where they left the Crystal of Lies!" said Garth. "In episode thirty-five."

"Bingo," said Lola with a grin. "So the professor uses the Crystal to rewrite time and bring back June's brother from the dead."

"I can't believe it!" said Becca.

"And then they all take the Interstellar Conveyer Belt back to the future, and rescue June from the space whale."

"Oh man, I bet that must have been awesome," said Becca.

"It was," said Lola. "So anyway, finally, they get back to the professor's home world of Megatraxis, and then . . ." Lola let the moment hang, let the Phan roil in their godlike anticipation. "On the floor of the Senate Hall . . . ," she said slowly. The Phan inched forward a few hundred miles in space. "In front of the entire Galactic Council . . ." The words dripped from her lips, the Phan quivering before her. "Professor Rivulon gets down on one knee . . ."

"No!" said Garth.

"Yes!" said Becca.

"And asks June to marry him."

The Phan erupted in the interdimensional equivalent of applause and joy.

"That's perfect!" thundered Garth.

"That's so perfect!" erupted Becca.

"And that," said Lola, "is how *Dimension Y* ends."

Hovering in space, protected by her space-time bubble, Lola Ray bowed.

The Phan exploded with delight. In their ultimate satisfaction they unwound themselves, unwound time, and in a kind of cosmic ecstasy, unwound reality itself . . .

. . . and then wound everything back up again.

Gasping, teary, filled with pleasure unending, the Phan sighed.

"Oh wow," said Garth. "Wow wow *wow*. I mean, not knowing was seriously killing me."

"Season six ended on such a cliffhanger!" said Becca. "I mean, we've been waiting . . . what, a thousand years to find out how it ends?"

"That is glorious," said Garth. "Thank you."

"You're welcome," said Lola. "Now." She brought herself up to full height—which is a funny thing to do when you're floating in space. "I think you owe us one."

"What's that?" said Garth.

"Hmm?" said Becca.

"I told you how it ended, I think you owe us one," said Lola. "Come on, without me you'd have *never* found out."

The Phan seemed to confer. "All right," Becca said after a moment. "What would you like?"

"Firstly, I want you to free all the Jeremys, Mr. Jeremy included. No more slave labor. Let them all go." Lola glanced at the Jeremys suspended in space and then quickly added, "I mean, *metaphorically* let them go."

"Fine by us," said Garth. "We don't need them anymore anyway."

"Great," said Lola. "Secondly, I'd like you to send me home."

There was a long silence. "You mean Hoboken?" said Becca, uncertain why any being would want to go there.

"In the twenty-first century," said Lola. "Yes, please."

"Oh," said Garth. "Yeah, we can't do that."

"We have no idea how to time travel," said Becca. "If we did, why would we need to ask *you* how *Dimension Y* ended? We could just go back in time and watch the DVDs ourselves."

"Yeah, sorry about that," said Garth. "Anyway, it's been real!"

"Thanks a lot, everyone!" said Becca. "Hope you have a great rest of your lives!"

"See ya!" said Garth.

And with that the Phan slipped back through their doorway and out of our universe, gone forever.

Lola remained suspended in space, her mouth agape.

She couldn't get home.

She didn't even know how to get down.

49

IN THE AFTERMATH OF the Phan, there was lots to do.

The galaxy had just experienced something totally unique. Forevermore history would be divided into *before* and *after* the Phan. It would be called the Day of the Answer. In history books and in university classrooms it would sometimes be referred to, inaccurately, as the Battle of Singularity City (historians being the type to throw the word "battle" in front of everything just to make their books and classes seem more exciting). Miniseries would be produced dramatizing the events, in which the galaxy's most famous actors would dress in giant spherical papier-mâché balls to portray the Phan. And across the stars, network showrunners would wake in a sweat, remembering what *they* referred to as the Great and Terrible Spoiler.

But that was all to come. Now there was work to be done.

Ten thousand Bog Mutants were left floating in a space-time bubble above Singularity City. While many could now return happily to their respectable jobs as floor sweepers and parking attendants, nearly half had been employed by the Temporal Transit Authority, which, now that the Phan had no use for it, was defunct. Thousands of Jeremys were now out of a job, a horrible thing for a Bog Mutant, and none of them were quite sure what to do with themselves.

As if in answer to their occupational anxiety, an enormous planetoid-sized fungal core floated toward them out of the night.

"*Come, my children*," said Mr. Jeremy, "*and let us be together again.*"

A family reunion was held on the surface of Mr. Jeremy, with all ten thousand Bog Mutants in attendance, as well as the population of mushroom people, their phenotypic brothers. Reunited with his children, Mr. Jeremy vowed to protect them and offered them a home on his surface. They were welcome to stay forever, or until they decided what they wanted to do with their lives. So long as they cleaned up after themselves and didn't let the laundry pile up.

In the hours that followed there was a great party on the surface of Mr. Jeremy. Bog Mutant DJs spun the latest tracks, Professor Donut served tea and scones and cucumber sandwiches for all, and the mushroom people showed the Jeremys a dance they'd invented that involved spinning on their dome-like little heads—which the Jeremys attempted without much success.

When the party was over, only four Bog Mutants decided

they wouldn't be staying. The first three claimed they had found their purpose in this universe, which was to open and run the galaxy's first interstellar taco stand. Mr. Jeremy gave them his blessing and out they went into the universe to seek their fortune.

The fourth was Gretta.

"Are you sure you don't want to stay with us?" Professor Donut asked as they stood in the shadow of a Temporal Transit Authority shuttle. "Now that the Triumvirate of Pong is disbanded, your father and I have all sorts of exciting projects we want to tackle," the little cat said excitedly. "There are so many questions cute science has yet to answer. We could use a mind like yours!"

"No thanks," said Gretta, not unkindly. "Someone needs to dismantle the Temporal Transit Authority, and with Bolus gone and the Bog Mutants freed, I guess it's up to me." She stuck her hands in her pockets and considered the stars. "Maybe I'll repurpose the fleet for something else . . . something better."

She kissed the professor on the top of his head, spit out a bit of fur, hugged her brother Mutants and brother mushrooms goodbye, and promised Mr. Jeremy she would call from time to time. Then she ascended the ramp into the little shuttle and flew up and out, toward her destiny, whatever that happened to be.

But in the moments just after the Phan had vanished, before all the hullabaloo with the Bog Mutants had a chance to begin, a sleekly red ship climbed into the massive reaches of space the Phan had only just occupied. In all that near emptiness it found a young girl, alone in the vacuum.

She was sitting in space, in her little bubble of space-time, her knees pulled to her chest, looking out at the stars, or at nothing in particular. The ship pulled alongside and opened a hatch, and after a moment, the figure of a young boy appeared in the airlock. Gingerly, he stepped out into space, testing the nothing beneath his feet and finding it sturdy.

The boy approached and stood a moment above the girl, who still sat, chin on her knees. The boy crouched. He might have been saying something to her. It could have been promises, reassurances, or even apologies on behalf of the big, uncaring, impossible universe.

The girl did not move or speak.

And then, the boy stopped speaking too, and simply wrapped his arms around her shoulders.

Suspended there, in a teardrop in space, they appeared to tremble.

EPILOGUE

A LOT OF PEOPLE had been preparing for the Phan for a very long time, and now that they'd come and gone, another question beat in their hearts.

What now?

The glittering towers of Upper Vancouver shone in the afternoon sunlight. Shuttles hummed between the skyscrapers. On the streets below, markets were closing for the day and cafés were switching to the lunch menu. In an alley not far from the shore, a small mangy dog peeked its nose out of a doorway and sniffed the air.

Cautiously, it stepped out onto the cobbled street on its morning search for lunch.

Just then a shadow passed over the alley. A steady hum filled the street as a downdraft scattered the scraps and sent the puddles left over from last night's thunderstorm rippling. The little dog barked and went scurrying back to the safety of its doorway as a spaceship descended, adjusted, and settled itself between the two brightly colored tenements in this, the oldest part of the city.

The ship was small, with a racing stripe down one side and what appeared to be cute little ears hot-glued to the roof. A hatch opened, and out stepped two figures in clean if slightly rumpled jumpsuits.

"This is it," Phin said, considering a readout on his tablet.

"Okay," said Lola. "Because you also said that about the shopfront in Gastown, and the empty lot across from the marina. In fact, that's what you said about the last five places we checked."

"Well, the records aren't exactly thorough," Phin grumbled.

Lola shot him a look.

"But I'm sure *this one* is it."

"Okay," she said, steeling herself. "Okay, let's do this."

Together the pair entered a darkened doorway, beyond which a staircase led them down, away from the sounds and smells of the city's historic district. Into the damp they descended, their flashlights sweeping over cobwebs and films of falling dust. Through basements and subbasements they passed until at last they came to a steel door. On it was emblazoned the seal of the University of British Colombia, and below it, the special research group of which Lola's father had been a part. Its image was faded by the wearing of time, but a slogan was still visible in flaking blue letters. *Move Ahead.*

"This is it," Lola said, her breath catching in the small, damp space. "That's the group Papa was working for when I, you know . . . blipped into the future."

Phin affixed the handle with a small device the size and shape of a pencil. There was a hiss and a pop, and the steel door opened. They were met with a gust as the chamber's hermetic seal was broken, and Lola felt a chill as she and Phin smelled air that had not been breathed in centuries.

Could she smell her father? Maybe. Under the stale, recycled smell was something else that might have been something familiar, but she couldn't be sure.

They followed a long corridor, passed empty rooms containing nothing more than broken glass and rubble, until at last they came to a final door. It was shut. It had a nameplate. The nameplate read *Ray*.

"Are you ready?" Phin asked.

They'd talked about this. Yes, she was ready. She was ready to find whatever remained of her family, and no, she didn't expect much. Her father, her mother and sisters, everyone Lola knew was long gone. Whatever might have outlasted them in Newark had been vaporized in the Great Pork Fat Meltdown in 2415. But if there was something, a scrap of paper or an old coffee mug, that once belonged to Papa—well, Lola wanted it. It had become her quest the moment she realized neither the Phan nor anyone else could send her home.

The door had its own, secondary hermetic seal, which Phin opened with his electronic lock pick. The room beyond was dark, cluttered, and unremarkable. The seal had preserved the papers and posters hanging on the wall, but a thousand years is a long time to wait.

"What are these?" Phin asked, shining his light on a shelf of slim volumes.

Lola grinned. "Those are DVDs. *Dimension Y*, seasons one through six," she said. "We used to watch it together sometimes. Papa loved it. He even wanted to name the dog Professor Rivulon—"

Phin had wandered away, already having lost interest.

Lola shook her head and ran her fingers along the dusty spines. "Too bad these are useless now."

"What was your father, er, Papa," said Phin, "researching?"

"Particles?" said Lola. "I think? I never really understood it."

Phin shone his flashlight on a whiteboard in the corner. Someone had been scribbling equations on it, and they were still mostly legible.

"He was working on *something*," said Phin. "It looks complicated."

"He came here on a research grant," Lola said, peering into a far corner.

"This can't be right," Phin mumbled to himself. "I mean,

I don't fully understand what he wrote here, and that's saying something."

Lola was no longer listening. She wasn't interested in Papa's business papers. She didn't care about his work. She wanted something personal, something *his*. A photograph maybe, or even (she didn't dare hope) a journal of some kind.

She shone her light in another corner of the laboratory. There were filing cabinets she could search. Plastic storage bins to upend. But something small and unassuming on a desk caught her eye.

Back home, Lola's father kept their important family documents—birth certificates and the like—in a small lock-box. A similar one sat on this table, here in the thirty-first century, under a thin layer of dust. *This* box, however, had the words *FOR LOLA* stamped on the side.

Lola hadn't been breathing much before. She stopped breathing now.

"It looks like your father was into some serious deep physics," Phin was saying. "He was fooling around with space-time. It's an interesting theory. Using alternate dimensions as a shortcut to travel through time. Looks like he'd even found one and named it." Phin sniffed. "Totally impractical though."

"This box," said Lola. "Phin, this box has my name on it."

Phin dropped what he was doing and came to her side. Lola ran her fingers across the stamped lettering. Whatever this box was, it had been built to last. Whoever had left it had intended it to sit here for a very long time indeed.

"Looks like it's for you," said Phin, and swallowed.

Lola was transfixed. As if in a dream, she turned the box, revealing a numbered combination lock. Lola entered her birthday, and the lid popped open on the first try.

Inside, untouched by the centuries, were two objects.

The first was so simple and homey in its familiarity it made Lola's heart hurt. It was a Twinkie, still wrapped in its protective cellophane, pillow soft and fresh as the day it was packaged, the same snack Papa used to sneak into Lola's lunch box when Momma was on one of her health-food kicks. Lola pressed the precious little confection to her nose. She could almost smell it through the wrapper.

"Still good after a thousand years," she said, beaming.

"That's disgusting," said Phin. "Look, there's something else."

The other object was a note. It was written on plain ruled notebook paper. The scrawl was unmistakably her father's.

"Here, shine your light on this," said Lola, holding up the note for them both to read.

"You're shaking, I can't read it."

"Just, shine your light!"

"Okay, okay!"

Together, breathless, they read Papa's last message to his daughter.

"Oh . . . ," said Phin.

"Yeah," said Lola.

"That's just . . . ," said Phin.

"Yeah," said Lola, and met his eyes. Her own were shining, for the first time in a long time, with hope.

Dear Lola Girl,

I'm so sorry for what's happened to you. I fear something may have gone terribly wrong and it's all my fault.

If you get this note, whenever you get it, your mother and sisters and I will be waiting for you.

Find us in Dimension Why.

Love,

Dad

PHIN AND LOLA WILL RETURN IN . . .

DIMENSION WHY:
REVENGE OF THE SEQUEL

Acknowledgments

I owe a lot of people gratitude for enabling me to take this spin around the galaxy.

Thank you to my agent, Melissa Sarver White, for believing in this silly book, and for allowing me to hang out in her office for extended wisecracking sessions. Thank you too to everyone at Folio Literary Management, especially my Folio Jr. team, helmed by the indomitable Emily Van Beek.

Thank you to my prince of an editor, David Linker, whose support and guidance steered Phin and Lola away from rougher shores and into safe harbor. Thank you to the entire team at Harper Collins, especially Vanessa Nuttry, Robby Imfeld, and Anna Bernard. Thank you a thousand times over to artists and designers Chris Kwon and Alison Klapthor for giving me the cover I always wanted (I said "make it wild" and you did, thank you). And thank you to my marvelous copy editors, Jon Howard and the delightful Megan Gendell, who made sure to laugh at my jokes, albeit in Track Changes.

Thank you to all of my clients—working with you is the

greatest privilege of my life, and you inspire me every day.

Thank you to Deborah Jaffa, without whose support and care the past three years would have been much more difficult. Seriously, Deborah, thank you so much for all you've done for me, and thank you for raising an incredible daughter.

Thank you to Ammi-Joan Paquette, whose notes on this book's sequel helped inform some vital changes to part one. Thank you to the many colleagues and fellow writers who also offered to read early versions of this manuscript, and thank you for not judging me when I was too self-conscious to take you up on it. Next time, I promise.

Thank you to my mother and father, who gave me everything, including my sense of humor. Thank you also to Katie Cusick and Andrea Hanley, two incredibly strong and inspiring women.

Thank you to my friends inside and out of the book business, especially those of you who have always held a place for me on the "writer's couch." Your love and support mean more than you could ever know.

Thank you, Zev Elman, for the spiritual and terrestrial guidance.

This book so clearly owes a tremendous debt of gratitude to creators greater than I: Thank you, Douglas Adams, Terry Pratchett, Neil Gaiman, Robert Asprin, Shinichirō Wantanabe, and Keiko Nobumoto, as well as perhaps less obvious inspirations and muses Kate Atkinson, Bruce Coville, Louis Sachar, and Bill Watterson.

Thank you to the staff at Krupa Grocery in Windsor Terrace.

And finally, thank you to my brilliant, beautiful, and courageous wife. Molly, you were quite literally the inspiration and impetus for this book. You encouraged me to share it with others. That day we edited the final draft from a hospital bed—I don't think I've ever laughed so hard in my life.

And thank you, reader. If you've enjoyed this reading experience, I highly recommend writing a book of your own.

—John Cusick